TWO SAMS
AT THE
CHALET SCHOOL

ELINOR M BRENT-DYER

Girls Gone By Publishers

COMPLETE AND UNABRIDGED

Published by

Girls Gone By Publishers
4 Rock Terrace
Coleford
Bath
Somerset
BA3 5NF

First published by W & R Chambers Ltd 1951
This edition published 2008
Text and Chalet School characters © Girls Gone By Publishers
Home, Sweet Home at the Chalet School © Helen Barber 2008
The Chalet School series: an introduction © Clarissa Cridland 2002
Elinor M Brent-Dyer: a brief biography © Clarissa Cridland 2002
Publishing History © Adrianne Fitzpatrick 2008
"Home is Where the Heart is" © Katherine Bruce 2008
Errors in the First Edition © Ruth Jolly and Adrianne Fitzpatrick 2008
Design and Layout © Girls Gone By Publishers 2008

Typeset in England by AJF
Printed in England by CPI Antony Rowe

ISBN 978-1-84745-055-5

CONTENTS

HOME, SWEET HOME AT THE CHALET SCHOOL

Two girls are exchanging confidences in the entrance hall at the Chalet School. It is the first day of term, both are new, and both have an uneasy feeling that somehow they are unwanted. Miss Annersley raises her voice to welcome back the School and the old girls respond with enthusiasm. Only Samaris Davies and Samantha van der Byl stand out. Lonely and at a loss in a large crowd, they have yet to discover that the Chalet School can be their home.

The opening scene of *Two Sams at the Chalet School* is a familiar one; its eponymous heroines undergo an experience common to the fictional schoolgirl (and perhaps to the real one, too). The experience is important. It evokes one of children's literature's recurrent themes, one found in books as diverse as *Anne of Green Gables* and *Harry Potter*: the theme of the 'displaced child'.

Displaced children have various literary guises, and their stories develop in different ways. Sometimes they are orphans; sometimes they live with unloving parents; sometimes they have been unavoidably separated from their 'real' families. Certain basic needs, however, are typically shared by them all. Lost and vulnerable, they long for security. Their chief desire is for a place—and often simultaneously for a family—which provides them with a sense of 'home'.

Elinor Brent-Dyer's long list of Chalet titles repeatedly caters for such characters. All the way through the series' three eras—the Tirolean, British and Swiss periods—lonely girls find comfort at the Chalet School. The leitmotif of the displaced child is not always handled in exactly the same way, but the theme reappears with enough continuity to make it a demonstrable characteristic of the books.

The story of the Chalet School begins with a real family, which consists of three orphaned siblings. Madge, Dick and Joey Bettany, despite their lack of parents, are far from being lonely outcasts: their familial unity is clear. Nonetheless, they arguably undergo displacement. Financial difficulties and health worries force them to sell their house in England. They move out to the Austrian Tirol, set up the Chalet School and before long the girls are comfortably established in their new environment.

Joey, after a skirmish with the villain Cosimo, thus looks round at her 'dear, familiar surroundings' and remarks on their loveliness. Her sister replies:

> "It's home, isn't it, Joey?"
> *The Princess of the Chalet School*, p257

The Bettanys' home is of great significance. It soon becomes home to many other persons, not a few of them 'displaced' children. The first, Grizel Cochrane, has been effectively rejected by her father and stepmother. "'Tisn't much of a home at *home*!" she tells Joey (*Jo of the Chalet School,* p170). Her longing to spend Christmas with the Bettanys and her obvious love for the school are indicative of the refuge she finds with both of them.

Other lonely and deprived children swiftly follow Grizel into the Chalet series. Like Grizel, they find themselves adopted, to some degree or other, by the school community. The Bettanys themselves often act as chief benefactors; their expandable family takes in Juliet and Robin as Jo's 'sisters'. But sometimes other members of the school offer their help: Mademoiselle La Pâttre gives Cornelia Flower some much needed 'mothering' and the Guides famously—if perhaps rather unrealistically—adopt Biddy O'Ryan.

Meanwhile, the school also provides for another sort of girl: the happy girl, who does not need a substitute family, but who looks upon the school as a second home. These characters play a vital role in the series. They help to create the familial environment that is so beneficial to the more vulnerable girls. In the Tirolean days, the school is still quite small, a factor which perhaps enhances its warm atmosphere. Domestic comfort is a key component in all of the early stories. EBD paints numerous scenes in which girls of all ages group together around the common room stoves or in the sunny garden, roasting chestnuts, sipping fruit drinks, exchanging ideas and telling stories. Importantly, the happy pupils' 'real' families are sometimes involved in creating significant 'homely' scenes—the Mensches, for instance, are responsible for the Bettanys' magical first Christmas in Innsbruck (*Jo of*). As the series progresses the ties between the school and these families strengthen. Girls leave school only to marry the brothers of their friends, at weddings attended by the entire School. Madge, herself now married to Dr Russell, finds herself the centre of a new community, built around the doctor's sanatorium on the Sonnalpe and consisting of old girls, colleagues and friends.

A familial atmosphere remains paramount in this community. It is a centre for much hospitality and, importantly, not only provides a welcome for old girls and their friends and relatives, but also for new, displaced children. When fatherless Gillian Linton arrives one cold January evening, torn from her London home by her mother's frightening illness and laden with the responsibility of her feckless younger sister, she is overwhelmed by kindness:

Gillian suddenly remembered her manners. "It's ripping of Mrs Russell to take us in like this," she said. "I never expected it, you know. Quite thought we'd have to camp out in some hotel or other."

"Oh, Madge wouldn't let people like you go to the hotel if it could be helped," said Jo cheerfully. "And even if we hadn't been able to take you, there are the Mensches and the Di Bersettis. Both Frau Mensch and Signora di Bersetti are old girls of the Chalet School, and it isn't likely they'd let new Chalet girls go to the 'Goldener Apfel' unless we'd mumps or measles or something like that."

The Chalet School and the Lintons, pp37–8

The message is clear: though Gillian has yet to attend a single lesson at her new school she already *belongs*.

So, the initial Tirolean period of the Chalet School series establishes a firm value system. It stresses the importance of domestic comfort, of sharing and of familial love in a wide community. Not long after Gillian Linton's arrival, however, huge changes take place in the series. In the real world, Hitler's imperialistic plans had begun to displace multitudes. After the Austrian Anschluss, the basis of EBD's idyllic setting was destroyed. Choosing to reflect this in her books, she sent her school into exile.

The series' carefully nurtured, close-knit community atmosphere might, of course, have suffered gravely as a result of this disruption. Fortunately, however, EBD managed it with ingenuity. She guided her principal old characters—interestingly, once more vulnerable and displaced—through various exciting adventures to the safe haven (and comfortable homes) first of the Channel Islands and then of the Welsh borders. And once she had them established there, she carried on promoting Chaletian values.

Whether at Sarres, Plas Howell or on St Briavel's, the school goes on acting as a comfortable home—the scene of much social interaction. Meanwhile, Madge and Joey both have their own households and both offer generous hospitality to old and new Chalet girls, extending the blessings of their domestic circle to the school. Once again, different sorts of girls are received: some have loving homes of their own and require only a friendly welcome into the school community; some are much more vulnerable—they are in want of more permanent shelter and perhaps of adoption. The diverse needs of all these persons are met. Madge and Joey persist in providing homes for people outside their immediate family circle; the population of Plas Gwyn, Joey's home, constantly changes and expands. The wider school-based community system also continues to operate; needy characters—such as Phoebe Wychcote and Jacynth Hardy—receive help from the school/Sanatorium population at large.

Several years after the war, the school moves back to Central Europe—to Switzerland—but domestic themes remain important. The school has evolved a whole range of customary communal activities. Girls work together to achieve common goals: gardening, entertaining their fellows on Saturday evenings, preparing for charity Sales, performing plays and pantomimes. The school is a cheerful place for girls to live in—and they are also blessed by Jo's continued hospitality.

She and her family have moved in next door to the school. Their new house, 'Freudesheim' (Happy Home), becomes the venue for many tea parties. Thanks to Joey's intervention, various guests find their social and familial problems resolved: Rosamund Lilley's worries about her background are assuaged (*A Problem for the Chalet School*); Richenda Fry learns to forgive (*The Chalet School and Richenda*); and Grizel Cochrane rediscovers that she can be loved (*The Chalet School Reunion*). Old-style family 'adoptions' also take place. Just after the move to Switzerland, Joey happily accepts Jo Scott as an unofficial goddaughter (*A Chalet Girl from Kenya*); towards the end of the series she admits two other girls into the family circle: Erica Standish and Marie-Claire de Mabillon. It is her husband, Jack Maynard, who expresses the family—and school—ethos at this point. As a sympathetic nun looks on, Joey asks him if they have room for one more child:

> The nun waited, breathless. If no one claimed little Marie-Claire she would not be thrown on the world, but how much better for her to have the kind of home it was clear she would have with the Maynards than to grow up in the orphanage!
>
> She need not have feared. Jack Maynard took the baby from Joey and kissed her in fatherly fashion. "Room for any baby left alone," he said.
>
> *Summer Term at the Chalet School*, p38

There is, then, a great deal of thematic continuity in EBD's Chalet series. In Austria, Britain and Switzerland, the school and the homes of its associated families persistently act as complimentary spheres of domestic bliss—havens for the lonely and displaced. However, over the course of the series, significant variations do occur in EBD's 'displaced persons' theme. I would suggest that the most obvious of these develop in the Swiss books.

This first change I wish to note is rather subtle and concerns both the communal atmosphere of the school and the manner in which it interacts with its associated families. I raise this matter very tentatively, as I realise that not all Chalet readers will agree with me. Nonetheless, I think it fair to express my opinion that *generally speaking* (there are exceptions, of course, both in the early books and the later ones!) the school's atmosphere is a little less intimate in the Swiss books, and its integration with its families less marked.

In the Tirolean era the school and the family are practically indistinguishable. The school *is* the Bettanys' only home; Madge combines a dual role—headmistress and mother/sister to Joey. Even after she marries and moves up to the Sonnalpe, she continues to be an important figurehead. Meanwhile, Joey, the series' central character, remains in the school. She provides a 'family' link to Madge's home, Die Rosen. When the School pays a visit to the Sonnalpe, the girls go there as pupils of Madge's school *and* as companions of her sister (think of the delightful baby-naming party in *Lintons*).

In the British books Joey becomes the chief hostess and she organizes a series of cross-form gatherings that closely resemble the earlier parties held at Die Rosen. She receives help from various family members—Robin Humphries, Daisy Venables and the young Bettany girls—who carry on providing a direct link between the school and home. In the Swiss books, however, things are slightly different. We see an influx of new girls who are not related to the main families and yet who take centre stage: Nina Rutherford, Rosamund Lilley, Richenda Fry etc. The books which tell their stories tend to concentrate on a few girls only—the girls in the same form as the newcomer and perhaps one or two others as well. The new girls make their visits to Freudesheim alone, or with only the Maynard Triplets as company, instead of in large, mixed groups.

The curious result of this is that we suddenly become aware of a significant increase in the school's roll. There have always been *some* pupils on the register who feature very little in the books, but where once they seemed to be a silent minority, they now sometimes give the impression of forming a majority. The school community is evidently still tightly knit together, but we now know less about it and see less of it in intimate domestic situations. Of course, the series still has some pivotal characters. Mary-Lou Trelawney and Len Maynard in particular engage the reader's interest. But neither functions in *quite* the same way as Joey did in the Tirolean days. Far away from Howells village, Mary-Lou cannot introduce girls to her own family, as she did in *Three Go to the Chalet School*. Len regularly accompanies girls on interesting visits to Freudesheim, but is rarely seen at home, surrounded by a group of schoolfellows of all ages. All this is indicative of a distancing that occurs between 'school' and 'home' in the Swiss era. The Maynard family and their home remain central to many of the books; but they now inhabit a more separate sphere.

The second change we see in the Swiss books marks a definite development in the 'displaced child' theme. Up till this point the school's most vulnerable displaced persons have commonly formed close attachments with people wholly unrelated to them. The resulting adoptive relationships have been as important, strong and lasting as any consanguineous one. Joey's deep love for Robin is proverbial, and Juliet's feelings for her new family become evident when she describes her university experience to Jo:

> "I was dreadfully homesick for Briesau and all you people. Remember, it was the first real home I'd ever had. You know how my own people regarded me—as an incubus, of whom they were only too thankful to be well rid. Then Madame came, with her heavenly kindness, and there were you and the Robin—in a lesser sense, Grizel. I had two years of that, and it was new to me. Can you

imagine how I felt when I went to England, and found myself alone for the first time after two years of love and fellowship, and—wanting?"

The Chalet School and Jo, p161

In the Swiss books, however, we meet a sequence of vulnerable girls—Nina, Ruey and Adrienne—who find an ultimate blessing in the discovery of 'long lost relations'. A basic pattern develops. The school or the Maynards—and sometimes both—administer some initial comfort, then 'real' kin are added to the girls as a bonus. Thus it is only after Joey and the School have helped Nina Rutherford to reintegrate into society that she learns—to her great joy—that the Emburys are her cousins. "I'm not alone any more!" she declares (*A Genius at the Chalet School* p154). Nina's experiences are closely paralleled by Ruey Richardson's and Adrienne Desmoines'. All three of them are orphans (or as good as orphans), desperately in need of care. And all three find sympathetic relations who offer them support and a home *outside school* (though always closely connected with it).

Mélanie Lucas's slightly different story is also worthy of note. When she meets the Maynards, she is *not* an orphan and does not need a new home. But she does have a problem: she feels displaced, having been wrenched from her old school. To achieve happiness she must accept the idea of a new one. The discovery that her aunt was an Old Girl of the Chalet School helps her to do this.

Commenting on the relationship, Irma von Rothenfels says:

"But now ... at least we know that Mélanie has every right to be a Chalet School girl."

A Future Chalet School Girl, p200

This statement reflects the Chalet books' new emphasis on blood relationships. In the early days, though unrelated to any of its members, Gillian Linton's right to the care of her future school was undisputed. Now it seems that Mélanie's familial connection gives her a *greater* claim on the school. As with Nina, Ruey and Adrienne, Mélanie's discovery of 'real' kin is of primary importance: it increases her sense of security.

There is an undeniable spate of 'long lost relative' plots in EBD's late books. It might be tempting to suggest that this trend points to a shift in attitude towards the family. Ruey's thoughts on the importance of blood relations are illuminating:

> She loved Joey and Jack with all the strength of her heart, but she knew that even their goodness was not quite the same as the goodness of her own family could be to her. There was no blood-tie between them and though she could never have explained it to anyone, not even herself, she felt the difference.
>
> *Joey and Co. in Tirol*, p210

Superficially, these ideas seem rather at variance with the experience of girls in the early books. Juliet would hardly have credited her own family with giving her *any* goodness: she received all her benefits from the Bettanys. Yet she might very well have agreed with Ruey in principle. Her adoptive family worked well because it reproduced the goodness that a real family *should* provide. In an ideal world, loving blood relations offer a person innumerable advantages. That EBD appreciated this fact is clear from the beginning of the Chalet series: it is illustrated by her portrayal of the relationship between Madge and Joey. Perhaps all that changes in the Swiss books is that EBD begins to focus on the idea of blood relations rather than adoptive ones and to use it as a plot device to create definitive 'happy endings'.

Quite what motivated this shift in focus is debatable. Perhaps it was slightly easier to write convincingly of girls forming deep and satisfying familial relationships without blood ties when the series had just begun: when the school and the family community were smaller and more closely integrated; in an era when children's stories in general were more sentimental. The overall idealistic tone of the early stories may have carried enough happiness to do away with the need for long lost relatives; but, despite variations, EBD's family ethos remains the same. Blood-ties or no blood-ties, what is important is that lonely girls should be made to feel at home; that they should be loved. This is admirably demonstrated in *Two Sams*.

The story of Samaris Davies and Samantha van der Byl begins with both girls feeling rather out of place in the school. Neither can be classed as a *very* vulnerable person; they are not orphans and enjoy good relationships with their parents. But both have been uprooted from their homes: Samaris's family has moved to Innsbruck; Samantha's is constantly travelling. Both are therefore in need of stability. They belong to the category of girl who needs a second home—and, in traditional fashion, the Chalet School soon provides that. On their very first evening, the two girls are welcomed into a hospitable society, share a meal and an evening's community dancing, in scenes which are familiar, warm and homely.

As the story progresses, the Sams become firm friends. Their friendship, we are told, is atypical: it ignores the discrepancies in their ages and forms (Juliet, Joey and Robin were not the same age either, but EBD appears to have forgotten that!). It is also so strong that, when cold shouldered by a few of their fellows, the two girls do not turn to some longstanding member of the school for comfort, but to each other.

EBD wants us to notice the curious nature of the Sams' mutual attraction. She mentions it several times and her final chapters provide an explanation. It transpires that there is a very good reason why the girls should like each other—they are 'long lost relations'. Once again in a Swiss book, EBD suggests that a blood-tie is a matter of overwhelming significance. Samantha says:

> "I guess if you're blood kin it makes all that much difference."

p222

Perhaps: it certainly makes a difference in this tale. Importantly, however, the plot of *Two Sams* does not abandon the other, 'older' type of relationship—the purely adoptive one. Unusually vulnerable (at this stage in the series), Joey has grave concerns about small Philippa's health. She is comforted by two friends, ladies whom her children have known since they were babies and whom they address as 'Aunt': Miss Annersley and Matey. Joey's scene with Miss Annersley is as tender and intimate as any family encounter:

> Joey dashed her hand across her eyes while Hilda brought her cloak and wrapped her in it. Joey kissed her.
> "I—I feel a little better. Thanks, Hilda; you always do me good."

p207

The Maynards' trouble over Philippa incidentally fosters one of *Two Sams'* most intriguing plot developments—one which has nothing to do with blood kin. Normally new girls receive comfort and advice at Freudesheim. In this story Samaris is asked back into their home to help Phil. In a reversal of roles, Joey and her daughter are comforted by the new girl. She—and her *alter ego*, Samantha—have evidently imbibed the ethos of the school. Caring and considerate and swift to identify with their new community, they are already totally at home—true Chalet girls.

Helen Barber

THE CHALET SCHOOL SERIES: AN INTRODUCTION

In 1925 W & R Chambers Ltd published *The School at the Chalet*, the first title in Elinor Brent-Dyer's Chalet School series. Forty-five years later, in 1970, the same company published the final title in the series, *Prefects of the Chalet School*. It was published posthumously, EBD (as she is known to her fans) having signed the contract three days before she died. During those 45 years Elinor wrote around 60 Chalet School titles, the School moved from the Austrian Tirol to Guernsey, England, Wales and finally Switzerland, a fan club flourished, and the books began to appear in an abridged paperback format.

How Many Chalet School Titles Are There?

Numbering the Chalet School titles is not as easy as it might appear. The back of the Chambers dustwrapper of *Prefects of the Chalet School* offers a simple list of titles, numbered 1–58. However, no 31, *Tom Tackles the Chalet School*, was published out of sequence (see below), and there were five 'extra' titles, of which one, *The Chalet School and Rosalie*, follows just after *Tom* in the series chronology. In addition, there was a long 'short' story, *The Mystery at the Chalet School*, which comes just before *Tom*. Helen McClelland, EBD's biographer, helpfully devised the system of re-numbering these titles 19a, 19b and 19c (see list on pp28–30).

Further complications apply when looking at the paperbacks. In a number of cases, Armada split the original hardbacks into two when publishing them in paperback, and this meant that the paperbacks are numbered 1–62. In addition, *The Mystery at the Chalet School* was only ever published in paperback with *The Chalet School and Rosalie* but should be numbered 21a in this sequence (see list on pp31–33).

Girls Gone By are following the numbering system of the original hardbacks. All titles will eventually be republished, but not all will be in print at the same time.

Apart from *The Chalet School and Rosalie*, Chambers published four other 'extra' titles: *The Chalet Book for Girls*, *The Second Chalet Book for Girls*, *The Third Chalet Book for Girls* and *The Chalet Girls' Cookbook*. *The Chalet Book for Girls* included *The Mystery at the Chalet School* as well as three other Chalet School short stories, one non-Chalet story by EBD, and four articles. *The Second Chalet Book for Girls* included the first half of *Tom Tackles the Chalet School*, together with two Chalet School short stories, one other story by EBD, seven articles (including the start of what was to become *The Chalet Girls' Cookbook*) and a rather didactic photographic article called *Beth's Diary*, which featured Beth Chester going to Devon and Cornwall. *The Third Chalet Book for Girls* included the second half of *Tom Tackles the Chalet School* (called *Tom Plays the Game*) as well as two Chalet School short stories, three other stories by EBD and three articles. (Clearly the dustwrapper was printed before the book, since the back flap lists three stories and two articles which are not in the book.) It is likely that *The Chalet School and Rosalie* was intended to be the long story for a fourth *Book for Girls*, but since no more were published this title eventually appeared in 1951 in paperback (very unusual for the time). The back cover of *The Second Chalet Book for Girls* lists *The First Junior Chalet Book* as hopefully being published 'next year'; this never materialised. *The Chalet Girls' Cookbook* is not merely a collection of recipes but also contains a very loose story about Joey, Simone, Marie and Frieda just after they have left the School. While not all of these Chalet stories add crucial information to the series, many of them do, and they are certainly worth collecting. All the *Books for Girls* are difficult to obtain on the second-hand market, but most of the stories were reprinted in two books compiled by Helen McClelland, *Elinor M. Brent-Dyer's Chalet School* and *The Chalet School Companion*, both now out of print but not too difficult to obtain second-hand. Girls Gone By have now published all EBD's known short stories, from these and other sources, in a single volume.

The Locations of the Chalet School Books

The Chalet School started its life in Briesau am Tiernsee in the Austrian Tyrol (Pertisau am Achensee in real life). After Germany signed the Anschluss with Austria in 1938, it would have been impossible to keep even a fictional school in Austria. As a result, EBD wrote *The Chalet School in Exile*, during which, following an encounter with some Nazis, several of the girls, including Joey Bettany, were forced to flee Austria, and the School was also forced to leave. Unfortunately, Elinor chose to move the School to Guernsey—the book was published just as Germany invaded the Channel Islands. The next book, *The Chalet School Goes to It*, saw the School moving again, this time to a village near Armiford—Hereford in real life. Here the School remained for the duration of the war, and indeed when the next move came, in *The Chalet School and the Island*, it was for reasons of plot. The island concerned was off the south-west coast of Wales, and is fictional, although generally agreed by Chalet School fans to be a combination of various islands including Caldey Island, St Margaret's Isle, Skokholm, Ramsey Island and Grassholm, with Caldey Island being the most likely contender if a single island has to be picked. Elinor had long wanted to move the School back to Austria, but the political situation there in the 1950s forbade such a move, so she did the next best thing and moved it to Switzerland, firstly by establishing a finishing branch in *The Chalet School in the Oberland*, and secondly by relocating the

THE CHALET SCHOOL SERIES: AN INTRODUCTION

School itself in *The Chalet School and Barbara*. The exact location is subject to much debate, but it seems likely that it is somewhere near Wengen in the Bernese Oberland. Here the School was to remain for the rest of its fictional life, and here it still is today for its many aficionados.

The Chalet Club 1959–69
In 1959 Chambers and Elinor Brent-Dyer started a club for lovers of the Chalet books, beginning with 33 members. When the club closed in 1969, after Elinor's death, there were around 4,000 members worldwide. Twice-yearly News Letters were produced, written by Elinor herself, and the information in these adds fascinating, if sometimes conflicting, detail to the series. In 1997 Friends of the Chalet School, one of the two fan clubs existing today, republished the News Letters in facsimile book format. Girls Gone By Publishers produced a new edition in 2004.

The Publication of the Chalet School Series in Armada Paperback
On 1 May 1967, Armada, the children's paperback division of what was then William Collins, Sons & Co Ltd, published the first four Chalet School paperbacks. This momentous news was covered in issue Number Sixteen of the Chalet Club News Letter, which also appeared in May 1967. In her editorial, Elinor Brent-Dyer said: 'Prepare for a BIG piece of news. The Chalet Books, slightly abridged, are being reissued in the Armada series. The first four come out in May, and two of them are *The School at the Chalet* and *Jo of the Chalet School*. So watch the windows of the booksellers if you want to add them to your collection. They will be issued at the usual Armada price, which should bring them within the reach of all of you. I hope you like the new jackets. Myself, I think them charming, especially *The School at the*

Chalet.' On the back page of the News Letter there was an advertisement for the books, which reproduced the covers of the first four titles.

The words 'slightly abridged' were a huge understatement, and over the years Chalet fans have made frequent complaints about the fact that the paperbacks are abridged, about some of the covers, and about the fact that the books were published in a most extraordinary order, with the whole series never available in paperback at any one time. It has to be said, however, that were it not for the paperbacks interest in the Chalet series would, in the main, be confined to those who had bought or borrowed the hardbacks prior to their demise in the early 1970s, and Chalet fans would mostly be at least 40 and over in age. The paperbacks have sold hundreds of thousands of copies over the years, and those that are not in print (the vast majority) are still to be found on the second-hand market (through charity shops and jumble sales as well as dealers). They may be cut (and sometimes disgracefully so), but enough of the story is there to fascinate new readers, and we should be grateful that they were published at all. Had they not been, it is most unlikely that two Chalet clubs would now be flourishing and that Girls Gone By Publishers would be able to republish the series in this new, unabridged, format.

Clarissa Cridland

ELINOR M BRENT-DYER: A BRIEF BIOGRAPHY

EBD was born Gladys Eleanor May Dyer in South Shields on 6 April 1894, the only daughter of Eleanor (Nelly) Watson Rutherford and Charles Morris Brent Dyer. Her father had been married before and had a son, Charles Arnold, who was never to live with his father and stepmother. This caused some friction between Elinor's parents, and her father left home when she was three and her younger brother, Henzell, was two. Her father eventually went to live with another woman by whom he had a third son, Morris. Elinor's parents lived in a respectable lower-middle-class area, and the family covered up the departure of her father by saying that her mother had 'lost' her husband.

In 1912 Henzell died of cerebro-spinal fever, another event which was covered up. Friends of Elinor's who knew her after his death were unaware that she had had a brother. Death from illness was, of course, common at this time, and Elinor's familiarity with this is reflected in her books, which abound with motherless heroines.

Elinor was educated privately in South Shields, and returned there to teach after she had been to the City of Leeds Training College. In the early 1920s she adopted the name Elinor Mary Brent-Dyer. She was interested in the theatre, and her first book, *Gerry Goes to School*, published in 1922, was written for the child actress Hazel Bainbridge—mother of the actress Kate O'Mara. In the mid 1920s she also taught at St Helen's, Northwood, Middlesex, at Moreton House School, Dunstable, Bedfordshire, and in Fareham near Portsmouth. She was a keen musician and a practising Christian, converting to Roman Catholicism in 1930, a major step in those days.

In the early 1920s Elinor spent a holiday in the Austrian Tyrol at Pertisau am Achensee, which she was to use so successfully as the first location in the Chalet School series. (Many of the locations in her books were real places.) In 1933 she moved with her mother and stepfather to Hereford, travelling daily to Peterchurch as a governess. After her stepfather died in November 1937 she started her own school in Hereford, The Margaret Roper, which ran from 1938 until 1948. Unlike the Chalet School it was not a huge success and probably would not have survived had it not been for the Second World War. From 1948 Elinor devoted all her time to writing. Her mother died in 1957, and in 1964 Elinor moved to Redhill, Surrey, where she died on 20 September 1969.

Clarissa Cridland

PUBLISHING HISTORY

Two Sams at the Chalet School was first published in 1967, with a dustwrapper and black-and-white frontispiece by D[orothy] Brook. The hardback was not reprinted.

A single paperback edition of *Two Sams* was published in 1993, at £2.99, with a cover illustration (right) by Gwyneth Jones.

Text

For this GGBP edition we have used the text of the original hardback edition, which contained a number of errors, typesetting and otherwise. The second appendix details how these errors have been dealt with.

Adrianne Fitzpatrick

COMPLETE NUMERICAL LIST OF TITLES IN THE CHALET SCHOOL SERIES

(Chambers and Girls Gone By)
Dates in parentheses refer to the original publication dates

1. *The School at the Chalet* (1925)
2. *Jo of the Chalet School* (1926)
3. *The Princess of the Chalet School* (1927)
4. *The Head Girl of the Chalet School* (1928)
5. *The Rivals of the Chalet School* (1929)
6. *Eustacia Goes to the Chalet School* (1930)
7. *The Chalet School and Jo* (1931)
8. *The Chalet Girls in Camp* (1932)
9. *The Exploits of the Chalet Girls* (1933)
10. *The Chalet School and the Lintons* (1934) (published in Armada paperback in two volumes—*The Chalet School and the Lintons* and *A Rebel at the Chalet School*)
11. *The New House at the Chalet School* (1935)
12. *Jo Returns to the Chalet School* (1936)
13. *The New Chalet School* (1938) (published in Armada paperback in two volumes—*The New Chalet School* and *A United Chalet School*)
14. *The Chalet School in Exile* (1940)
15. *The Chalet School Goes to It* (1941) (published in Armada paperback as *The Chalet School at War*)
16. *The Highland Twins at the Chalet School* (1942)
17. *Lavender Laughs in the Chalet School* (1943) (published in Armada paperback as *Lavender Leigh at the Chalet School*)
18. *Gay From China at the Chalet School* (1944) (published in Armada paperback as *Gay Lambert at the Chalet School*)

19.   *Jo to the Rescue* (1945)
19a. *The Mystery at the Chalet School* (1947) (published in *The Chalet Book for Girls*)
19b. *Tom Tackles the Chalet School* (published in *The Second Chalet Book for Girls*, 1948, and *The Third Chalet Book for Girls*, 1949, and then as a single volume in 1955)
19c. *The Chalet School and Rosalie* (1951) (published as a paperback)
20.   *Three Go to the Chalet School* (1949)
21.   *The Chalet School and the Island* (1950)
22.   *Peggy of the Chalet School* (1950)
23.   *Carola Storms the Chalet School* (1951)
24.   *The Wrong Chalet School* (1952)
25.   *Shocks for the Chalet School* (1952)
26.   *The Chalet School in the Oberland* (1952)
27.   *Bride Leads the Chalet School* (1953)
28.   *Changes for the Chalet School* (1953)
29.   *Joey Goes to the Oberland* (1954)
30.   *The Chalet School and Barbara* (1954)
31.   (see 19b)
32.   *The Chalet School Does It Again* (1955)
33.   *A Chalet Girl from Kenya* (1955)
34.   *Mary-Lou of the Chalet School* (1956)
35.   *A Genius at the Chalet School* (1956) (published in Armada paperback in two volumes—*A Genius at the Chalet School* and *Chalet School Fête*)
36.   *A Problem for the Chalet School* (1956)
37.   *The New Mistress at the Chalet School* (1957)
38.   *Excitements at the Chalet School* (1957)
39.   *The Coming of Age of the Chalet School* (1958)
40.   *The Chalet School and Richenda* (1958)
41.   *Trials for the Chalet School* (1958)

42. *Theodora and the Chalet School* (1959)
43. *Joey and Co. in Tirol* (1960)
44. *Ruey Richardson—Chaletian* (1960) (published in Armada paperback as *Ruey Richardson at the Chalet School*)
45. *A Leader in the Chalet School* (1961)
46. *The Chalet School Wins the Trick* (1961)
47. *A Future Chalet School Girl* (1962)
48. *The Feud in the Chalet School* (1962)
49. *The Chalet School Triplets* (1963)
50. *The Chalet School Reunion* (1963)
51. *Jane and the Chalet School* (1964)
52. *Redheads at the Chalet School* (1964)
53. *Adrienne and the Chalet School* (1965)
54. *Summer Term at the Chalet School* (1965)
55. *Challenge for the Chalet School* (1966)
56. *Two Sams at the Chalet School* (1967)
57. *Althea Joins the Chalet School* (1969)
58. *Prefects of the Chalet School* (1970)

Extras

The Chalet Book for Girls (1947)
The Second Chalet Book for Girls (1948)
The Third Chalet Book for Girls (1949)
The Chalet Girls' Cookbook (1953)

COMPLETE NUMERICAL LIST OF TITLES IN THE CHALET SCHOOL SERIES
(Armada/Collins)

1. *The School at the Chalet*
2. *Jo of the Chalet School*
3. *The Princess of the Chalet School*
4. *The Head Girl of the Chalet School*
5. *(The) Rivals of the Chalet School*
6. *Eustacia Goes to the Chalet School*
7. *The Chalet School and Jo*
8. *The Chalet Girls in Camp*
9. *The Exploits of the Chalet Girls*
10. *The Chalet School and the Lintons*
11. *A Rebel at the Chalet School*
12. *The New House at the Chalet School*
13. *Jo Returns to the Chalet School*
14. *The New Chalet School*
15. *A United Chalet School*
16. *The Chalet School in Exile*
17. *The Chalet School at War*
18. *The Highland Twins at the Chalet School*
19. *Lavender Leigh at the Chalet School*
20. *Gay Lambert at the Chalet School*
21. *Jo to the Rescue*
21a. *The Mystery at the Chalet School* (published only in the same volume as 23)
22. *Tom Tackles the Chalet School*
23. *The Chalet School and Rosalie*
24. *Three Go to the Chalet School*
25. *The Chalet School and the Island*

NEW CHALET SCHOOL TITLES

In the last few years several authors have written books which either fill in terms in the Chalet School canon about which Elinor did not write or carry on the story. These are as follows:

The Chalet School Christmas Story Book edited by Ruth Jolly and Adrianne Fitzpatrick—featuring short stories by Helen Barber, Katherine Bruce, Caroline German, Heather Paisley and more (Girls Gone By Publishers 2007)

The Bettanys of Taverton High by Helen Barber—set immediately before *The School at the Chalet School* (Girls Gone By Publishers 2008)

Juliet of the Chalet School by Caroline German—set in the gap between *Jo of the Chalet School* and *The Princess of the Chalet School* (Girls Gone By Publishers 2006; out of print)

Visitors for the Chalet School by Helen McClelland—set between *The Princess of the Chalet School* and *The Head Girl of the Chalet School* (Bettany Press 1995; Collins edition 2000)

Gillian of the Chalet School by Carol Allan—set between *The New Chalet School* and *The Chalet School in Exile* (Girls Gone By Publishers 2001; reprinted 2006; out of print)

The Chalet School and Robin by Caroline German—set after *The Chalet School Goes to It* (Girls Gone By Publishers 2003; out of print)

A Chalet School Headmistress by Helen Barber—set during the same term as *The Mystery at the Chalet School* (Girls Gone By Publishers 2004; out of print)

Peace Comes to the Chalet School by Katherine Bruce—set in the gap between *The Chalet School and Rosalie* and *Three Go to the Chalet School*; the action takes place during the summer term of 1945 (Girls Gone By Publishers 2005; out of print)

New Beginnings at the Chalet School by Heather Paisley—set three years after *Prefects of the Chalet School* (Friends of the Chalet School 1999; Girls Gone By Publishers 2002; reprinted 2006; out of print)

FURTHER READING

Behind the Chalet School by Helen McClelland (essential)*

Elinor M. Brent-Dyer's Chalet School by Helen McClelland. Out of print

The Chalet School Companion by Helen McClelland*

A World of Girls by Rosemary Auchmuty*

A World of Women by Rosemary Auchmuty*

*Available from:
Bettany Press, 8 Kildare Road, London E16 4AD, UK
(http://users.netmatters.co.uk/ju90/ordering.htm)

TWO SAMS AT THE CHALET SCHOOL

ELINOR M. BRENT-DYER

CONTENTS

Chapter I

FIRST NIGHT

SAMARIS stood shyly to one side as the school took up its position in long lines across the wide entrance hall of the Chalet School. She was new that term and, so far as she could see, the only new girl. How simply ghastly!

"If only I could have travelled with the rest it would have been *something*!" she thought miserably.

Unfortunately, it hadn't been possible. She had been with her parents in Innsbruck where her father had a post as British representative of a big manufacturing firm. That had meant flying to Lausanne with him when he made one of his periodic trips to England. She had been met at the airport by the wife of the Swiss representative of the firm and put on the train for Interlaken. There she had been taken in charge by a young mistress who was quite pleasant but who, she could see, regarded her as something of a nuisance for having to be met specially. Miss Smith had whisked her off to a pâtisserie where she had been treated to coffee and cakes before they made their way to the Ostbahn whence started the mountain railway up to the Görnetz Platz where the school stood. Arrived at the school, they had found that the big coaches which brought the girls from Basle, by way of the road through the mountains, were just arriving, and Miss Smith had time only to take Samaris into the entrance hall and tell her to stand to one side on the stairs for the moment. Someone would tell her what to do later. Then the mistress had hurried off and her charge stood wondering how long she must remain there.

A moment later and she was no longer alone, for a tall girl, whose russet-brown hair was drawn up into a long, curling ponytail, came up, bringing with her another girl who was clearly older than Samaris and who was looking almost as scared as the younger girl felt.

"You're new, too," said the eldest girl with a vivid smile. "What is your name?"

"Samaris Davies," Samaris gasped.

The big girl's eyebrows rose and she laughed. "Not really? Well, here is Samantha van der Byl—only she's not Dutch but American. Just stand here for a moment, you two, and I'll try to find out where you ought to be— Oh, no! There isn't time now. Never mind! Stay here and I'll fetch you when our welcome is over. You'll be all right here." She flashed another smile at them and departed, leaving the two new girls looking at each other doubtfully.

Samantha was the first to speak. "I guess we're a bit of a bother, coming like this," she said in a pleasant voice only faintly tinged by an American accent. "I know, for a friend of Mama's told her, that the school don't like new girls this term. It couldn't be helped in my case. I've two small sisters at home and they started with mumps two days before I was due to fly to Switzerland last September, so that spoilt me for coming then. Ermina began it and Manela followed on three weeks later. By the time she was well again and it was plain I wasn't going to get mumps, it was past half-term and not worth the long journey. So here I am—a term late."

"Oh!" said Samaris. "Well, Mam didn't want me to speak anything but German—we're living in Innsbruck and I went to school there—and someone told her about the Chalet School at Christmas, so they sent me."

A bell tinkled at that moment and the buzz of laughter and

chatter which had been going on all round the hall ceased at once. Samaris and Samantha followed suit and stopped talking as a tall, graceful woman suddenly appeared on the great flight of stairs that swept down to the hall. She paused halfway down and smiled at the assembled school before she spoke.

"Welcome back, everyone! Had good holidays?"

An enthusiastic assent rose from everyone and she laughed. "Excellent! I hope this means that you're going to make it a good term." She paused as the girls joined in her laughter. Then she went on in the lovely voice that Samaris, at least, had already noted. "Now I know that many of you must be tired after your long journey and all of you are hungry—at least, I hope so. Karen has made her usual special effort for Abendessen and she will be very hurt if you don't appreciate it!—so I won't keep you any longer. Any news I have for you will keep till after Prayers tomorrow morning. School—turn! Lead on, Len!"

As one girl, the school swung round while one of the mistresses, seated at the big grand piano standing to one side of the hall, struck up a brisk march. The big girl who had brought Samantha led off, though when she reached the entrance to one of the corridors which ran off the main hall, she stopped and the rest marched on smartly, followed by the mistresses who had all been gathered at the foot of the stairs. When the Head had gone, Len came swiftly across the hall and smiled at the two new girls.

"Now I can see to you. I've spoken to Miss Dene who is our secretary and she tells me that you are in Inter V, Samantha. Samaris, you are to be in Upper IVb. Come along and I'll take you to your several splasheries."

"Splasheries?" the pair demanded in startled tones.

"Yes; we don't call them cloakrooms, you see. Samantha, you're in Senior school; you're a Senior Middle, Samaris." She stopped to laugh. "How odd that you should both have names beginning with 'Sam'! But they're very pretty, I can see my mother being all over them." She laughed again, while the pair wondered why Len's mother should be pleased with their names. "No matter! I'll explain later. Down here, and here you are, Samantha," as she paused before an open door. "Wait outside, Samaris, will you, splasheries aren't vast apartments and a pack of girls milling around doesn't make it easier."

She vanished, Samantha following and Samaris was left to stand on one leg and wonder how she was going to manage here. One thing wasn't too bad. Fräulein Hamel, her mother's friend had said that the school spoke German and French as well as English. After eighteen months in Innsbruck, Samaris could chatter in German freely enough though her French was still rather a shaky affair. Still, with two languages more or less on the end of her tongue she had decided that things shouldn't be too bad. As she waited for Len to return, she wondered what Samantha would do.

Len was gone only a minute or two. Then she came back and tucked a hand through the younger girl's arm. "Come along, Samaris! This way and down this corridor. Here we are!" And she pulled Samaris into a long, narrow room with pegs on the two side walls and two peg-stands running down the middle. At the bottom the wall was lined with shoe-lockers. Under the windows at the other end were six toilet basins. A crowd of girls, mainly of Samaris's own age, were milling about, hanging up coats and berets, changing shoes for house-slippers, or crowding round the basins to wash faces and hands.

Len looked round and singled out a sturdy girl with a bush of brown hair cut in a short straight bob and dark eyes twinkling merrily in a round, freckled face.

"Robina!" she called. "Robina McQueen!"

Robina turned, hurriedly pushed her way through a cluster of people near the door and came up with a beaming smile.

"Oh, Len! Nice to see you! Did you have decent hols? And how is Phil?"

"Hols were tops," Len returned, "and young Phil is going ahead. But I haven't time to talk now. Look, Robina, this is Samaris Davies, a new girl. Sheepdog her, will you?" She turned to Samaris as Robina nodded. "You'll be all right now. Robina will look after you for the present." Then, with a nod, she hurried away, leaving Samaris to look questioningly at Robina. What on earth did Len mean by "sheepdog her"? It had a queer sound.

She was not long left in doubt. Robina grabbed her arm. "Come on—Samaris, did Len say? I say! That's a new one on me! But never mind now. There isn't a minute to spare. The gong will be going in a sec." She raised her voice. "Any spare pegs, anyone? One with S. Davies under it. Next to you, Mathilde? Good! Come on, Samaris!"

Still clutching Samaris's arm, she wriggled her way through the mob, most of whom looked up to get a glimpse of the new girl. When they had reached the far end of the room where an unmistakably French girl was standing beckoning, Robina heaved a deep sigh.

"Here we are. This is your peg, Samaris. Hang up your coat and beret on the pegs. Shove your gloves and scarf into the bag. Then come on and we'll find your shoe-locker. Hurry up!"

Thus adjured, Samaris pulled off her coat and beret, tucked gloves and scarf into the bright blue bag hanging from the lower hook of the peg, and then followed Robina to the lockers, into one of which she was bidden to put her shoes when she had changed into house-slippers.

"You've got your nightcase, of course, with your slippers?" Robina asked.

Samaris shook her head. "I—I left it in the hall," she faltered.

"Oh, gosh! Whatever did you do that for?" Robina exclaimed.

"Oh, well, you're new so no one will say anything and you can change later. What about your hair? Want to borrow my comb?"

"I've got one—in my coat pocket," Samaris gasped. She was feeling breathless with all this rush.

"We'll get it. Come on back to the pegs."

Samaris was hustled back to her peg where Mathilde was putting the finishing touches to her own neat coiffure. Robina regarded the new girl's crop of short thick curls as the latter found her comb and grinned.

"Aren't you lucky! Curls never look so untidy as straight hair."

Samaris raked the comb through the said curls, put the comb into her bag and faced her mentor. "Will I do?"

Robina eyed her critically. "You look O.K. Come on! They're beginning to line up for the Speisesaal."

Meekly, Samaris went with her, though inwardly she was thinking that Robina resembled the Red Queen in *Alice*—she was perpetually telling you to come on. Robina pulled her into the line forming beside the door, pushing her into place between herself and a girl whose long flaxen hair hung in two plaits down her back. At the same moment there came a mellow booming which seemed to ring all round and at once the noise in the splashery ceased. Those girls who had still been fiddling with hair or towels gave it up and rushed to their places in the queue. A short, stout girl in glasses, obviously one of the Seniors, came to the door and said in German, "Ready? Then follow on, please. Lead the way, Agneta."

The girl at the head of the line instantly led off and the rest followed her. They went along the short corridor where the splashery was, turned up another much longer, and then into a narrow passage and through a big double door into a hall-like room. Long tables covered with gaily checked cloths and peasant chairs closely set on either side gave promise of a meal. Samaris felt she could do with it. She was really ravenous and the savoury odour coming through the hatches at one side of the room intensified her hunger. Then she found she was standing behind a chair about the middle of one of the tables. While she waited for the others to fill up she looked round to see if she could see Samantha. She must be there, but if so it was at a table behind her own. She gave it up and looked quickly to the top of the room where one table stood across, running from side to side of the low daïs there. Here, the mistresses were taking their places and she recognised Miss Smith as that young lady entered with a big, jolly-looking person and a much smaller one whose golden-brown head shone out under the lights.

She had no time to see more, for at that moment Miss Annersley came in. She was followed by a dark, vivacious little Frenchwoman and a tall, fair person who was smiling as she came. The Head took her place and struck a small bell before her place. At once all heads were bowed, the words of a brief Latin Grace rang out in that beautiful voice which Samaris had so admired in the entrance hall. Everybody said "Amen", and then they were pulling out their chairs and sitting down. The maids appeared, bearing trays laden with bowls of savoury soup and the meal began.

Soup was followed by slices of beef, cooked in a way that Samaris had never tasted before, with tiny potatoes and equally tiny carrots served in a rich gravy. Samaris enjoyed it. What she also liked was the fact that though the other girls seemed to have plenty to discuss, they tried to draw her in when they could and saw that all her wants were supplied.

"They're so *friendly*!" she said to herself. Then the girl on her other side who was addressed as "Sigrid" was offering her more potatoes and she had to stop thinking. Later, she was to learn that one of the strictest unwritten laws of the school was that new girls were to be made to feel welcome and one with the others as quickly as possible. Certainly by the time she had finished her sweet—a bunlike affair with a delicious sauce poured over it— she was beginning to feel that she was going to like being here.

Towards the end of the meal the bell rang again and Miss Annersley stood up.

"Just a moment, girls! You've arrived in such good time that we have nearly an hour before Prayers. After we finish, you may go to Hall and dance or play games. Prayers will be at 19.30 hours as usual on our first night. After Prayers everyone under Lower IV will go to bed. The three Senior Middle forms will go at 20.45 hours and the Seniors an hour later. Most of you have had a long, tiring journey and will be glad to be in bed once you are there. That is all for the moment. Finish your sweet now."

She sat down and everyone turned to finishing the sweet. When they had done and Grace had been said, the Staff headed by Miss Annersley left the room and the prefects took charge. Not that there was much need for them to tell anyone what to do. Service is as difficult in Switzerland as it is everywhere else and the girls were expected to help with clearing the tables after meals.

Robina directed Samaris to bring her table-napkin and place it in the drawer with the others from their table.

"And mind you see which is ours," she said. "Each table has its own drawer for cloth and napkins and then if you get any spills they're your own and not someone else's—see?"

Samaris saw. She also saw that the prefects were piling cutlery and dishes on the shelves of the big three-tiered trolleys to a height that made her wonder however anyone could wheel the trolleys to the hatches without upsetting a good half of what was on them. Then she saw Len Maynard pulling up sides of wire netting when her trolley was full and was so delighted that she spoke her thoughts aloud.

"Oh I say! What a nifty idea!"

Len overheard and gave her a smile of amusement. "We had to do something to prevent wholesale smashes," she said, while Samaris went red.

Robina, who had been busy collecting peppers and salts and putting them away in one of the upper cupboards of the big press whose drawers held the linen, came and slipped a hand under the new girl's arm.

"That's all. Come on! We're going to Hall for games and dancing. Be my partner for the first dance, will you?"

Samaris reddened again. "I'd love to, but I don't dance much."

"Oh well, we'll teach you. We all dance here. Come on!" And Robina hauled her off along more corridors and into a great room where already one of the mistresses was seated at the grand piano on the daïs at one end and was turning over a pile of music lying on a side-table.

Len, who seemed to be in charge, mounted the daïs and went to speak to her. Then she turned to the girls and said, "Take your partners for a polka."

"Come on!" Robina said. "You can polka, can't you?"

"I—yes," Samaris said. The music rang out and she was whirled away with much goodwill if less skill.

The polka was followed by a game of *Wallflowers* for the little ones. It was new to Samaris, but she quickly caught the idea and joined in as gaily as anyone. When it was over and they were all waiting for the next item to be announced, Sigrid, who had been near, gave the new girl a nod of approval. "You will do," she said.

The next was a country dance—*Jenny Pluck Pears*—and Samaris had to confess that she did not know it and would rather sit and watch.

"Oh, well, if you're sure," Robina said. She turned to a very

51

attractive girl seated next to them. "Be my partner for this, Guita?"

Guita nodded, and when the music brought most of the others on to the floor Robina and she caught hands and ran to make up a set near by.

Further along, Samantha, who knew no more about the dance than Samaris, saw her fellow-novice sitting alone and moved to join her.

"Been O.K.?" she asked. "I saw you dancing and playing in that ring game. Who's the girl who was partnering you?"

"Robina McQueen. She's sheepdogging me," Samaris said with a giggle.

"Say, what d'you mean by that?" Samantha asked curiously.

"Well, that's what they seem to call it. Giving me a hand and showing me the ropes, you know. Haven't you got someone to look after you until you know?"

Samantha nodded. "Yes; someone called Val Gardiner. She's over there—that girl with the red hair dancing with the tall dark girl. I was asked to join in, but I don't know the dance and I guess I've no fancy for making a fool of myself." Samantha chuckled comfortably. "I said I'd watch and maybe I could manage to do it another time."

"It looks rather jolly, doesn't it?" Samaris said. "I'd like to learn it."

"Don't you worry! I can see that they don't leave you to sit and mope on your own here; I guess we'll have to join in sooner or later."

"Yes; they're jolly matey," Samaris agreed.

The dance ended and at the same time a great bell boomed out overhead. At once the others were running to pull the long forms set round the sides of Hall into place across it. Robina came with the rest and promptly took charge of Samaris once more.

"Prayers now," she said. "Help me yank this form into place, will you?" She glanced at Samantha, but at that moment the red-headed Valerie arrived and took the elder girl off to join her own form.

"Who is she?" Robina asked curiously as she and Samaris helped by two or three others pulled the form into place. "Did you know her before you came? She's new, too, isn't she?"

"Never seen her until this evening," Samaris said. She giggled. "Yes; we're both new and, believe it or not, we've got names alike."

"You mean she's Samaris, too?" exclaimed one of the other girls, a gangling youngster named Brigit Ingram.

"Oh, not the *same* name," Samaris hastened to assure them. "I'm Samaris; *she* is Samantha!"

"Gosh!" they exclaimed as the bell rang again and they hurriedly sat down. Samaris had given them a sensation!

Chapter II

SETTLING DOWN

BOTH Samaris and Samantha fell asleep almost as soon as they lay down that night. Samaris took it for granted, but Samantha, rousing up early next morning, thought it over. At home she frequently lay awake reading till after midnight. Dropping off to sleep like this was something new in her experience.

"I guess I was tired to death," she mused as she lay comfortably snuggled under her blankets and the big plumeau which had kept her so cosy during the night. "Goodness knows it isn't like me! I hope it goes on. I hate lying awake in the dark, and it's my bet there'd be a fuss if I asked for a bedside lamp. Oh, well, I knew when Mama sent me here I'd have to put up with a lot I'm not used to. It'll come in time, maybe. I certainly do hope so." She yawned widely and turned over. A low whisper from one side of her startled her.

"Are you awake, Samantha? Quite warm and comfy? No; we can't talk—not until the bell goes. Don't forget you're second on our bath-list and be ready to fly the instant Jack Lambert gets back. No time to waste in the mornings here!" There was a low chuckle and instantly a sleepy voice from the far end of the dormitory said, "Who's that talking—you, Val? Pipe down, then. It's another quarter of an hour to bell-time."

Val grunted and silence fell again not to be broken until, from overhead, the big bell which had summoned them to Prayers the evening before pealed out loudly. Then came a chorus of groans from the other cubicles.

"Time to get up? It can't be!"

"Moi, je préfère à me reposer dans mon lit jusqu'à huit heures."

"Moi aussi."

"Stop chattering, all of you, and get up!" came from the upper end of the room. "Out, everyone! Show a leg—show a leg!"

There came a series of thuds and Samantha, not very sure what to do, hissed to Val, "What does she mean?"

The curtain was pulled back at the foot of her cubicle and Val Gardiner's red head and dancing, very blue eyes appeared. "Out of bed and shove a leg through between your curtains into the aisle," she said. "Buck up!"

Samantha slipped out of bed and went to stick out one leg between the gay, poppy-sprayed curtains. She giggled softly to herself as she visioned the picture, a series of pyjama'ed legs sticking out into the aisle.

"O.K.; get cracking, everyone!" ordered the voice, and Samantha drew in her leg and looked round, not very sure what to do. Her front curtains were parted and Valerie looked in again.

"Strip your bed as soon as you've collected your bath things," she directed. "Take all the clothes off and throw them over the chair—"

"The featherbed thing, too?" Samantha asked, startled.

"Of course! Hump your mattress up in the middle and buck up about it. Jack's gone already—and so have most of the first bathers." Valerie withdrew to attend to her own duties and Samantha, after pulling on dressing-gown and bedroom slippers, set to work to strip her bed. By the time she had finished, her curtains were pulled apart again and a slim, black-haired girl whom she had noticed the night before looked in to say briefly, "You're next on the list. Scram!" Valerie had pointed out to her charge the night before which bathroom and bath-cubicle she must use. Samantha grabbed her towels and sponge-bag and fled.

Val had also warned her that she might take her morning bath either cold or lukewarm and she must leave the bathroom as tidy as she found it. She shivered as she forced herself into the water for a hurried splash. Then she was out and towelling vigorously before scrambling into her pyjamas and collecting her belongings together after a scrub at her teeth. She glanced hurriedly round the place before she sped back to her dormitory. On the way she was stopped and recognised her fellow new girl who was making for the long narrow passage where the bathrooms were.

"Hello, Samaris!" she said.

"Hi!" said Samaris. "Isn't it a scrum?"

"It's worse than that," Samantha said. "You O.K.?"

Samaris nodded. "All right so far." Then she dashed off and Samantha made for her dormitory, where Valerie met her at the door.

"Samantha's back, José! Come on, Samantha!"

José Helston, an ornament of Vb, appeared with her towels slung round her neck and her sponge-bag dangling from one wrist as she frantically twisted up her long brown curls.

"Not a moment too soon!" she gasped as she fled.

Valerie chuckled. "Poor old José! She's a dawdler at best, so try not to keep her waiting, Samantha. Now you hang up your towels on their pegs and get dressed. Don't forget to hang up your dressing-gown and put your slippers on the rail below the bureau. Matron does the rounds as soon as we've gone down, and heaven help you if you've left your cubey in a mess!"

She vanished on the last word and Samantha did her best to obey instructions. Her hair was the worst problem. Long and waveless, it took some brushing and combing before she could begin on the heavy pigtail she wore during the day. Her fingers flew, but before she had finished, Valerie was with her again.

"Ready? Let's look at your bed. You haven't humped your mattress properly. You finish your hair and I'll do it for you. Like this—see? It has to be so that the air can pass under it as well as over it." She readjusted the mattress and nodded. "That's better. Hurry and finish! Lesley Anderson will be calling for prayers in a moment, but you'll be all right when you've finished your hair. What a mane you've got! Thank goodness mine's short!"

She finished on that and Samantha finished her pigtail, examined herself in her mirror and then looked round to make sure that her cubicle was in proper order.

The voice of the dormitory prefect rang out: "Prayers, everyone!"

There came the sound of girls kneeling down and Samantha followed suit.

"They seem to go a lot on prayers here," she thought as she buried her face in her hands. For a few minutes there was silence and Samantha, having repeated OUR FATHER, wondered what else she could say. She could think of nothing, so she remained kneeling until the sound of the bell seemed to bring everyone to their feet. She got up, wondering what to do next, then light footsteps sounded in the aisle and Lesley Anderson was beside her.

"Good morning, Samantha," she said briskly. "You managed all right? Yes; I thought Val Gardiner would see to you. She's a capable creature when she likes."

"Thanks for the flowers!" came from Valerie as she appeared with stunning suddenness from between the curtains. "I think I've seen to everything, Lesley."

"I see you have. Go and line up, you two. The second bell will ring in a moment and I must take a dekko at José, she's a born slowcoach." Lesley laughed and went off and Val, after pushing the window open and showing the new girl how to toss up her cubicle curtains over the rods which held them, drew Samantha off to join the line already forming by the door.

"Why do we do all that?" Samantha queried.

"Do all what? Oh, the curtains! To get the place properly aired. Are you cold?" for Samantha had shivered. "The air's nippy, I'll admit. What do you expect in January? There goes the bell! No more talking until we get downstairs."

Samantha smothered the question she had been about to ask and they marched out of the already chilling dormitory and down to what she had been told the night before was the Senior commonroom. As she went she caught sight of Samaris standing in line at the door of another dormitory and gave her a smile. The younger girl's face lit up, but she had evidently been warned about the silence rule for she made no attempt to speak. Further, she was not in the same commonroom and Samantha recalled that Len Maynard had told her that Samaris was only a Senior Middle.

"I'm sorry," Samantha thought. "I like that kid more than a little."

In the Senior Middle commonroom, Samaris was thinking along much the same lines.

"Weird!" she told herself. "Somehow I've taken a complete yen for Samantha. Wonder why? P'raps it's because we've both got the same name more or less and they're rum names however you look at them."

She got no further in her wondering. At that point Robina was saying, "Samaris, are you always Samaris or how do you shorten it?"

Samaris laughed. "They call me 'Sam' at home. Will they do it here? They didn't allow it at my last school—in Innsbruck. I was 'Samaris' all the time."

"Oh, the staff will call you that," Robina said easily, "just as they call me 'Robina'. Otherwise, I'm 'Bobbie'." She cocked her head on one side. "I like 'Sam'. We'll call you that out of school."

At the same time Meg Walton, a shining light of Inter V, was saying to Samantha, "Do you always use your full name or do they make 'Sammy' of it at home?"

"Either that or 'Sam' if they're in a hurry," Samantha said with a laugh.

"Like us to do the same?" asked Jack Lambert who was standing beside them.

"I guess so if you like," Samantha said, smiling. "I'll take it as real friendly of you. Will the teachers do it?" she added.

"Rather not," Valerie chimed in. "They don't allow nicknames in form and only a few shorts. For instance, Jack is really 'Jacynth' and Meg is 'Margaretta', but you couldn't always use a mouthful like that, could you? And as for Jack, well, *can* you imagine her as 'Jacynth'?"

Samantha looked at boyish Jack with her cropped black head and laughed again. "I guess not. But 'Jacynth' is a real pretty name though I don't know as I ever met it before."

Jack reddened. "I'm called after an aunt and it fits *her* all right, but it's too girly-girly for me. I'm 'Jack' and don't you forget it!"

"O.K.," Samantha said easily. "It suits you, as Valerie said." She changed the subject. "Say, I was told you speak in three languages here. How do you manage that?"

"Easily! French one day; German the next; English the next," said a very pretty girl from Vb whom the others called Anne. She was fair, with light-brown hair, blue eyes and a pink and white skin. She was very feminine. Later, when Samantha heard that she was Jack Lambert's elder sister, she could scarcely believe it, the two were so unlike. Later on she discovered that they were as unalike in character as in looks, for Jack was more than half-boy and Anne was all girl.

There was no time to say more just then for the gong sounded and they all hurried to form their lines and march to the Speisesaal, as the new girls had been informed it was called. Breakfast, known to the school as "Frühstück", was, so Samantha found, quite unlike what she usually had at home. There was no chilled fruit-juice to start with, but a big, bowl-like cup of milky coffee, a dish of porridge or other cereal, and bread twists with butter and honey. But the cereals were served with milk that was yellow with cream, and there was no stinting of twists, butter or honey. Samantha contrived to make a good meal though she missed her usual eggs and fruit.

After clearing the tables, they all hurried off to make their beds and dust their rooms which must be left in perfect order.

"What next?" Samantha demanded of Valerie who was finishing off her dusting.

"Walk, since it's a fine day," Valerie informed her. She went to the window which she had closed when they first came up, opened it again, and shook out her dusters. "Finished? Let me have a dekko. I'd better warn you now that Matron makes the rounds when Prayers are over and if your cubey isn't just so, she yanks you out of lessons to put it right and no one loves you."

Samantha laughed. "I think it's quite O.K., but take a peek. I should hate to be called out of class to tidy up here. I guess the teachers would have a lot to say."

"They would—they do! And while I think of it, we don't call 'em teachers here, but mistresses or staff. Don't know why, but it just is so."

"I'll remember if I can. Way back home we always called them teachers—not that I've had much of school these last five years. My father is always on the move and he likes to take Mama and me with him."

"What fun!" said a leggy, brown-eyed girl whose cubicle was on the other side of Valerie's. "Oh, I like school all right, but it must be fabulous to keep moving about and seeing all sorts of other countries."

"Maybe; but you get tired of it after a time. I'm glad to be settled for the next two or three years. Papa"—she pronounced it "pappa"—"will likely be in Switzerland for the next year and when he leaves I'm to be left here. I can always fly to wherever he and Mama may be."

"Ready, you folk?" Lesley called. "Then downstairs and be quick about it. We want as long a walk as possible."

The entire dormitory hurried, even the dawdling José. Presently they were all outside, clad in big coats, berets, enormous scarves and nailed boots.

"Does the whole school go together?" Samantha asked Valerie who was partnering her.

"Goodness, no! Usually the two Sixths make one croc with Va. We go with Vb and the Middles make another two crocs— Senior and Junior Middles—and the Juniors do the same. The prees—prefects, I mean—split up among the different crocs and either one or two of the mistresses act as escort, too."

At this point, two or three of the elder girls arrived to join their ranks and a pleasant-looking mistress came a minute or so later.

"Are you all here?" she asked. "Yes? Then lead on, Janice and Adrienne. Across the playing-fields and out of the back gate and then round by the road to the big gates. That's as much as you've time for today."

Janice and Adrienne, two important members of Vb, led the long line and they set off at a smart pace along a narrow path which ran through a shrubbery and came out at a gate to the playing-fields at present covered with snow frozen to an iron hardness. The paths had been heavily sanded and their nailed boots gave them a grip on the otherwise slippery surface. In addition, every girl carried an iron-spiked alpenstock to help her to keep from slipping. Samantha had spent a winter in northern France and after the first few minutes she ceased to watch her step and joined in Valerie's gay chatter. That young woman was renowned in the school for having a tongue that wagged at both ends. Furthermore, this was the first time she had been trusted to "sheepdog" a new girl and she felt very responsible. By the time they had finished the round Samantha was glowing from the swift movement through the sharp air and was also feeling completely muddled by all the information her partner tried to cram into her. They met the Senior Middles' crocodile at the big gates and the two Sams were able to exchange smiles as they tramped up the short drive. At the great door they parted company, the Middles going round to the right-hand side of the house and the others turning left.

"Why don't we all go round together?" Samantha inquired.

Valerie grinned. "Gosh! What a scrum it would make! There are over fifty of us and about as many of them. Is that other new girl a relation of yours, by the way? You have names fairly alike and I saw you grinning at each other."

"Not so far as I know. We came together and I like her. She seems good fun."

"Oh, I just wondered. She's Samaris and you're Samantha and though I like both names they aren't exactly ordinary."

"I'm called after my grandmother—Mama's mother. I don't know where Samaris got hers. But we certainly aren't any kin to each other."

By this time they had reached the side-door and talking had

to stop. They hung up their coats and berets, changed back into house-shoes and then, after hastily tidying themselves, marched off to Inter V formroom. Valerie dashed for a certain desk, pulling Samantha down into the next one.

"Done it!" she said with a smirk. "I wanted us to sit together so that I could keep an eye on you when you wanted it. But you'll soon know all about it. Prayers come next and then we have token lessons so that the staff can set us prep in their subjects for next week. In between, we go for unpacking."

"How? What do you mean?"

Brown-eyed Celia Everett from their dormitory who was seated on the other side gave a giggle. "Poor you! Has Val been pouring information into you? I wonder you aren't *exhausted*!"

A small, very lovely girl whom the rest addressed as "Wanda" and who was sitting behind Valerie, leaned forward. "But it is simple, Samantha. As soon as Prayers are over the Sixth Forms go up to the trunkroom where all our trunks are put and unpack. When they have finished, the next batch goes, and so it continues until all are finished. Das ist richtig, nicht?" she smiled at Valerie.

"You've said it. That's the way it's managed," Valerie assented. "If you are slow in unpacking and putting things away and miss anything, you get the prep from one of us. They take us in alphabetical order, you see, and only twenty or so at a time, so that no formroom is completely empty all the time."

Jean Abbot, the form prefect came up, holding out a slim book. "Here's a hymn-book, Samantha. Stick your name in it when you get your labels and keep it."

She had no time to say more, for the bell rang and everyone sat up properly, Jean scuttering hurriedly back to her own desk. There came the sound of quick, springy footsteps outside, the door opened, and the mistress who had been in charge of their walk arrived. The girls rose and Jack Lambert who was nearest the door closed it. Miss Moore walked briskly up to the small platform on which stood the mistress's chair and table, seated herself and gestured to them to sit down.

"Sit down, girls. The register won't be ready till Monday, so we can't take it this morning. Has anyone seen that our new girl, Samantha, has a hymn-book?" She smiled at Samantha.

"I gave one to her just now, Miss Moore," Jean said.

"Good! Now, girls, I know this is the first full day of term and rules are not yet in full working order; but you know what we always say. You *may* use your own languages, but it's wiser to use the language of the day to get you into working order. How many of you have remembered?"

A stifled giggle arose and Miss Moore laughed sympathetically. "I see. Well, try to remember. It really is much the best way. Samantha, this is German day. Do you speak any German at all?"

"Very little indeed," Samantha said promptly.

"Ah, well, you'll soon learn. Has anyone explained to you how we do it here?"

"Yes, Miss Moore. Valerie told me—some, anyhow."

"Right! Then do your best to pick it up. If you want to know any words or phrases, ask someone. Everyone will be ready to help you. Valerie must take you to Miss Denny who teaches German here and she'll give you lists of words to learn. Don't be too worried about it. You'll soon find you can get along if you try." She flashed a friendly smile at Samantha. "What about French?"

"Oh, I speak French," Samantha replied. "I had a French nurse when I was little and Mama has a French maid."

"That will be a great help. There goes the bell! Girls—stand! Line up at the door! Lead on, Barbara!"

The girls lined up and then headed by the form prefect, one

Barbara Hewlett, marched off to Prayers. About half went to Hall, but Samantha saw quite a number branching off at the end of the long corridor to vanish down another passage. She wondered about it, but there was little time for talk, for almost as they took their seats on one of the long forms running from side to side of Hall a mistress seated at the piano began to play and even the low murmuring which had been filling the room died down.

Chapter III

NEWS FROM NINA RUTHERFORD

PRAYERS were taken seriously here, the two Sams discovered. Once they were over, the girls in Hall sat back and almost immediately came the steady tramp of marching feet and all the Catholic girls and mistresses came in to take their places among the rest. Later, the girls discovered that this was the rule of the school and very rarely did they have Prayers together.

When they were all sitting quietly, the Head rose from the big chair in which she had been seated, chatting softly to the sundry members of the staff. She came forward to the big lectern and stood behind it, smiling down on the upturned faces of the girls.

"I'm very glad to be with you once more, girls," she said in the deep, beautiful voice which was one of her greatest assets. "I can't begin to tell you how much I missed you all last term, even though I enjoyed my journeys about the various countries and their schools. I've come back with quite a number of new ideas, some of which I'll discuss with you later on in the term. At present, we will continue in our old way. Meantime, I have several bits of news for you. For one thing, there is a new school opening down by Lake Thun in Thun itself. The Head is an old acquaintance of mine and she hopes that as soon as her school is settled—next term, you'll be pleased to hear—it will be possible for us to arrange for matches with them. Her girls play netball, hockey and tennis. She hopes to begin cricket when the school starts."

She paused a moment and the girls applauded. She laughed. "Yes; I thought that would please you all. Furthermore, she proposes that we should arrange for a gym contest at either the end of next term or the term following. She tells me her girls are very keen—yes, Len?" for Len had risen from her seat.

"I just wondered how big the school is," the Head Girl said.

"Well, nothing like as large as we are. There are eighty or so girls, ranging between the ages of fourteen and eighteen. You will be glad to know that I've already proposed that during the winter months they should come up here twice a week for ski-ing and tobogganing."

A quick outburst of clapping greeted this. Evidently the school was delighted at the idea. Valerie muttered to Samantha, "That's O.K. We can do with a spot more competition." Then she stopped, for Miss Moore had seen and was glaring at her.

The Head continued serenely, "St Mildred's are hoping to give their annual pantomime this term. I understand they want to borrow a good many of our Juniors to act as elves, fairies, imps and so on." She smiled down on the small fry, who beamed back at her but managed to restrain themselves from further demonstration. "Lastly, I wonder how many of you remember Nina Rutherford?"

A forest of hands waved in the air at this. It was only four years since Nina had left school at the age of seventeen to give all her time to her music. She had been at the Vienna Conservatoire since then, but the previous year she had begun on her longed-for career and already she was making a name for herself not only by her piano-playing but by her compositions. She had a long way to go before she would reach the full strength of her powers, but she had made a good beginning and the school was very proud of her.

As it happened, Samantha had not heard of her. Samaris not only knew her by name but had also attended two recitals she had given in Innsbruck. She was thrilled to learn that the young pianist she had so much admired had actually been a Chalet School girl herself.

Marie Huber of VIa, who was also very keen and intended to teach when her training was ended, looked up eagerly and caught Miss Annersley's eye. "Oh, is Nina coming to give us a recital here?" she asked in her native German.

The Head laughed. "I wish I could say yes, Marie. Unfortunately, Nina is off on a tour of Canada, Australia and New Zealand next week. That will occupy her time fully for the next year or so, so we must wait for that, Marie. No; the reason I asked you is that Nina wants to do something for her school. She tells me she was very happy here and now that she is of age and has control of her own money, one of her first ideas was to endow a prize to be awarded annually. She is also endowing a scholarship to be competed for by musical girls but, as she says, while for her and others like her music is the be-all and end-all of life, she learnt at school that it isn't so for the majority and she wanted to give us something that would appeal to everyone. She offers a prize of £20 annually to be spent by the winner on books dealing with her own—the winner's—special subject. The competition will take the form of an essay on *My Life and what I Hope to do with It*. It will be open to all girls except the Juniors. Age will be taken into account by the judges, so you younger girls will have an equal chance with the Seniors. Essays are to be written in your own free time and must be handed in a fortnight before the end of term. The music scholarship will be open to girls in their last term at school. It will be for £100 annually for three years. Nina realises, as she was told when she first came to school, that a good general education is of the utmost importance for everyone. She seems to have thought it all out very thoroughly," the Head added. "The scholarship will be awarded to the girl who has made the most of her musical opportunities here. It will be competed for every three years and you will know by half-term during the summer term who has won it."

There was a pause. Then black-headed Ted Grantley stood up. "Miss Annersley, may we know who is to judge—for both things, I mean?"

"The music staff here will decide on the scholarship," Miss Annersley said. "As for the essays, they will be judged by Mrs Maynard, Dr Benson and myself. In the event of any difficulty in deciding on the winner of that prize, we shall call in a stranger to decide. And now, girls," she went on in a different tone, "I think that will be all for the present. I've given you a good deal to discuss and time is flying. We ought to be in our formroom or unpacking." She glanced across at the piano where Miss Lawrence, head of the music staff, was seated.

Miss Lawrence at once swung round on the piano-stool and struck a chord. The girls came to their feet on a word, turned, and led by the tinies, marched out of Hall to their various formrooms where they hurriedly took their seats and began to discuss all the latest news as hard as they could go until the mistresses should arrive.

Samantha listened to what the rest of Inter V had to say, but made no comment until Valerie turned to her to ask, "What do you think about it, Sammy?"

"Which do you mean?" Samantha asked. "If it's the music, it won't affect me. I'm not musical though I like a good tune. If it's the essay, I guess that's going to take some thinking about. I can't say I've ever given much thought to what I want to do with my life. Travel around and have a good time and marry later on, maybe."

"Glorianna! Is that all? How dull!" exclaimed tomboy Valerie.

"It's what happens to most girls," Samantha said.

"Oh, not to me!" Jack Lambert cried. "I mean to go in for

motor engineering when I leave school. Some day I mean to have my own garage."

Wanda von Eschenau laughed. "How like you, Jack! For me," she said in her prettily accented English, "I must work, of course. My parents are not rich and there are five of us. I should like to be an air hostess. But later I should wish to marry. I would not like to be an old maid."

Samantha laughed. "I guess there's not much danger of that for *you*," she said with an admiring look at lovely Wanda. "You'll be having them chasing you in rows before you're much older."

Wanda went pink. "But how horrid!" she said in her own language. "I should not like that at all, so I hope you are wrong, Sammy."

"Cavē!" hissed Arda Peik who sat near the door. "Miss Moore's coming!"

Everyone stopped talking and straightened up in her seat while Arda held the door open and Miss Moore entered. She gave them a sympathetic smile. "Well, all agog about Nina's prize?" she asked. "I hope everyone here means to enter for it. I should like my form to send in 100 per cent. essays. It's an easy subject, too. You must all have some idea of what you *hope* to make of your lives."

"Isn't that the same as what we *want* to make of them?" Barbara Hewlett asked. "Or is it?" she added as she saw the expression on the mistress's face.

Miss Moore sat down on the edge of her table. "Not quite," she said.

"But what's the difference?" Jack Lambert asked in startled tones.

"What you *want* may be far beyond what you are likely to get," Miss Moore said seriously. "For instance, some of you may *want* to become famous artists or writers or musicians. That will depend on whether you have the requisite gifts for such things. Again, it might not be possible for you to obtain the necessary training. What you want can depend on a number of things."

"Then what about what we hope?" asked Emilie Gabrielli, a Swiss girl who was the daughter of a well-known Advokat or barrister. "Must that also depend on circumstances?"

"Not necessarily. Wanting and wishing frequently lead one into extremes. Hope depends very much on what you yourselves are. Think it out!" She nodded and then turned to other things. "Now for work. This term we are doing Australasia in detail. I have your synthetic maps here, so come and get them, Jean, and give them out—"

She got no further. There came a sudden crash outside, followed by a loud explosion and the girls jumped to their feet.

"There's something wrong!" Valerie exclaimed.

"Car collision!" Jack added knowledgeably. "Oh, gosh!"

Miss Moore had run to the window. "You're right, I think, Jack. Now don't go rushing off all of you. You'll be more nuisance than help. Yes; there goes Gaudenz with the big fire-extinguisher!" She glanced back at the imploring faces of her pupils and laughed. "You may come and see, but you won't see much. The hedge hides most of it—and Gaudenz is evidently coping with the fire. I only hope no one is badly hurt!"

The girls thronged to the windows but found that she was right. All they could see were columns of black smoke and occasional flames. But it was evident that people were rushing to the rescue, for they could hear the sound of many voices.

"Oh, I *must* go and see what's happened!" Jack ejaculated, making for the door.

Miss Moore acted at once. She bounded forward and caught Jack's arm in time to stop that young woman from hurtling out to the scene of the accident. "Stop, Jack! Did you hear me say you were to stay here? Go back to your seat at once!"

Jack went. After all, obedience was reckoned as one of the major virtues at the Chalet School. When Miss Moore spoke to you in that tone, you did as she told you or woe betide you! But Miss Jack looked very glum as she sat down. So did the others when Miss Moore ordered them back to their seats. But though she deprived them of the excitement of watching she had enough sympathy with them to send Celia Everett along to the office to ask Miss Dene, the school secretary, for any news there might be. At the same time she remembered thankfully that all the Junior and Middle School formrooms were at the back of the building. They must have heard the explosion, but they could see nothing.

Other people had also seen nothing for at that moment Ted Grantley appeared to ask that the first batch from Inter V might go to the trunkroom to unpack.

Miss Moore looked round. "Jean Abbot to Celia Everett, go for unpacking," she said. "Oh, you've unpacked already, Celia. That's the best of living up here. You, too, Valerie. Then you are the last, Emilie. Hurry up, girls! Matron doesn't like to be kept waiting, you know."

They did know. They also knew that people who did keep Matron waiting were liable to get the rough edge of her tongue and the girl who had no objections to that had still to become a Chaletian. The twelve people called jumped to their feet and hurried from the room, Samantha among them.

They raced upstairs to the top of the house where, in a long, narrow attic room, the trunks were waiting. So was Matey, as everyone called Matron, head of that side of the school and, to quote Val Pertwee of Upper IVb, a terror to snakes. With her were the six senior prefects, each of whom seized two of the newcomers and marched them off to their trunks.

"Keys—where are your keys?" demanded the prefect in charge

of Samantha and a French girl, Michelle Cabràn. "Unlock your trunks and give me your inventories and quickly, please! There isn't a moment to waste!"

She spoke with a certain imperiousness that made Samantha open her eyes, but Michelle was hurriedly kneeling down to unlock her trunk and pull out the printed list attached to the inside of the lid, so the new girl felt she had better do likewise.

Meanwhile, a plump Dutch girl, Renata van Buren, was speaking to her own prefect. "Oh Con, did you hear that awful crash?—yes; I've got it open; here's the inventory!—Jack said it was a motor smash."

Con, slim, dark, and extremely good-looking, was startled. "I can't say I did. What crash!"

"A terrific one just a few minutes ago. There must have been a fire for Miss Moore saw Gaudenz go tearing down to the road with one of the big fire-extinguishers." Jean Abbot, at work next door to them, had chipped in. "Oh, I do hope nobody was badly hurt!"

"Oh, so do I!" Con was all sympathy at once. She turned to glance at Matey, who was demanding with some point to be told why Sarah Akerman had elected to pack her shoes in the tray of her trunk on top of her frocks.

"Can't you ask Matey?" Jean urged in an undertone. "She's sure to know something. Oh, do go on, Con!"

Before Con could do anything about it, the door opened and Miss Dene appeared. "Matron here? Oh, thank heaven! You're wanted at once, please. A car accident, just outside our gates. One car skidded into another and both overturned. Three people are hurt, at least two of them badly we fear. We've rung for a doctor, but in the meantime there are cuts and bruises and burns and shock to deal with and it's a case of all hands to the rescue. The girls will be all right with Len and Co. Len, take charge, please!" as Matron sped off. "You know what to do. Finish with these girls, send them back to their formrooms and have up the next set. No girl may leave the building. I must go. I shall be needed in the office for telephoning." She left the room hurriedly and Len proceeded to take charge.

"You've all heard what's happened. There isn't much *we* can do to help at the moment except get on with our jobs without fuss. Sarah, take those boots and shoes off your trunk tray and begin to load your carrier. The rest of you get on with unpacking. Now, Angela!" and she turned back to Angela Carton with whom she had been dealing.

It meant an effort for the girls were dying to know more. For instance, who was so badly hurt? How had it happened and were the unfortunates anyone they knew? But no further news came to them and the prefects had worked through a good half of the unpacking before the school was sent for to go to Hall. By that time, it was nearly time for Break and both the Sams had met several of the mistresses who, like the prefects, had realised that the best help they could offer was to go on with the usual first-morning jobs and keep the girls as fully occupied as possible.

"Now we shall hear something *at last*!" Valerie murmured to Samantha as they left their formroom and marched off to Hall. "The Head's bound to tell us *something* or she wouldn't have sent for us. Oh, I do hope it's no one we know!"

But her hope was belied. When they were all seated Miss Annersley came to stand on the daïs and break to them the news that the occupants of one of the cars had been Nina Rutherford, her cousin Lady Rutherford who had been driving, and her own eldest girl, Alix, as well as one of the twins who had followed Alix—Anthea. Lady Rutherford was slightly burned and suffering from bruises and cuts. Alix had bad bruises and a sprained wrist and Anthea was also cut and bruised; but Nina had struck her head on a stone and it was feared her skull was fractured. She and her two elder cousins had all been taken to the Sanatorium which stood at the further end of the Görnetz Platz. So had the driver of the other car, a young American who had been caught by his steering wheel and injured internally.

"Is it—is it very bad?" Len asked fearfully. "And what's become of Anthea? Is she here?"

"Need you ask? Your mother has taken charge of her for the present," Miss Annersley said. "She has also rung up Brettingham Park, the Rutherfords' home, and Sir Guy is coming out as fast as possible. Lady Rutherford was in a good deal of pain, though the doctors have seen to that with alleviating drugs. Alix is suffering from severe shock, but should soon recover. But Nina— no one can say how things will go with her yet. Pray for them all, girls, and especially for Nina. That is all we can do for the present. And now you had better have your elevenses. As it's such a fine day, you will all go for a walk after that, so change into your outdoor clothes as soon as you leave the Speisesaal."

She gave the signal and they left Hall for the Speisesaal for biscuits and hot milk or chocolate as they chose. They were too shocked by the news to do much talking just then. They were sorry enough for Lady Rutherford and the two girls, but Nina had been one of them not so long ago and this sudden ending, for the present, to all the bright future everyone thought lay before her horrified all but the younger ones, who did not yet understand just what that accident might mean.

Chapter IV

SAMANTHA HELPS

DECIDING that it would be as well to give the elder girls something else to think about, Miss Wilmot, who was in charge at the moment, had, for once, mixed up the walks well and truly. Only the Juniors went off by themselves as usual. For the rest, Seniors were sent off with Middles. Vb were paired with Upper IVa and Inter V were told to take Upper IVb.

"Choose your own walks," the maths mistress said, "and remember that you elder girls are directly responsible for your juniors. Seniors, stop any gossip about the accident if you can. Dr Maynard will let us know how Nina and the others are going on as soon as possible and there's nothing we can do for the present except, as Miss Annersley said, pray for them all—especially Nina. Now lead off, Solange and Jane. Inter V, you and your gang follow them. Don't do too much yelling, any of you."

The two leaders of Vb set off and the rest followed in a long tail, chattering together in subdued tones. Samantha and Samaris were together. They had met outside in the path where they lined up, and Samantha scurrying forth had been stopped by a light touch on her arm. Turning round, she saw Samaris looking up at her pleadingly.

"Please, Sammy, may I be your partner?"

"O.K. I guess you can," Samantha said. She smiled down into the dark eyes. "Not scared, are you? Your crowd are decent to you?"

"Very decent; but—well, it's this ghastly accident. I don't really know Nina Rutherford, of course, but I've heard her play and she's marvellous. Somehow—well—well I know you better than the others and I'd—I'd like to be with you," Samaris blurted out.

Privately, Samantha thought that apart from the fact that their names were somewhat alike and they had had those few words at the very beginning they didn't really know each other at all. But she was quick to understand that Samaris might feel a more personal interest in the young pianist than the rest of her form and the names did form a link if a slender one.

"I'd try not to fuss yourself," she said kindly. "I guess Nina What's-her-name will be O.K. I was talking to Val Gardiner just before we came out and she says some of the surgeons at the Görnetz San are simply wizards!"

"Oh, I know. What's bothering me is supposing this means she can't go on with her music."

"Why ever not? It isn't as if she'd hurt her arms or her hands."

"No; but she's given her head a complete crasher and couldn't that upset things—her brain, I mean?"

"I don't see why it should. Oh, I guess it'll be quite some time before she can play again, and that tour we heard about will definitely be off for the time being. But she'll practise as soon as she can and come up again. Cheer up, Sam! They can do wonderful things nowadays."

There was no time for more. Miss Ferrars, who was acting as escort, came up that moment and called to them to straighten their lines before she marched them through the shrubbery and across the snowbound plain of the playing-fields. The ground was hard as iron with a deep frost, and slippery as glass, but they all wore heavily nailed boots and carried alpenstocks so, though there was a certain amount of sliding, it was not so bad as it might have been.

With an eye to Samaris's feelings Samantha bore her off from the others as soon as she could. At first they talked very little. Samantha was not sure how to deal with Samaris and Samaris was still thinking too much about Nina Rutherford's accident to want to chatter. But once they were across the fields and had passed through the back gate on to what, in summer, was rough pasture, the younger girl heaved a deep sigh and looked up at her elder.

"It does seem a frantic shame!" she said.

"I know it does, but you chewing it over and over won't make it any better. Snap out of it, Sam!" Samantha said bluntly. "Anyway, I don't see why you feel about it as you obviously do. Nina Rutherford can't be anything to you—not really."

Sam sighed. "I expect it seems mad to you, but in a queer way she is. I just love her playing. She—she seems to make the piano *talk*. I'd never loved it much until I heard her and now I'd give a lot to be able to play like that. And then she was *here*—as a schoolgirl, I mean. That makes her belong to the school. And—and—oh, I don't know. I just feel awful about it."

Samantha glanced at her. "It's partly the shock it's been that makes you feel like that. Anyway, she wasn't the only one hurt. I guess that aunt or whatever she is who was driving is pretty bad. Miss Annersley said she was in such bad pain they gave her drugs. And there was the man in the other car. I guess he's real badly hurt if it's internal injuries, and there were those two girls as well."

Samaris nodded. "That's what the Head said; but they're only cut and bruised. One of them hasn't even gone to the San. Didn't the Head say she'd gone to Mrs Maynard—whoever she is. Len's mam, I know."

Samantha had heard a good deal about Mrs Maynard from her form-mates. "She is the school's very first pupil," she said impressively, thankful for a change of subject. "Val Gardiner—that red-headed girl over there with Solange de Chaumontel and Celia Everett—told me that the school was started by her sister in Tirol. She's the one they call 'Madame'. Actually, she's Lady Russell, I believe."

"Which is she?" Samaris asked. "I don't think I've seen her."

"She isn't at the school, honey. Val says she's with her husband in Australia now though they're expecting her back any day. She should have come last term, but she has twin boys—just small kids—and they decided to let them finish the term in their Australian school. And then it's the hot-weather season there and I guess no one would want to come straight from that sort of heat to the weather we have here. So they're waiting until the spring begins—March or sometime."

Samaris shivered. "March isn't much fun in England as a rule. It can be as cold as Christmas—colder, in fact." She went back to the accident. "I wonder how it happened?"

"What—the accident? Goodness knows! My guess is that someone skidded and barged into someone else. I'd say it would be real easy for that to happen with the ground like this."

"Finding it slippery?" asked a sympathising voice behind them. "But you're wearing nailed boots and you've got your alpenstocks. I can't say I've noticed either of you sliding about much."

They turned to see one of the Vb girls coming behind them with two others. It was the central one of the trio who had spoken and she was smiling at them. She had a most attractive smile.

"You're all right, aren't you?" she said. "By the way, I do know you're both Sams—Samantha and Samaris. Which is which?"

Samantha laughed. "I'm Samantha van der Byl and this is Samaris Davies. We're no kin to each other though our names are quite a lot alike, if that's what you want to know."

"I'll bet my Auntie Joey leaps on both names with howls of joy when she hears them."

"Why on earth?" Samantha asked involuntarily.

"She writes books, you know, and she's always on the look-out for unusual names. By the way, I'm Ailie—Aline Russell. These two are Solange de Chaumontel and Janice Chester."

Samaris looked eagerly at her. "Are you any relation to Madame—the Lady Russell who started the school?" she asked.

Ailie nodded, her grey eyes dancing in her small attractive face. "Got it in one! That's Mummy! How did you guess?"

"Girls! Keep away from the trees!" came a warning voice, and Miss Ferrars came hurrying up to draw them away from under the heavily laden pine branches under which they had been walking. "Ailie and Janice," she said reproachfully, "*you* ought to know better. Some of those boughs are very heavy and if one broke off and came down on you it would give you a nasty knock. We've quite trouble enough on our hands with Nina and the others without you adding to it!"

"Oh, goodness, I'm sorry, Miss Ferrars. I didn't think of it," Ailie said apologetically. Then she added eagerly, "Have you heard any more about them?"

"Now is it likely considering I came out when you did? I've met no one from the San and any news will go straight to School. By the way, where are the rest of your crowd?"

"Somewheres behind," Samantha replied.

Miss Ferrars frowned. "Not 'somewheres', Samantha. We don't say that in English. It's 'somewhere' without the S."

Samantha blushed. "I guess I'm real American at times, Miss Ferrars. It don't really matter, surely? Some day I'll be going home and then I want to talk like other folks."

Miss Ferrars laughed. "It all depends on where you live. I

know that in Boston, for instance, the English is as pure as anywhere in England itself. It's more the accent and intonation that differ. Yes, Samantha. I think it does matter that you should speak correctly. Do your best with it, anyhow. Remember, both of you, that one reason for your being here is that you may learn to speak all of our three languages properly. And while I remember, try to keep with the others. You girls aren't supposed to wander off by yourselves just now, as you two, Ailie and Janice, very well know." She finished with a smiling nod and went back to act as whipper-in to another group which had strayed away from the main body.

Samantha frowned and then laughed as Janice and Ailie ran off ahead of herself and Samaris. "I guess she's right. But it's a mite surprising to be hauled up for using your own language. I didn't know I did speak American until these last few days, anyway." She glanced at Samaris. "Do me a favour, Sam. Stop me if I get too bad. Papa and Mama are real keen on me speaking nicely."

"Well, that's one thing you do say nicely," Samaris said bluntly.

"What thing?" Samantha raised her eyebrows.

"You don't say 'Poppa' and 'Momma'; you say 'Pappa' and 'Mamma' and it sounds *much* better." Then she added somewhat irrelevantly, "The Maynards say 'Papah' and 'Mammah' and that's how they're usually called in England I believe. Mostly, though, the girls I knew at my English school said 'Mummy' or 'Mum and Dad'. I'm Welsh, so I've always called my mother 'Mam', but it's more or less the same thing."

By this time they had reached the others and Samantha was claimed by Val Gardiner and Celia Everett while Samaris was collected up by the bunch which was led mainly by Robina McQueen, Val Pertwee, and a French girl, Marie Angeot. They were walking across the road side of the playing-fields and Robina

81

waved a mittened paw towards a deep dip in the ground not far away.

"That," she told Samaris, "was made by a landslide last summer."

"Not really?" Samaris was duly impressed. "What a size it must be! Even after all the snow we've had it's quite a pit, isn't it? How did it happen?"

"Rain, mainly," said Rosemary Wilson who was close behind them. "There was a spring there, too, though no one knew anything about it. D'you know Erica Standish in Upper IVa—that girl with the long fair hair like *Alice in Wonderland*? Well," as Samaris nodded, "she fell into it and they had to rescue her. She'd hurt her foot and couldn't do much by herself. She was walking along there when the earth gave a heave and fell in. That was how it happened."

"And is it a pond now?" Samaris asked eagerly.

Rosemary shook her head. "No fear! It was only a tiny spring and they concreted it up though I *believe* that at first they did think of making a swimming-pool of it. Then they didn't—*I* don't know why—but they had it plastered up with concrete and filled it in. It's odd it still makes such a hole, isn't it?"

Miss Ferrars, who was again at hand, overheard and joined in. "That was the earth settling, Rosemary. It takes time, you see. They'll have to fill it up again when the snow has gone in order to level the ground. In fact, I shouldn't be surprised if it needed doing two or three times. Meanwhile, you girls get all the swimming that's good for you when we go down to Lake Thun in the summer. You couldn't hope to use an outdoor swimming-pool this weather."

"No-o; I suppose not," Rosemary agreed. "But we might have been able to skate on it."

"We might! On the other hand the water might have caused

more landslides and we don't want to lose any more of our playing-fields. It's best as it is."

"I see." But Rosemary looked dissatisfied.

Miss Ferrars laughed again and glanced at her watch. "Time to turn, girls!" she called; and the long files turned and plodded back to school.

It was not until they were walking through the shrubbery dividing the playing-fields from the garden that Samaris saw Samantha again. Then, as they reached the garden gate, they formed into pairs again. The path through the shrubbery was too narrow for more than two to walk abreast with any ease and they must arrive at the school in proper order.

Samaris claimed her new friend with a shy smile and Samantha returned it.

"Enjoyed yourself?" she queried.

"Oh, yes; but I do hope there's better news of Nina Rutherford waiting for us," Samaris said earnestly.

"Well, don't worry if there isn't. No news is good news, you know. I guess they'll tell us as soon as there's anything to tell," Samantha said comfortingly. "They were saying that she's had a hard crack on the head. I guess once she comes round she'll be O.K."

They had reached the side-door here and had to part, but Samaris felt happier for the elder girl's words. Even when the Head, in reply to a question from Len Maynard, could only tell them at Mittagessen that so far there was no more news from the Sanatorium, the younger girl managed to feel fairly happy.

News, in fact, did not come till early next day when, Prayers ended, Miss Annersley told them that Nina had had an operation, was still unconscious, but it was hoped she would do well though it must be a long time before she was fit again. As for Lady Rutherford, her burns were giving her pain, but she was going on satisfactorily. As for Alix and Anthea, no one was really anxious about them. Wisely, the Head said as little as possible about the driver of the other car. He had been very seriously injured and was lying between life and death at the present moment. All the school was told was that he was very ill and no one could say how things were likely to go with him.

The girls accepted this. After all, he was a total stranger to them; but Nina and Anthea were Old Chaletians, and though Alix had never been at the school, quite a number of the Seniors had got to know her while she was a patient at the Görnetz Sanatorium three or four years ago, and they tended to reckon her as one of their own. Three days passed and they heard that Nina was still unconscious though all her cousins were doing well. By that time, school was in full swing and though the elder girls inquired about the young American, their juniors had almost forgotten him, which was as well. The surgeons at the Sanatorium had operated on him, but even then there was no good news of him and he was in the gravest danger.

"More I cannot tell you at the moment," Miss Annersley said. "Meantime, girls, pray for him. It is all we can do and the best we can do. And now we must give our attention to school matters. Don't forget that this is German day and rules are in full swing. That is all for the moment. School—stand! Turn! Forward—march!"

Miss Lawrence, head of the music staff, struck a chord and, to the music of an inspiriting march, the school swung off out of Hall, form by form, ready to start on the day's work.

Chapter V

A New Friend for the Sams

"Hi, Samantha!"

Samantha, walking across the commonroom to choose a book from the shelves, pulled up and stared at the doorway, where Margot Maynard, the Games prefect, was standing.

"You want me?" she queried.

"You and the other Sam," Margot said, coming in briskly. "I've a message for you two from my mother. She wants you and Samaris to go to English tea tomorrow."

It was the second Saturday of term and there was no hope of going out. A heavy mist veiled everything. The girls had had their usual early-morning programme of prep, mending, and letter-writing. Normally, they would either have gone for a walk or had games, but no one was going to send girls out into that sort of fog. The Seniors were congregated in their commonroom, reading, playing table games, or otherwise amusing themselves. Samantha, brought up short, stared at the tall, strikingly handsome girl who was by the door. She knew now that there were three Maynard prefects—triplets; that Len, the Head Girl, was someone to apply to if you were in difficulties; that Con, the second of the trio, was conscientious enough about her duties, but that her real interests lay in the way of writing and she was unusually gifted; that Margot, youngest of the three, was Head of the games and that she was not only regarded as the best-looking, but was, in many ways, the most forceful by reason of her determination and her temper. She was tall, with red-gold hair curling all over her head, brilliant blue eyes, and the sort of complexion to be found in beauty advertisements. Len was a general favourite and people had a deep respect for Con's gifts; but Margot, though she could be fascinating when she chose, was very much a problem. You never knew when her hasty temper would flash out, and then, beware! She had a tongue that could cut like a knife.

The other girls had informed Samantha that Mrs Maynard, who lived next door to the school in a house called Freudesheim, was the school's earliest pupil and still in many ways remained a Chalet girl. The triplets were the first of a long family of eleven, but in spite of that Mrs Maynard was also a writer who managed to produce at least two books a year, published under her maiden name of Josephine Bettany. Thanks to her wandering life, Samantha had never come across any of them until she came to the school. Then Meg Walton had insisted on her borrowing an historical novel, *Swords for the King!* and the new girl had been thrilled by it.

"Do you really mean it?" Samantha asked doubtfully.

"Of course I do. Mother always has the new girls to tea on the first Sunday of term that she can manage. She couldn't do it last Sunday. She was too busy with our youngest, Phil. You do know that Phil has had polio and is just getting better, don't you?" Margot said, coming to join Samantha. "Poor mite! She's had a bad time for she had to have a mastoid operation only the Easter before. We nearly lost her in the summer, but she's pulling up now, thank goodness! Only she has off-days and then Mother is completely tied up with her. However, she seems to be on the upgrade again, so you two are to go to tea. Go and ask the Head if you may. It'll be O.K., but it's good manners to ask. Now I must find young Samaris. Upper Middles, isn't she? Good! I'll get her. Don't forget to ask the Head, Samantha." She nodded and left the room.

"Lucky you!" Jack Lambert exclaimed. "Tea at Freudesheim is worth having!"

"Freudesheim? Oh, that's the Maynards' house, isn't it?"

"It is. You know the name means 'Happy Home', don't you? Freude means happiness," Jack said. "Mrs Maynard says that she wants us all to look on it as a happy home for us as well as for them. You'll have a *stupendous* time!"

Samantha looked puzzled. "As how?"

Half a dozen voices answered her.

"Oh, it's such a lovely place to begin with!"

"Tante Joey ist eine treue Herzensfreude!"

"*What?*" Samantha exclaimed above the chorus.

Wanda von Eschenau blushed. "I mean she is a real darling. Say him, Samantha, and that is another German word for you."

Samantha laughed, but she repeated the phrase four or five times before she attended to Jean Abbott who told her, "There are three babies and they are all sweet."

"Cecil is scarcely a baby," Barbara Hewlett said. "She's six in April. The twins will be three in June. But you'll see them all tomorrow."

"They sound real cunning," Samantha said.

"What you *will* like is Bruno," Celia Everett added.

"Bruno? Who's he?"

"Mrs Maynard's St Bernard. He's a pet!"

Samantha looked alarmed. "Oh, but I'm not real crazy on dogs—not *big* dogs."

"Not?" exclaimed Celia who *was* literally crazy about all dogs and had fully made up her mind to become a kennel maid when she left school.

"I guess I'm just not. I've not had much to do with them, anyway. You can't take dogs around with you when you're always on the move."

"You'll like Bruno," the girls assured her. "No one could help it."

Samantha looked sceptical but said no more. Instead, she went to choose her book and the chatter ceased.

Samaris, on the other hand, received the news joyfully. She loved dogs and had caught a glimpse of big Bruno during one of the early-morning walks when Mrs Maynard had been giving the gentleman his early-morning run. She had wished aloud then that she could speak to him, but morning walks at the school were fairly formal affairs and you might not break ranks for any but a very good reason. Going to speak to a dog could hardly count as that.

On the Sunday afternoon Len arrived to collect her mother's guests.

"I'm coming with you," she explained. "Wrap up well, Samaris. It's bitterly cold! One thing; we always have a roaring fire in the salon at this time of year. Mamma said she must have *one* open fireplace, so it's in the salon and we burn logs there. Oh, we've central heating, too, of course, but we wouldn't be without our fire in the winter for a good deal."

She led them out of the side-door, but instead of turning to go round to the front and down the drive, she took them along a path which had a shrubbery on one side and a low brick wall on the other. Beneath lay a garden with rose bushes swathed in straw and sacking and looking like huddled old women. Len waved her hand towards it.

"Our sunken garden," she said. "We made it ourselves and though it looks a desert now it's a picture in summer when all the flowers are out and the fountain—there in the middle, Samantha— is playing. Turn up here and through this gate. Welcome to Freudesheim, both of you!"

They climbed a little sloping path, bordered by low bushes,

and came out above a second sunken garden. To one side of it stood the house, once a pension, but now a real home. The Maynards occupied the central part and one of the wings. The other wing was, as Len explained to the two, the home of a friend of her mother's, Dr Eustacia Benson.

"You won't see her today," she said as they turned the corner and went along a terrace across the front of the house to the far side where what appeared to be two steps leading up to the front door. "She's in England for a few weeks."

The top step was sheltered by a deep porch with a steeply-pitched roof and sides made of half-logs, banded closely together. Len opened the door and ushered in the guests, remarking that when the snow had gone they would find that there were six steps up, but at present they were buried.

"Here we are!" she said, tossing off her coat and cap. "Drop your coats, etcetera, on that chest and change your shoes. I expect we'll find the family in the salon. Anna and the Coadjutor have Sundays free from Mittagessen onwards, so the babies will be with Mamma. Ready? Then come along and meet her!"

They went along a wide hall with a highly polished floor that made Samaris yearn for a good slide. At the far end was a big double door. Len opened it and the glow of blazing logs welcomed them. A tall, slim woman appeared and held out both hands in a warm welcome.

"The two Sams!" she cried in a golden voice that thrilled Samaris the musical. "Sorry I couldn't ask you before, but my Phil was having an off-day last Sunday and took up all my attention. Today, though, she's very well for her." She drew them into the room and looked at Len. "Well, my Len?"

"All very well," Len said as she kissed her mother. Then with a sudden change of tone, "Oh, mercy! Down, Bruno—down, old man! Yes; I love you very dearly, but I don't like being knocked down and your kisses are so wet!" She was laughing as she warded off the advances of a magnificent St Bernard at sight of whom Samantha shrank back.

Joey Maynard noticed it at once and laid a restraining hand on his harness. "Quiet, boy! You're a lot too boisterous for a gentleman your size. He's all right, Samantha. He's very friendly and he means well, but if you aren't accustomed to dogs I admit he can be quite alarming. Ah, you don't mind him, Samaris?"

Samaris was on her knees beside him, hugging him fearlessly. "I've been dying to make friends with him," she said, looking up into the soft black eyes that were laughing down at her. "Oh, he *is* a darling! Pat him, Sammy! He's as matey as can be. Oh, you angel!" She planted a kiss between his eyes.

Bruno was clearly delighted. He swept her face with a warm red tongue and his tail went like a flail.

"Zowie!" exclaimed Len as she rescued a bowl on a nearby table just in time. "Bruno, you're a menace where knicknacks are concerned. It's O.K., Mamma. I got to it in time."

"Come and sit down by the fire," Joey said, leading the way. "He'll settle down then. Well, Len?"

"Where are the babies? I thought they'd be down here with you."

"The twins are having their nap and Cecil was busy with La Maison des Poupées. She promised to be good so I left her."

"I'll pop up and take a dekko," Len said, making for the door. "Cecil is good as kids of her age go, but you never know!"

"How true!" Joey chuckled, a deep, rich chuckle. "Look in on the twins, Len. If they're awake, bring them down. Geoff probably is, but Phil may still be asleep. Don't rouse her if she is. The more sleep she gets the better for her just now."

Len nodded and went off. Joey turned to her guests. "Quite

comfy there? Like a screen for your face, Samantha? The fire's pretty hot."

Samantha accepted the Japanese fan her hostess handed to her with a murmured, "Thank you!" Samaris had Bruno beside her and was burying her face in his great ruff and whispering love-words to him. Joey looked at her and laughed.

"He can take any amount of that. Regular old sentimentalist, aren't you, boy? Well, now how are you two settling down at school? Enjoying life?"

Samaris sat up and nodded. "I am—but then I knew I should. Fräulein Hamel who told Mam about the school said I would."

"Fräulein Hamel? You *don't* mean Sophy Hamel? She's a very old friend of mine! How is she—chubby as ever? Poor old Sophy! When she was at school she was always known as Fatty. Not that she minded. She's one of the most good-natured creatures that ever trod this earth. I knew you came from Innsbruck—Rosalie Dene told me so; but I didn't know you knew the Hamels."

"Only Fräulein Hamel. Her sister has moved away to Kufstein. She's Frau Bernigger, you know. Herr Bernigger's firm sent him to take charge of their branch there before we came to Innsbruck. I've seen snaps of her, though. She isn't a bit like her sister, is she?"

"Not a scrap! Berta was always a scrag and Sophy tells me she's scraggier than ever since her babies came. What she can be like I can't imagine—definition of a line, length without breadth, I should say!"

"Well, her family must take after Auntie," Samaris said with a giggle. "Three fatter kids you couldn't wish to see!"

"They'll thin down in time, I expect. And how did *your* people hear about us, Samantha? By the way, I do like your two names, but life's short. How do we abbreviate you? Do we say Sam I and Sam II?"

91

"I'm generally Sammy," Samantha replied with a chuckle. "Not in class, of course. Out of it, no one but the prefects calls me Samantha. Oh, Mama picked the school from a whole list of others."

"I see. Well, I hope you'll both be as happy as I was—still am, for the matter of that. Oh, yes!" as they stared at her. "I may be the proud mamma of eleven and a writer to boot, but I'm still a Chalet School girl and always will be if I live to be a centenarian, deaf, blind and gaga!"

"Goodness! I hope it won't come to that!" Samaris cried.

"So do I; but you never know what lies before you. Ah!" as her quick ear caught a sound. "Here comes Len with our small fry! I'd better warn you two that though Cecil and Geoff are matey enough, Phil, poor poppet, has grown very shy since her illness. We're hoping she'll grow out of it as she gets stronger and like herself again. Before that she was as friendly as a puppy. Here they come!"

The door opened and a small, black-curled creature danced in, followed by a sturdy small boy whose straight hair was bright red and whose square-jawed face wore a liberal sprinkling of freckles. Tall Len followed, carrying another little girl who struggled as she saw their mother.

"Put me down, Len! Wants Mamma!"

Len set her carefully on her feet and the two Sams saw to their surprise that she was even taller than the black-haired Cecil. She was very thin and her little pointed face was pale under the chestnut fringe which crossed her brows. She walked slowly towards Joey, clinging to the furniture as she went.

"That's the girl! Better and better every day!" Joey exclaimed as she lifted the child in her arms. "Now here are two new friends for you, and—listen, Phil!—they're both called Sam, and they're both new this term. Isn't that funny?"

Phil clung firmly to her mother as she peeped at them from under long black lashes; but when they tried to coax her to shake hands, she buried her face in Joey's shoulder and refused to have anything to say to them.

Cecil came to them willingly, her face held up for kisses, and Geoff followed suit. Cecil glanced back at her little sister. "She's not being *rude*," she said anxiously. "It is just that since she was ill she doesn't like strangers."

Samantha nodded. "I guess she'll grow out of it soon. You aren't a bit shy, are you?"

"No; and I'm coming to school next term," Cecil said eagerly. "Not the *big* school you know, but St Nicholas where Felicity is."

"Felicity?" Samantha asked.

"She's the next sister before me. She's quite big now—going on nine."

"I know her," Samaris put in. She looked at Cecil. "You and she aren't a bit alike to look at, though."

"No; but Con and me are," Cecil said. "Mamma says we're the Brownies of the family. We've four brothers, too, but they go to school in England."

"Chatterbox!" Joey laughed. "Suppose you come and help me to bring tea in. *No*, Bruno; *not* you! You stay here and look after everyone. Come, Cecil!"

Cecil skipped off obediently while little Phil took instant refuge with her eldest sister. Len sat her on her lap and smiled down into the beautiful brown eyes that seemed too large for the thin little face. "Do you know what, Phil? Sam the Second loves Bruno nearly as much as you do. What's more, he looks like loving *her*."

Phil said nothing, but she looked at Samaris and gave her a tiny smile.

"I think Bruno is an utter pet!" Samaris said. She rubbed the ears of the large gentleman stretched out at her feet and he beat the floor ecstatically with his tail.

"Me like Bwuno," said Phil. "Tum to Phil, Bwuno!"

Bruno got up and came to stand by Len. The fragile-looking child patted him with her tiny clawlike hands. The two Sams saw that he seemed to realise that he must deal very gently with little Phil. Len saw the comprehension in their faces and nodded.

"Bruno knows he can't bounce at Phil as he does the rest of us," she said. "He's as cute as they come, aren't you, boy? Never mind; when the summer comes we hope Phil will be almost as sturdy as Geoff himself. Meantime, she's making progress. Here comes tea! Open the door for Mamma, Geoff."

Geoff scampered across the big room to open the door and Joey arrived, trundling before her a big, three-tiered trolley laden with tea, fancy cakes of the most enticing kind and bread twists.

Samaris jumped to her feet. "Oh, let me help!"

The next moment she was grabbing at a nearby chair, for Bruno had followed and, pushing most rudely past her, made his way to his adored mistress and nearly sent her flying.

Cecil, who was following with a silver muffin-dish, gave a yell.

"Bruno! Mamma! Stop, Bruno!"

Joey laughed whole-heartedly. "*Down*, Bruno! It isn't done to knock our guests about like that! You all right, Sam? Good! Come and help me push. This thing takes some manoeuvring between the rugs. Put the hot-cakes in the hearth, Cecil. Geoff, you shut the door, will you, and then pull up your chair and Phil's at your own table. That's the boy! Now sit down, all of you, and let's begin. Who takes cream and who takes sugar?"

It was a luscious tea, and small Cecil, assisted by her eldest sister, waited very prettily on the visitors. Geoff ate with an appetite, but little Phil had to be coaxed all the time. When the meal was over, Len packed the trolley again and wheeled it out to the kitchen before she came back to claim the three babies and take them up to the playroom at the top of the house. Left alone with her guests, Mrs Maynard set to work to get to know them properly.

"So you've been living in Innsbruck, Samaris? How did you like it?"

"Oh, love it!" Samaris said promptly. "I didn't exactly love the school, though. For one thing there aren't any proper winter games, though we did play tennis in the summer. For another you have to slog so at your lessons and such long hours!"

"Don't you like lessons?" Joey asked curiously.

Samaris grinned. "Some, quite a lot. Others, not at all." She glanced at the delicate, mobile face smiling at her. "Did *you* like all your lessons?"

Mrs Maynard giggled like a schoolgirl. "Not I! Anything to do with languages or history or literature I was all over it. Most other things bored me to tears. Believe it or not, Sam, I was never a model pupil. I was slung out of all art classes quite early in my career; and Bill—I mean Miss Wilson—flatly refused to have me in science lessons after I'd sat down on a new case of test-tubes and smashed the lot!"

"No! Did you?" Samaris exclaimed in awed tones.

"Oh, it was an accident. *I* didn't mind. I always loathed science. The only part of it I really objected to was having my pocket-money docked by half each week until those blessed test-tubes were paid for. How are you with regard to science?"

"I don't mind it though it isn't my favourite lesson."

"What about you, Sammy?"

"I've never done any. I'd have liked to start it here, but my folk thought not. Mama said she guessed I'd find it would take me all my time to pull up on ordinary subjects. When you're forever travelling around you don't get down to things real *solidly*. I'm doing maths instead."

"D'you like that?" Samaris asked.

"I don't mind it. What I *am* crazy about is the English branches. History, now, really is something the way Miss Charlesworth teaches it."

"I hope this means you're going in for Nina Rutherford's prize," Joey said.

Samantha nodded. "It's right up my street. The only thing is I'm not just sure I know what I want to do with my life. Have a good time and get married while I'm still young enough to enjoy it. But I guess that isn't quite what she meant."

"So far as I know Nina—and that's pretty far—unless you mean to make a very good thing of your marriage, I don't suppose it is. Nina, poor lamb, has always been dedicated to her music. It comes first with her all the time."

Samaris looked up quickly. "Mrs Maynard, how is she *really*?"

"Difficult to say. She's never fully recovered consciousness."

"But—but—the accident happened days ago!"

"I know; but she was very badly injured and they had to trephine—the telephone! Excuse me!"

Joey leapt to her feet and hurried from the room. Bruno followed her and, except for the crackling of the log fire, there was silence for a minute. Then Samaris turned to Samantha. "Don't you really want to do anything but get married?"

"I guess not. I don't need to work. Papa has plenty of money and there's just me and my sisters. What about you, Sam?"

"What I'd like best is to go in for music properly, but I'm not good enough. Anyhow, I don't play anything much. I'll have to work, of course. We aren't rich so I must get a job and keep music for an extra. Just what job I'll go for, I don't know."

"What about teaching?" Samantha suggested.

Samaris made a face. "No *thank* you! I'd rather do something outdoors."

"What? Gardening—farming—"

Samaris shook her head. "No; something to do with animals, I think."

"A veterinary, then?"

"Oh, no! You need science for that. Besides, I think it's almost as long a training as a doctor's and we couldn't afford it."

The daughter of wealthy parents considered. Suddenly her face lit up. "Are you keen on riding?"

"Quite keen, though I've never done much. But one summer we had a holiday on a farm and the boys there taught me to ride one of the ponies. I've had some since, but not much. I told you we couldn't afford luxuries."

"But you're keen?"

"Oh, quite keen. Who wouldn't be?"

"Then I'll tell you what. My papa has a horse ranch in Kentucky. What say I get him to take you on as an apprentice? You'd get all the riding you want and training, too. If you did well you'd ride for him and you'd get jolly good pay and a share of the prizes as well."

Samaris stared at her. "Gosh, Sammy! You do go ahead! I'd never be good enough. I haven't had enough practice. But it's decent of you to think of it," she added.

What more might have been said remained unknown. Joey came back into the salon. Her face was alight and her eyes glowing.

"Girls! Good news for you! Nina has roused fully at last and though it will be a long time before she's really fit again, the doctors all say she will be all right in time. I've been on to the Head to give her the good news. And now," she added briskly, "what about coming upstairs and helping to put the babies to bed. No; *not* you, Bruno. Your idea of helping is to lick them lavishly and that's not much help. Stay here, old man. Missus will be back before long. Come along, you two! Upstairs and help with tubs and hair-brushing and all the rest of it. When we come down we'll have a good natter about the school. I can tell you all the legends. Remember: I'm the first pupil and the oldest Old Girl! What I don't know about it isn't worth knowing!"

Chapter VI

A SHOCK FOR UPPER IVB

"YOUR turn, Samaris. Read the next lines until I tell you to stop, please, and let me see if you can put a little meaning into them."

Miss Stone, who was responsible for literature in Upper IVb, cast a glance at Robina whose rendering of the previous dozen or so lines of *The Pied Piper of Hamelin* had been as uninspired as it could be, and that young woman turned red.

"It's all very well," she grumbled under her breath to her nextdoor neighbour, "but reading aloud isn't my gift." Then she stopped short for Miss Stone was looking at her again and there was a warning in her glance.

Samaris stood up, not without a quaking feeling. As it happened she knew the poem, having learned it two years ago in her English school, but she was not at all sure that her rendering would satisfy Miss Stone, who had proved herself a mistress of gentle mockery at the efforts of one or two of the girls.

"Begin!" Miss Stone said; and Samaris began.

> "Into the street the piper stept
> Smiling first a little smile
> As if he knew what magic slept
> In his quiet pipe the while."

Her voice, which had begun quaveringly, steadied as the well-known lines continued and when she reached the last one—

"And out of the houses the rats came tumbling!" it positively clanged.

Miss Stone had listened with a smile broadening as Samaris

reached this climax and when the girl finished, she nodded.

"*That's* more like it! Now, girls, if one of you can read like that, others can." She looked round the form. "Lysbet Alsen, take the next verse and see if you can continue in the same way."

Lysbet stood up looking alarmed. Dramatic reading was no more in her line than in Robina's, and though she had enjoyed Samaris's reading, she was wishing devoutly that the new girl wasn't so good. "Rocky", as her unregenerate pupils called her among themselves, would expect far more of them now. Mercifully for her, the greater part of her lines contained the descriptions of the various rats and demanded little effort at drama. Even more mercifully, the bell rang for the end of the lesson as she finished the last line. Miss Stone, who was something of a stickler for punctuality, told them to finish reading the poem for preparation, gathered up her books, and sped off to her next class.

Upper IVb had algebra with Miss Ferrars next, and while they waited for her to arrive, Lysbet turned to the new girl to demand, "But why did you read like that? None of *us* ever do and now see what you have done! Rocky will expect all of us to read like you. It is not fair!"

"*What's* not fair?" Samaris cried, flaring up at this unwarranted accusation. "I just read in the ordinary way. You've got to put *some* sort of expression into it or it's the most boring thing on earth. Besides, I love poetry!"

What she was not to know was that during the previous term Miss Stone had wrestled long and furiously with Upper IVb over this very thing. As a form they were not given to love of poetry or prose. They much preferred netball to any of their lessons and, with one or two exceptions, looked on all lessons as an ingenious form of torture especially invented for schoolgirls.

What, again, none of them knew was that at the end of the previous term every member of staff who had had anything to do with them had complained formally about them.

"Games-crazy!" Miss Ferrars had said bitterly.

"Mentally lazy!" was the even more bitter complaint of Miss Stone.

Other people's comment had all been along those lines. Two or three years before there had been the same trouble with the Inter V of that day. Miss Annersley had vowed then that she would not permit another form to work up through the school with a similar reputation. Unless they reformed, Upper IVb were in for some nasty shocks this term. Now that they numbered among them a girl who at least seemed to be able to read aloud with interest and understanding, Miss Stone remembered this and made up her mind that she was going to refuse to be satisfied.

As for the girls themselves, they had managed very nicely so far with work that just passed muster as a general rule. Robina McQueen was keen on maths and slogged at them, and one or two of the others were interested in history and geography and showed up quite good average marks; but taken as a whole, Upper IVb were a poor form with a low standard of work. Lysbet, in particular, objected to having to use her brain more than she must, though she was good at games and gymnastics. The same applied to Marie Angeot, Brigit Ingram, Celia Thornton, Emmy Friedrich and Hilda Wendt. The rest followed this crowd like a flock of sheep.

Samaris, on the other hand, was a real live wire. She had an excellent brain and had been trained to use it. She was keen enough on games, too, but they were by no means the be-all and end-all of her existence. In fact, during her year at the Innsbruck school she had had no organised games worth mentioning, though she had learned to ski and skate during the winter months and enjoyed both thoroughly. But she was an ambitious young thing, and she was determined to make good in whatever she decided to make her career.

Lysbet regarded her with dislike. "Oh, are you a *worker*?" she asked with a sneer. "A marks-hunter, eh? Well, you had better know first and last that we have no use for your sort in *this* form."

"But that's a lot of rot!" Samaris protested. "You've got to work at school if you want to get anywhere later on and I jolly well mean to. I'm not going to be a stick-in-the-mud all my days. If I want to work, I jolly well will!"

"Delighted to hear it!" remarked a new voice; and the form as a whole jumped violently and sprang to its feet in short order. None of them had heard Miss Ferrars coming until she was in their midst, and goodness only knew how much she had heard of the argument.

Miss Ferrars made no comment until she was standing at the Mistress's table. Then she looked round at the girls with twinkling eyes and a smile that most of them rather disliked.

"Sit down, girls," she said, speaking in the English which was the language for the day.

They sat down and looked at her with some trepidation. Ferry, as she was known throughout the school, was liked by everyone, but she kept a firm grip on the reins and some of her remarks last term to sundry members of the form had stung badly at the time. What was coming now?

She waited until they were all seated. Then she said, "I have some news for you. Miss Stone is taking over Upper IIIa as form mistress in my stead. I think it may be as well for us to understand each other from the very beginning. Put down your pencils and sit back and listen to me."

They had to obey of course, but more than one of them awaited her next remarks with some anxiety. *Why* were they to have a change of form mistress in any case?

Miss Ferrars set her hands on the edge of the table and leaned back on them, her smiling brown eyes roving from one troubled young face to another. Suddenly she nodded.

"No; I don't see one of you that looks *mental*," she informed them; and they blushed wildly. "*That* can't be the cause for your consistently poor work. Therefore, I'm driven to the conclusion that the trouble with you is laziness. Well, that is something that can be conquered. Make no mistake, girls. You are going to get the better of it this term if it means giving up all your free periods for work. I've always been proud of my forms so far, and I don't mean to be shamed by you."

She paused there to let her words sink in and the appalled form sat staring at her, wondering what was coming next. Robina raised her hand.

"Yes, Robina?" Miss Ferrars said.

"It's just—I'm keen on maths and I do work at them," Robina said, reddening furiously, "but—but—well, it's different with history and English. F'rinstance, I can't write compositions—not decent ones, though I try."

Kathy Ferrars smiled. "Yes; so I have heard. I know we aren't all gifted with language. But you can go on trying, Robina. Don't be defeated by a thing like that. You may never be able to write like—say—Con Maynard writes, but you can always do your best to make people see the pictures you see." She turned to pick up the mark-book which was lying on the table behind her. She looked through the various subjects while the form, feeling more and more uneasy, watched her. "Yes," she said after she had glanced down the last page, "as a form your marks are disgraceful. We must alter that. Half a dozen girls seem to be able to manage B+ and there are even one or two who achieved A–. Now that must cease. And to help you to realise it," she added blandly, "for the next two weeks instead of games you will have short, brisk walks and spend the rest of your games periods in working up those subjects in which you are weakest." She nodded at them. "We'll see how that answers for the moment. Oh, by the way, you have games with Upper IVa, so those girls who show signs of working well at lessons will be excused the extra work with me and will go to games as usual. That is all for the moment. It is time we were busy with algebra. Open your books at Example 15 and we'll work the first sum together on the board."

Without a word the form opened their textbooks and then sat with eyes glued to the blackboard, following her as well as they were able while she helped them to solve the problem of a simple equation. When it was finished, she wiped the board clean and told them to work it out for themselves in their roughbooks. It is on record that not a girl thought of anything but algebra for the rest of the lesson though more than one of them was fuming deep down inside. The worst of it was they could not accuse Ferry of being against games. She was one of the coaches for lacrosse and she was in the Staff hockey team and had proved herself a good player. As for tennis, she had a demon service as they all knew.

"Oh, whatever have they changed us for?" Lysbet muttered to herself as she struggled with the second problem. "Rocky was bad enough but whoever would have thought that Ferry could be so revolting?"

A good many of the others felt the same. Even at this early date it was plain to them that their days of ease were over for the time being. Not one of them wanted to miss games practice so that meant that they must take their school work seriously. Ferry had a well-founded reputation for doing exactly as she said.

Miss Ferrars kept them hard at it until the bell rang and there was no chance of discussing the latest. Mdlle came to them next and, since the previous period had been a "free" for her, she was waiting outside the door when Miss Ferrars left the room, and started them off at once on their translations of *Le Chien du Capitaine* which was their set book.

Little Mdlle de Lachennais was a favourite with them but very few girls ever cared to risk badly-prepared work for her. She was endlessly patient with those who were naturally dull, but she had no mercy on slackers and on this occasion she gave her tongue free rein.

The truth was that at a staff meeting the previous evening Miss Stone had let herself go on the subject of her form. She had wound up by wishing aloud that she might change with someone else—anyone else! The Head had promptly taken advantage of her remarks and requested Kathy Ferrars to hand over Upper IIIa and take hold of Upper IVb. She had already decided on this and discussed it with Miss Ferrars in private.

"We must do something about Upper IVb," she had said. "I won't have them continuing in their present idle, careless way. I think Linda Stone isn't quite the right person to tackle them. Will you exchange with her and see what *you* can do, Kathy?"

"But why me?" Kathy Ferrars had asked in dismay.

"Because you are very much of a live wire. Also, that crowd are games-mad and you are good at games. Linda isn't really keen and hasn't the hold on them that that would give you. Take them over and *wake them up*! I'll back you to the limit in whatever methods you choose to use; but something must be done if we are not to have the same trouble with them later on as we had with Inter V four years or so ago—remember? They're young enough to respond without much bother if you pull them up sharply now. Will you do it?"

"What does Linda think of it?" Kathy asked.

"She will be only too thankful to be relieved of them. She will do much better with IIIa who are a keen set; but I doubt if she has the right approach towards people like Upper IVb. I think you have."

Kathy Ferrars had laughed. "IIIa are a set of mark-hunters at the moment. Upper IVb couldn't care less—or that's the impression I get."

"I think," the Head had said thoughtfully, "that they are lacking in any really outstanding leaders in that form. Robina McQueen could be one, but she lacks the nerve to take hold. That form had a large number of new girls last term and none of them seems to have the requisite qualities."

"I'll tell you one new girl who might do it when she's really found her feet, and that's Samaris Davies. But she only came this term."

"And the term is barely a fortnight old. I agree with you. What is more, she seems to be friendly with Robina in her own form, though the girl she's most friendly with is that other new girl in Inter V—Samantha van der Byl. Still, if you will take hold and Samaris and Robina back you up I think we shall have an Upper IVb who are quite average by the end of the school year. At the moment they are well *below* the average."

"I'll do my best. I may use any methods I choose?"

"So long as you remember that your first consideration is the girls' health. They must have their full amount of exercise out-of-doors—when possible. You know what this term can be like!"

"Do I not!" Kathy laughed ruefully. "Very well; I'll take it on, but whether I'll be more successful than Linda Stone is another question."

"It's an experiment, I agree, but I think we must try it. Upper

IVb must not continue along their present lines if we can prevent it."

That had ended the interview and the result had been the preliminary shock the form had had administered to them that morning.

Chapter VII

Samantha Takes a Chance

WHILE Upper IVb were unwillingly digesting the fact that work during school hours they *must*, whether they liked it or not, and Samaris and one or two of the others were rejoicing in the fact that the rest must pipe down on nagging at them because they did work consistently, Samantha was experiencing quite other difficulties. Inter V were a keen form on the whole. They were keen on games and, within reason, on lessons, too. They had leaders who preferred to get their work well out of the way so that they had time for other ploys. Jack Lambert, for instance, had no use for slackers in any shape or form. Backing her up were Jean Abbott, Celia Everett, Barbara Hewlett, and the two Dutch girls. Her own chief friend, Wanda von Eschenau, was very average, but she was a worker and did the best she could. This little crowd led Inter V and it was the fashion there to work.

Samantha, having led a wandering life for the last few years with continual changes of governess, found it hard to settle down to steady, regular study. She was bright enough, and in those subjects she enjoyed she could shine. In others she had made little effort hitherto. She could produce an essay that was well written so long as it dealt with surface matters and description. Given such a topic as "Account for the hold Elizabeth I had on the imagination and loyalty of her people", she was completely flummoxed.

"What *can* you say about a thing like that?" she queried

plaintively of Celia Everett on Wednesday when they were settling down to their afternoon prep. "You can't say she was beautiful. To judge by that effigy of her in Westminster Abbey she was a real shocker for looks."

"Never seen it. Is it so very ghastly?"

"Ghastly? I guess you'd have run a mile if you'd met her out after dark!" Samantha said flatly. "And it can't have been just because she was a woman. So was her sister Mary I who came before her, but the folk didn't run around after her as they did after Elizabeth. Religion might have had something to do with it, of course."

"And Mary insisted on marrying Philip of Spain and the English loathed the Spaniards at that time," Barbara chimed in. "There was the Spanish Inquisition, you know, and the Smithfield business and all that."

"Yes; but under Elizabeth the Catholics were treated just as awfully," Samantha objected. "If they weren't burned to death they were hung, drawn and quartered and the hanging was only in name. They were still alive when they were cut down and hacked open. I think it was a beastly thing to do!"

"I wish you people would stop talking and let other folk go on with their work!" Jean complained at this point. "Anyhow, we are not supposed to talk during prep."

Thus reminded, Jack, who was form prefect this term, interfered. "Jean is right. Stop talking, you two, and get down to it. I'm sorry, Sammy, but you'll have to work it out for yourself."

Samantha heaved a gusty sigh, picked up her pen and set to work as well as she could while the others, thankful for the respite, also plunged in. The resultant essay Samantha presented was bald in the extreme. She had never been taught to reason from cause to effect and she was unable to see that what gave Elizabeth her hold over her people was that she was a Tudor of Tudors. With all her faults she *reigned* and reigned right royally. Neither was she above using what femininity she had to influence her men—something that her stepsister could never have done. Also she knew what the half-Spanish Mary never learned—when to give in to her advisers. She had clever men in her government who knew how to handle an imperious Tudor, something that Mary never had. There was a great deal more to it, of course, but even so much would have enabled Samantha to hand in an essay which would *not* have made Miss Charlesworth demand plaintively of her colleagues if the American girl had ever been taught the rudimentary elements of essay writing!

Lessons apart, the two Sams were enjoying life at the Chalet School. Oddly enough, considering the difference in their ages and positions in the school, their early friendship grew and flourished. Samantha was a good mixer, but it was mainly on the surface. She was chummy with half a dozen girls in her own form, but for some reason unknown to herself, she preferred Samaris to any of them. They were unable to be much together, but they seized every opportunity. Samaris knew no more than her elder why she liked Samantha so much more, even, than the girls she chummed with in form. She only knew it was so.

"Probably it's because she's a bit like me—has travelled about," she said to herself. "We've quite a lot in common that way. Anyhow, I *like* her!" Beyond that she was unable to go.

The Saturday after the Wednesday when Samantha had so much trouble with her essay broke fine and dry. Previously, the Görnetz Platz had been largely shrouded in mists since the beginning of term. There had been one or two falls of snow, but when they ended the mists came down again and no one was going to allow schoolgirls to do more than take brief, brisk walks in that. The lights burned night and day, and even the central heating seemed inclined to go on strike—or so Jack Lambert said.

"I'm sick of this!" she had grumbled the previous night after Abendessen when they were all working hard at Hobbies. "When are we going to get out for ski-ing or coasting, I'd like to know?"

No one could tell her then. However, next morning they woke up to find that the mists had departed, and during Frühstück a pale sunshine crept through the windows, rendering the electric lights unnecessary. Everyone cheered up at this. When the Head rang the bell on the staff table, there was no need for anyone to ask why. They all knew that she was going to announce that there would be no schoolwork that morning. It was the policy of the Chalet School to take full advantage of good weather during the winter months because so often the girls were house-prisoners for lengthy periods.

"After Prayers, you will all go out," she announced. "Wrap up warmly and don't forget your coloured glasses. People who want to ski, be in your lines with skis strapped on. The others may have their toboggans ready. That is all." She sat down to the sound of clapping and then they applied themselves to finishing their meal in short order.

It was barely 09.00 hours when they assembled in their various lines in the drive and along the side-paths. Questioned, both the Sams had said that they could ski. Samaris had learned during the previous winter in Innsbruck and Samantha had done some while with her parents in Bergen. The experts were thankful to know that there was no need to worry about them. There were plenty of girls who had come to the school the previous term who were complete tyros.

They set off for the meadow halfway along the Platz where they usually did their practice work. It lay at the foot of the great mountain slope where there were runs which they might use after Gaudenz, the school's man-of-all-work, had made sure that there would be no risk of falling branches from the nearby fir trees. They went by forms to begin with, but once they reached the meadow they broke up into little groups and either helped beginners or enjoyed themselves in their own fashion. Most of the mistresses were with them and the rules, though few, were strictly adhered to. No one might stand about. When the recall whistle blew, they must respond at once. Girls disobeying its call lost the fun next time. No one wanted that and it was rarely that the rule was broken.

So far as tobogganing was concerned, they had definite boundaries beyond which they might not go. Sleds designed to take two or three girls only might not be overloaded. The school had four or five big ones on which the younger girls were taken down by older people; the others either had their own or shared with friends.

The two Sams had elected to ski and as soon as the word was given to break ranks, they paired off by mutual consent.

"How far may we go, please?" Samaris asked Len Maynard eagerly.

The tall Head Girl paused to laugh down into the small, glowing face. "From our own railings to that chalet over there, and the run down at that side. Keen, are you?"

"I'm mad keen!" Samaris laughed back. "This is what I've been yearning for ever since term began."

"Then yearn no longer but be off! You, too, Samantha?"

"I guess so. I'm real mad about it," Samantha said.

"Good! You two keeping together at the moment? Then keep an eye on Sam the Second and see she doesn't do anything mad," Len said with another laugh. "You're the elder. Samaris, mind you do what Samantha tells you. I must fly. Erica Standish seems to be in difficulties." She waved to them as she swung round and sped off to where Erica Standish of Upper IVa appeared to be trying to perform somersaults of a complicated nature.

Samantha looked round at their bounds. "Not much room for a really good run," she added. "Oh, well, I guess we must make the best of it. Come on, Sam!" And they set off side by side at a speed that made one or two of the novices look after them enviously.

Of the two, Samantha was the better, but Samaris was not far behind her. If her style left something to be desired, she was ready to learn, and when Samantha gave her one or two tips, she grasped them eagerly.

"Just look at those two!" Lysbet Alsen said to Marie Angeot when she paused once to recover her breath. "What on earth a big girl like Samantha can see in a kid like Samaris is more than I can think. Anyhow, I don't think it's the thing for anyone in our form to suck up to a Senior like that."

Marie shrugged her shoulders. "Perhaps they are relations," she suggested. "Their names are very much alike. In any case, ma chère, what can you do about it? Nothing!"

"I wonder some of the Inter V haven't spoken to Samantha about it," Lysbet growled.

"They may have done, but I do not think Samantha will listen unless she desires it," Marie said shrewdly. "Come, Lysbet! Miss Ferrars is looking at you and you know we may not stand still for more than a minute or two." Thus warned, Lysbet set off again and in her enjoyment of the swift movement, forgot about the two Sams for the time being. Meanwhile, the couple in question had ski-ed to the furthest boundary and were swinging round to come back. At this point there was a fairly steep downhill run where some of the Seniors were disporting themselves. They set their course for the foot of it where Con Maynard was standing for a few moments, her deep brown eyes on the scene, but mind miles away from her surroundings.

"Come on, Sam!" Samantha cried. "Let's have a go at this! It's a mighty lot better than that baby run at the other end!"

"I'd love to; but do you think it's O.K.?" Samaris asked.

"I guess so. There are the Dawbarns coming down, and there's Con Maynard watching them." Then, as Con suddenly swung round in a perfect curve and came towards them, "Gee! How that girl can ski!"

"All the Maynards can," Samaris panted, trying to keep pace with Samantha. She was beginning to tire a little and finding that even last winter's experience had not made her nearly as expert as her friend.

"Oh, well, they've lived out here for donkey's years," Samantha said easily. "Val Gardiner told me they'd lived here since they were small kids. I guess it comes as natural to them as walking. Gosh! Look at that," as Con swung round on her skis in a beautiful turn and came up to them.

"Whither away?" she asked in her slow, rather dreamy voice.

"I thought we'd try the run," Samantha explained. "We can both ski."

Con nodded, her mind still far away from the Görnetz Platz. "Very well. You certainly may, but I think Samaris had better not risk it just yet. It's on the tricky side." Then as she saw Samaris's face fall, "I'll tell you what, Samaris, you shall come for a turn with me. Go on, Samantha if you're sure you can manage it."

"I did a lot of ski-ing when we were in Bergen," Samantha said.

Since ski-ing was born in Norway, Con accepted this—later, she was very sorry. But a sonnet on the beauty round her was teasing at her and she was still not altogether with the two Sams in mind.

"Very well," she said. "I'll see to Samaris and we'll meet you around here. Come on, Samaris!"

Samantha glanced at Samaris. "Would you care a lot if I went, Sam?"

"No; of course not. You've been with me all the time up to now, anyhow. You go and have a good go at it," Samaris replied promptly; so Samantha went.

"Sorry I couldn't let you have a go," Con said as she and Samaris swung off on their run, "but no Junior is allowed to go on that run, and only Seniors who can really ski. You do understand, Samaris?" Then she broke off to laugh. "Oh, glorianna! It's a bit muddling you two having names so alike!"

Samaris laughed. "It *is* rum, isn't it? I mean, both of us with names like ours and turning up at this school the same time."

Con pushed the sonnet to the back of her mind. "My mother will be all over your names. Don't be surprised if one or both of them figures in her next book."

Samaris laughed again. "Is she busy with a new one?"

"Thinking about it. She sent one off a month ago—that's about as long as she usually likes to be between books." She changed the subject. "Look, Samaris, when you are making a turn like that, lean back a little further—like this." And she executed a beautiful turn.

Samaris watched her enviously. "Wish I was as good as you. It's a treat to watch you—or any of you Maynards! Even Felicity is good."

"My dear, we've lived out here for ages and the twins have ski-ed since they were little more than babies. As for us three, we learned in Canada before that. We've been at it quite a long time. And that's a lot better," she added as Samaris finished a good curve. "You'll soon get into it. Now come on. It's much too cold to stand about."

Side by side they swung off towards the run where Samantha, having finally clambered to the top, was preparing for the downward run. Con watched her with a little anxiety. "I hope she knows what she's doing," she murmured, more to herself than to Samaris.

"Oh, I'm sure she does," Samaris said. "She told me she'd spent two winters in Bergen and did lots of ski-ing."

"I dare say. Just the same, that run isn't exactly nursery slopes."

Up at the top Priscilla Dawbarn, Carmela Walther and Henriette Zendl, all sixth formers and all experienced ski-ers, were giving the new girl hints about the difficulties. It was not really dangerous except to novices, but there were leaps, one in particular demanding a good spring off and careful direction. The curves were not too hard except at one place where there was a sharp hairpin bend. They warned Samantha of these snags and she listened. Then she nodded.

"O.K. I guess I'll take a chance with it, just the same. And if I fall and break anything," she added, laughing, "you don't have to blame yourselves. I guess you've told me just everything there is to tell."

With this she began to skim down the steep slope with perfect confidence. The other girls watched her with some uneasiness, but she certainly seemed to know what she was doing. She reached the first bend and took it beautifully, swinging back into the straight almost at once. The next, a left hand curve was not quite so good.

"I'm going after her!" Carmela exclaimed suddenly. "The little jump comes next and then there's the hairpin. We desire no accidents."

She was off and Henriette followed her, leaving Priscilla to keep watch at the top and also to warn the four or five girls who were toiling upwards for another downward run.

Samantha managed the little jump quite well, but although she would never have owned it, she was tiring after all her previous exercise. She contrived to swing round the hairpin bend without a mistake, though it was with her heart in her mouth. Now came the big jump and she gathered up all her force to take it cleanly. She took off, but her spring was not good enough. She jumped short and furthermore forgot what she had been taught about keeping her legs well under her. Even as Con Maynard shouted, "Keep your legs up—keep your legs up!" she realised that she could not make it. She panicked and fell, landing on one shoulder and rolling over just as Henriette, ski-ing for her life, came flashing down to take the jump, swing round and prepare to turn back. Carmela, using her sticks, contrived to brake herself though she ran off the run on to the snowy mountain slope. Luckily, being thoroughly experienced, she swiftly righted herself and came skimming back to where Henriette was already stooping over Samantha lying white and still on the snow.

"What has she done?" gasped Carmela, speaking in the Swiss German which was the native tongue of both girls. "Not her neck, I pray!"

"Thank God, no! But I fear—I greatly fear she has injured her shoulder. We must get her down and someone must ring up the Sanatorium to send an ambulance for her at once."

"I'll do that!" It was Con who had just reached the scene of the accident.

"Just a moment!" She stooped down over the unconscious Samantha. Then she straightened up. "Nothing serious, I fancy; but the San's the place for her so that they can find out what she really has done. You two stay with her and I'll fly to Die Hütte and 'phone!" She swung round on her skis and went down at top speed while the other two waited with Samantha who was beginning to come to a little.

At the foot of the slope, Samaris, white and big-eyed, was waiting. She had seen the accident but she dared not move from where she was after the imperative command Con had flung at her as she set off up the slope. When the prefect reached her, she caught at her hand.

"Con! Samantha isn't—isn't—"

"She's not killed, but she seems to have broken either her collarbone or her shoulder," Con replied. "You go and find Willy or Mdlle and tell them there's been an accident, but not really serious, I think. Scram!"

They had been ski-ing while she talked. Now she simply shot ahead and Samaris was left to seek a mistress to whom she might break the news. As it chanced, none of them had been near at the time, being fully occupied in other parts of the area. They trusted to the prefects, all of whom were good, experienced ski-ers, to keep an eye on the far quarter. Luckily Mdlle, a veteran ski-er and a member of the French Alpine Club was not too far off and she skimmed away at a speed that even the Maynards could not rival. Ted Grantley, the Second Prefect, was also there and took charge of Samaris, who looked all in by this time.

Ted got her story and then led her off to Miss Wilmot, who decided that since the girls had already had nearly two hours, and elevenses would be ready and waiting, they had better return. So the school knew nothing beyond the fact that there had been an accident until word came from the Görnetz Sanatorium that the damage was not as bad as it might have been. Samantha had broken her collarbone and twisted an ankle. She also had sundry bruises; but that was all. They were keeping her at the Sanatorium until the morrow, but she would return to school then.

"Thank God it's no worse!" was the Head's reaction when she heard.

Later on, Carmela summed it up in the prefects' room. "Well, she said she was going to take a chance, and my goodness, she did! I thought at first she was killed and she is fortunate that it is not so. But tell me, anyone, will this put a stop to our ski-ing in future?"

Chapter VIII

CONSEQUENCES

MISS ANNERSLEY had sent for Priscilla, Carmela and Henriette. They came into the study and somewhat quakingly faced her. She was looking her grimmest and there was nothing in her chilly, "Come in, girls!" that encouraged them to think that she was likely to accept any excuses they might offer for having let Samantha go her own way over the ski-run before they knew that a mistress had passed her.

"Well," she said when they were seated, "what have you to say about this morning's happenings?"

There was a pause and she waited their pleasure, still regarding them with the steely look that most girls found it hard to face. Then Carmela spoke up.

"Bitte, I know it is no real excuse, but—but Samantha did tell us that she was accustomed to ski-ing in Norway."

Henriette instantly backed her up. "Indeed, that is true. We could see for ourselves that she could manage skis well."

"Yes?" It was all the Head said, but its effect was of a piece of ice dropping from her lips.

Priscilla tried. "Truly, Miss Annersley, she looked awf—very good to us."

"You know the rules?"

They did. No girl was ever supposed to try that particular run unless one of the experts on the staff had given permission. How they could have overlooked it none of them could state. The run was not dangerous unless attempted by beginners, but the invariable rule was that any girl, however good she might be, and however she might say that she was, must first have permission to make it.

"Which mistresses were with you?"

"Mdlle—Miss Wilmot—Miss Ferrars—Miss Derwent—and some of the mistresses from the Junior school," Henriette said slowly. "Miss Annersley, I know we should not have taken it for granted that Samantha was as good as she said she was. Mdlle was at our end of the meadow, but she was at the further side. We should have asked her—but—but we did not think of it."

"And in consequence Samantha has suffered a nasty accident which might have been fatal. Have you thought of that?"

Carmela, an emotional girl, bit her lips to prevent herself from bursting into tears at this awful pronouncement. Priscilla and Henriette looked at the Head in horror. They had feared in that first moment that the girl might have broken her neck, but since then they had consoled themselves by saying that it hadn't happened and the jumps were not difficult enough for it. But it *might* have ended in just that. The three young faces whitened and this time not all the lip-biting in the world could prevent the tears from filling Carmela's eyes.

"Oh, Miss Annersley," she faltered, "indeed we never thought about it."

"And yet you are prefects!" The biting comment went home.

They sat silent, Carmela dabbing her eyes with her handkerchief and the other two not far from tears. Then the Head spoke again and this time her tone had altered.

"I don't know if you girls have ever considered how much we mistresses rely on you. It is for that reason that you are so free from staff supervision. We don't ask you to shoulder heavy responsibilities, but we do expect you to see that rules are kept. You three are well over seventeen—no; you were eighteen last week, weren't you, Henriette? At that age quite a number of girls are married and have babies for whom they must be responsible. It may be that in another three or four years that may happen to you. If you can't be answerable for a simple thing like seeing that the younger girls keep to rules, how can you be answerable for the lives and souls of tiny children who must rely on you for everything?"

She waited a moment, but she had no need to ask if they understood her. The faces of all three told her that what she had said had gone home. She left that subject and went on to the consequences of the affair.

"I'm sorry, girls, but this means that so far as ski-ing is concerned, we can no longer trust you. In future, anyone wishing to try the run may only do so when a mistress who is qualified to judge a girl's ability to use it is with you. And this must apply to *all* the prefects. After Prayers tonight I shall give out this new rule and it will be added to the lists on the noticeboards during the weekend. So far as Samantha herself is concerned, I'm afraid she has put paid to any further participation in winter sports for the rest of the term. I shall speak to her about that when she is well again. In the meantime, try to realise that you girls are rapidly reaching adulthood and are expected to behave accordingly. That is all I have to say to you."

The girls glanced at each other. Carmela and Henriette, at least, had expected to be told that they had lost their prefectships over the affair. Priscilla had not reached that, but she had expected a severe punishment for her carelessness and lack of thought. That the Head's words would recur to her at intervals throughout the term with a sting of which she could not easily rid herself hadn't occurred to her as yet. But the Head knew all about it. She dismissed the trio, shelved her other work, and then wrapped up and ran across to Freudesheim for a few words with Joey Maynard.

But if it was finished so far as the Head was concerned, the three found that their own clan had a good deal to say on the subject.

"Whatever possessed you to let Samantha try the run until Mdlle or somebody had passed her for it?" Margot demanded. "It was enough to get it banned altogether and a nice thing that would have been!"

"As it is we've got to have a staff with us if we want to try it," Ted Grantley growled. "That's something that's never happened before. I wish you'd managed to think before you said Silly Sammy could go down it!"

"I also," Jeanne Daudet put in. "And for Samantha, I am told that she will have no more winter sports this term, la pauvre!"

"Well, what did you expect?" This was Joan Dancey. "With a broken collarbone and a twisted ankle it isn't likely she could manage anything for weeks to come. I'm not worrying about *her*, though. She deserves all she's got. What I do object to is the Head thinking we prefects aren't capable of shouldering our responsibilities without being supervised like a set of babies. That's never happened before, not in this school."

Len's comment was the unkindest cut of all. "And what," she asked, "are the Middles and especially the Senior Middles going to think of us?"

This had not occurred to the others and their faces lengthened.

"Oh, bother you three!" Eve Hurrell exclaimed. "As though Senior Middles weren't the outside of enough at any time!"

"Who gave Samantha leave to try it out, anyhow?" Ted demanded. "I know it was you three at the top, but didn't anyone do anything about it when she was on the meadow? Surely the young ass didn't just go shooting up the hill without a word to anyone?"

"I saw Samaris Davies with her," Jeanne said doubtfully.

"Oh, come off it!" Ted ejaculated. "I didn't mean a kid like Samaris—and new at that!—and you know it. Wasn't there a pree or a staff around that she could have asked?"

No one could tell her that at the moment. The three had been chattering and had not seen Samantha until she was halfway up the hill. No one else in the prefects' room seemed to have noticed the girl.

Margot thought. "I'm not sure, but wasn't Con somewhere there. I seem to remember she told me she was going to give Samantha a rest from Samaris and take the kid on herself. Not that she seems to mind having the kid hanging round her. Anyone would think they were dearest sisters!"

"Not even cousins," Eve said positively. "I asked Samantha about that and she said that so far as they knew they weren't any sort of relations."

"But I find that easy to believe," remarked Marie Huber, who had hitherto been silent. "Samantha is fair and tall and slim and Samaris is short and dark and rather plump. They are not at all alike. But why trouble? It is no different from Jack Lambert and Len." She smiled at the Head Girl.

"I should say it was very different," Len returned. "Jack latches on to me because she thinks I can answer her endless questions. I doubt if Samaris is the living question-mark young Jack is. There *couldn't* be two of that kind in one school!"

The others laughed and then Carmela, looking round, remarked, "But where, then, *is* Con? I have not seen her since we came up here after Mittagessen."

"Oh, she'll be off somewhere reading," Ted said easily. "Probably in the library. Go and look there for her if you want to question her."

But the library was far from being where Con was. She was

in the Head's salon, confessing her sins of omission with all her might and thoroughly miserable about it.

She had heard nothing about the trouble of the other three until halfway through the afternoon, when she had met Samaris looking deeply unhappy. Being a kind-hearted girl when she was not in the throes of composition, she had paused to ask what was wrong and try to comfort her junior. Samaris was not to be comforted. Far from it! When Con had done her best, she said wretchedly, "It's rotten luck on Sammy, but it's almost as tough on Carmela and the other two."

"What on earth do you mean?" Con asked in amazement.

"The Head's been having them in the study and talking to them. I met them coming out and Carmela looked as if she'd been howling."

"What? Oh, nonsense!" Con said. "You're imagining things, Sam. Why should those three——" She stopped and her face changed. "Oh, my goodness! Of course! And the blame is actually mine. I told her she might go. No; don't stop me! I must go to the Head at once!" And she rushed off, leaving Samaris staring after her with her mouth open.

Con went straight to the study, but found no one there. Nor was the Head to be discovered for a good hour when she returned from Freudesheim after a refreshing visit from Joey, who had contrived to soothe her. In the meantime, Con had been wandering about the Annexe, as the Head's quarters were called, deeply unhappy and wishing that Miss Annersley would hurry up and come back. So it was that when that lady finally returned and had just settled down in her own quarters there came a tap at the door, and in answer to her, "Herein!" Con entered.

One look at her told the Head that something was badly wrong. She had no need to ask any questions, however, for Con was standing before her, her cheeks crimson, her long lashes drooping over her eyes as she said, "I—I've something to tell you. It was all my fault."

"What was?" Miss Annersley demanded.

"It was my fault that Samantha tried that run."

"What? But you weren't there—or not till it had happened. Carmela and Henriette and Priscilla all told me so. What are you talking about, Con?"

"Oh, that was right enough. The thing is that I met the two Sams at the foot and told Samantha she might have a go on it. I never thought of asking if she had been tested. So, you see, I'm the one really to blame. If the other three saw us talking I expect—"

"From all I can gather they saw nothing of it," the Head interrupted. "They seem to have taken it for granted that she had been tested and had permission. Neither did it dawn on them to make any inquiries."

"And it didn't dawn on me," Con said in a low, ashamed voice. "Oh, Auntie Hilda!" She dropped on her knees beside the Head's chair. "I'd been thinking up a sonnet and I only half attended to the Sams. If I'd been fully on the spot as I should have been it *couldn't* have happened. Oh, will I *ever* get over this habit of dreaming at the wrong time?"

"Yes; I think this will prove a sharp lesson to you," Miss Annersley said gravely. "It's happened once or twice before. I hope this last one will help you to learn to break yourself of your trick of going off into a daydream and giving only half your attention to what is going on round you. As it is, I'm bitterly disappointed in you, Con. I thought you were really improving in that way."

"So did I." Con spoke in a low tone.

"Well, there's nothing for it but to go on trying. Of course you must acknowledge your share of the accident to the others—

the prefects, I mean. I know they are blaming those three severely for my latest rule. You must take your share of the blame. But Con, you really must try to overcome this tendency to neglect positive duties for delightful dreams. It is selfish. What is more, it is wrong. I think you had better talk it over with your mother when next you go home. She will be as sorry and disappointed in you as I am, but that's something you must bear. Now, if that's all you have to say to me, you had better go. The gong will be sounding for Kaffee und Kuchen."

The Head stood up and Con stumbled to her feet. "I'm most horribly sorry and ashamed of myself. I did think I'd got over it more or less, especially after all Mary-Lou said to me years ago, but it seems as if I just *can't* break myself of it."

"That's rubbish! Of course you can! Oh, I know it's not easy. Breaking oneself of bad habits is never easy. But you must try. I think that after today you will find it less difficult for a time. But remember, Con, it won't come at once. Now you really must go, for the gong is sounding."

Con nodded. "Th-thank you, Auntie Hilda. I'll do as you say— about talking it over with Mamma, though I'd a lot rather *not*! And I will try."

She left the room and the Head sat down again. "Poor Con!" she said to herself. "In her own way she has as hard a row to hoe as Margot. It's part of her make-up, of course. All the same she must learn to control it as Margot is learning to control her temper. Neither of them is going to find life very easy, I'm afraid. Still, I think Con has learnt a lesson from today. And I can trust Joey to talk seriously to her and make even more impression than I have. Thank goodness her girls look on her as a friend as well as a mother! She and Jack have been very wise in their training of their long family."

Chapter IX

LEN ADMINISTERS JUSTICE

SAMANTHA came back to school early in the following week, her shoulder and ankle firmly strapped up. She had run a slight temperature during the first day or two after the accident, but once that had settled down, the Sanatorium authorities pronounced her fit for school and no one wanted her to miss more than she must. She found, to her dismay, that most folk blamed her for the new rule. The prefects came in for their share, of course, but, as Lesley Anderson of Va pointed out, none of it need have happened if Samantha hadn't imagined she was so much better at ski-ing than she really was. Inter V in particular were indignant. That run was the aim of every girl in the form, and now they might not try it unless a mistress was present. The school at large greatly valued its freedom from supervision, and to have any part of it curtailed annoyed them beyond words.

"You *were* an idiot, Samantha!" Val Gardiner said bluntly.

Samantha had a temper, and this remark roused it. "How was I to know we were supposed to pass a test?" she retorted. "No one ever told me."

"Your own common sense should have told you," Barbara said severely. "Well, it's done and can't be undone, but another time you want to do a mad thing, you might find out first if it's against the rules or if you have to be tried out."

Samantha was intensely proud and she hated this forthrightness. At home she would have been told that the result of her foolhardiness served her right and it would have been left at that. The comments of her own form-mates infuriated her. In consequence, she left them severely alone and went about with Samaris as much as the fact that they belonged to different divisions of the school would permit.

Samaris made no comment beyond asking anxiously if she had any pain and commiserating with her on the loss of her winter sports. But Samaris had different hours for a good many things and, however much she might sympathise with the elder girl, no one was going to cause her to miss her own winter sports. Samantha was kept to the house for the first few days, but as soon as she might go out, it meant walks with whoever was free to take her. Miss Annersley had not been sparing in her strictures as soon as she felt that the girl was well enough to be spoken to on the subject. Like Barbara, she remarked that Samantha's own sense should have told her that she ought to have asked permission from a mistress and undergone a test as well before she was allowed even to try that run.

"Such stupidity might be excusable in one of the Juniors," she said. "In a girl of your age it is sheer absurdity. Well, you have punished yourself, I'm sorry to say. There will be no more ski-ing for you this term and we must see how your hurts mend before we can let you play games next term."

She ended there and Samantha left the study fuming inwardly.

Meanwhile, the school, after the first ten days or so, turned their attention to other things. The "Millies," as the members of the finishing branch, St Mildred's, were always called, were preparing in real earnest for their annual pantomime. A number of the Juniors and Junior Middles had been borrowed for fairies, elves, goblins and so on, and the school was longing to know what story had been chosen this year. The cunning Millies had sworn all the young fry to secrecy—not even the smallest girl would do anything but grin and look knowing when questioned.

It was known that Felicity Maynard, Jean Morrison and Lucy Peters from St Nicholas, the Junior house, were to dance a pas de trois. All three had firmly made up their minds to make ballet their career and all three were, to quote Joey Maynard, "rather more than crackers over it."

"Lucky them to have the chance of ballet classes!" Samaris remarked one day. "I've always longed for it but never had it."

Robina, to whom this was said, grinned. "Rather you than me! I'd hate to do all the exercises and foot positions and things those kids are forever practising. I don't see you going mad over it either, Sam. You don't *want* to be a ballet dancer, do you? Well, then, what's the good of it?"

"I'd like to be able to do it. I've seen ballet quite a few times and I just love it—it's so beautiful, and graceful."

Lizette Thomé who was listening, laughed. "But you are too stout, my Sam, for that," she remarked teasingly. "Ballet dancers are slim and elegant."

"Well, all the work would probably thin me down," Samaris returned, unperturbed by the comment. She knew that she was chubby, to put it kindly.

"You'll slim down when you get older, I expect," observed Miss Ferrars who overheard this. "It's just what's called puppy fat, Samaris. And now run along to prep, you three. There goes the first bell. Have you got your work out?"

They hadn't. They scurried off at her words and forgot ballet and plumpness for the time being. The noses of Upper IVb were being kept well and truly to the grindstone just now, and Samaris and Robina, at any rate, had no mind to get into trouble for ill-prepared lessons. Those awful two weeks when their main outdoor exercise had consisted of prim and proper walks with a mistress lay not so far behind them, and many of the girls were working more or less steadily. Robina and Samaris and one or two others had been permitted their games, but Lizette, who greatly preferred games to lessons, had been one of the sufferers from Miss Ferrars' edict. In fact, as a form, they were beginning to pull up though it meant hard work for all concerned.

Prep that evening consisted of three sums in compound fractions, a question on ocean currents which had to be answered by a sketch-map, and repetition. Samaris decided to get the geography out of the way first. She hated sketch-maps, and even though Miss Moore was prepared to accept very rough maps of the kind, they must show the five continents more or less adequately drawn. She had given them the last ten minutes of the lesson to make a start on the outlines of the said maps, but there were still at least six of the great currents to be put in from memory.

Samaris finished her map and then set to work with her red and blue pencils to show the direction of the currents. She was hard at it when a scuffle suddenly took place at the back of the room. Everyone stopped work at once and Len Maynard, the prefect in charge of prep, called the combatants to order in no uncertain tones.

"Fredrika and Brigit! What are you doing?" she demanded as she left the mistress's platform and stalked down the room.

The pair stopped dead and said nothing. Looking her grimmest, Len stood before them. "Eh bien, qu'est-ce que vous faisiez?" she demanded in the fluent French spoken by all members of the Sixth Forms.

No reply; but Fredrika was scarlet and Brigit scarcely less so. Len looked at them sharply. She noted that Fredrika kept her eyes down, but Brigit was glaring at her fellow-tussler.

"Come up to the table," she said. "Bring your work with you. The rest of you, please go on with what you were doing."

There was nothing wrong with Len's discipline. The rest of the form promptly glued its eyes to its own work and the two culprits followed Len up to the mistress's table.

"What were you doing?" she demanded again.

Silence! Brigit had no idea of telling, and Fredrika didn't dare, for the truth was that she had been taking sly peeps at a loose map. Brigit, sitting next to her, had glanced up and caught her at it though Fredrika tried to smuggle the map away once she realised that she was being watched. Brigit was no telltale though she was one of the most featherheaded young creatures in the school. Fredrika, knowing quite well what a good number of the others would think of her action, didn't dare. They stood in silence before the Head Girl while the rest of the form worked for dear life. Len was a favourite with most of them, but she expected to be obeyed. Besides, only Brigit knew what had been happening.

"Well," said Len when the silence had lasted a full two minutes, "for the fourth time, what were you doing?"

Still no reply. Len glanced at her wrist-watch. "I'll give you five minutes to make up your minds to tell me what all this is about," she remarked; and turned back to her Latin.

Those five minutes seemed never-ending to the culprits, but when they came to an end and the Head Girl, setting aside her Livy, requested to be told the cause of the trouble for the fifth time, neither replied.

Len nodded. "Very well. In that case you will remain where you are until you do decide to tell me."

Brigit was horrified. She had begun with arithmetic and had got into a thorough mess with her second fraction. It would take her all her time to rework it and do her map and repetition. Furthermore, apart from the trouble that would ensue if she turned up at lessons next day with her prep undone, she had a stern father whose comments on her last report stuck in her mind.

She made an effort and hoped Len would not inquire too closely. "S'il te plaît," she began, "je suis bien fâchée, mais c'est moi qui l'a commencé."

"Vraiment?" Len leaned back in her chair and looked at her. "Mais pourquoi?"

Brigit was gravelled. She would not tell tales and yet how was she to get out of this mess? She wished heartily that she had let Fredrika alone until after prep. Fredrika herself said nothing. She knew just what the rest of the form would say if she owned up to cheating. At the same time, how was she to get the rest of her prep done? It was a horrid impasse. Neither dared speak, so each remained silent.

Len gave them plenty of time. Then she nodded. "Very well. You stand there as I said. Any time you like to tell me you may and I'll listen—Emmy Friedrich! Turn round and go on with your work, please."

After that, Upper IVb, with the exception of the sinners, worked as if their lives depended on it. They had come across Len Maynard in this mood once or twice before and they had no wish to get across her. Len returned to her Livy, though privately she kept an eye on the pair. It might have gone on to the end of prep, but Robina dropped a pencil which rolled away to the back of the room. Quaking inwardly, for Len in this mood was very stern, she held up her hand and asked if she might get it in the best French she could muster.

Len nodded. "Yes; but be quick."

Robina scudded on tiptoes to the back of the room where the pencil had fetched up against a screwed-up ball of paper. Robina picked both of them up and brought the paper to the table. "Shall I put this in the waste-paper basket?" she asked.

"No; leave it on the table and go back and get on with your work. You have none too much time left," Len said. She gave Robina a smile and that young woman went back to her desk and proceeded to bury herself in her repetition.

Meanwhile, Len continued with her own Latin and the delinquents beside her stood there and wondered what would happen if neither of them spoke up. And what, oh, *what* would happen tomorrow when they had done next to no prep?

Len finished her Latin. She had brought nothing else down to the formroom, so she closed her book, sat back, and surveyed the form judicially. Most of them seemed to be working for all they were worth. Robina was sitting with closed eyes, apparently gabbling something to herself. Len nearly grinned. She could guess what was up. Samaris Davies was doing arithmetic and counting on her fingers—nor was she the only one. Len, having set Livy aside and made sure that everyone was at least appearing to work, picked up the screwed-up paper Robina had brought to the desk and idly opened it. The next moment she was tapping with her pen.

"Attention, please, everyone!"

Everyone looked up. Len was looking very stern.

"Robina! where did you find this?" she asked, holding up a crumpled sheet which they all recognised as a map.

"D-down there at the b-back of the room," Robina stammered.

"Was it beside any desk in particular?"

"Er—er no. It was—between—those two." Robina half-turned, flinging out her hand. Celia Morton, sitting behind her, was unprepared for it and gave vent to a smothered howl as the hand caught her cheek.

"Oh, sorry!" Robina gasped, speaking in English in her agitation. "I didn't mean to hit you!"

"It—it's all right," Celia replied, likewise speaking in English. She caught Len's eye and turned into French in a hurry. "Ça ne fait rien, I mean!"

"That is better," Len said, suppressing a grin. She turned to the two by the table. "To which of you does it belong?"

Giving herself no time to think, Fredrika said hurriedly, "It is not mine. It must be Brigit's."

Len glanced at Brigit in time to catch the glare that young person was bestowing on her fellow-sinner. "Well, Brigit?"

"It's not mine," Brigit replied, adding to her sins by speaking in English.

"En français, s'il te plaît," Len said inflexibly.

"Oh—" A pause. Then Brigit collected her thoughts and said, "Ce n'est pas le mien—I mean la mienne—at least—" She stopped there, too flummoxed to remember whether the French for map was masculine or feminine.

Len realised this and in mercy passed it. "It is not yours?"

Brigit looked up. "No; it is not. I have not a loose map like that." She cast a scornful glance at Fredrika, who reddened but said nothing.

"Well, it belongs to one of you two, I imagine," Len said; but there came an interruption. Val Pertwee was waving a hand madly.

"What do you want?" the prefect asked coldly.

"Pup-please, Len, I think it must be mine—I mean, je crois que c'est la mienne," Val said, hurriedly changing from English to French. "I lost it this morning."

"I see. Very well, Val. Sit down and go on with your work." Len gave her a smile. Then she turned to Brigit and Fredrika. "That means that one of you two must have been using it." She smoothed it out on the table and looked at it. "What was your geography prep, Robina?"

"A map of the world and put in six of the great ocean currents."

"I see. And this is a map of the currents. Which means," Len said awfully, "that one of you two was cheating. I suppose you had to do it from memory?"

"Only the currents. We drew the map from the atlas," Robina said.

135

Samaris came to her aid. "Please, Len, we did most of the drawing in geography. It was only the currents we had to do from memory."

Len nodded and glanced at her watch. "There are ten minutes left of prep. Get down to it, you people. As for you two," she turned to Brigit and Fredrika, "you may stay where you are until the one who was using this likes to tell me. Oh, the rest of you, if you don't finish, I'll explain to the mistresses concerned. That is all."

She sat down and for the remaining ten minutes of prep sat quietly watching the room. It was very still. Everyone kept her eyes glued to her work and no one looked at anything else until the bell rang. Then Len spoke again.

"Put your work away and go to your commonroom—*quietly*, please," she said. "No; not you two," as Fredrika made a move towards the desks. "You will stay here until the one who was using that map owns up."

Very quietly the rest put their work away. Equally quietly they lined up by the door and when Len gave them the word to march off to their commonroom they went as silently as they could. When the last girl had gone and the door was shut behind her, Len picked up the map and looked at it. A sudden idea occurred to her.

"If neither of you will confess to using it, I must get it powdered and take your finger-prints," she said, her eyes fixed firmly on the pair.

That did it! With a howl, Fredrika broke down. Fingerprints sounded horrible and Len had the reputation of doing exactly what she said she would.

"I—it was me!" she wailed, using her own language in her agitation.

"En français, s'il te plaît," Len pulled her up. "Very well,

Brigit. Put your books away and go. I see you were not to blame. Fredrika, stop that noisy crying. You are too big to behave like a baby."

Brigit hurriedly gathered up her belongings. "Please, Len, what about my prep?" she asked in her best French.

"I'll get leave for you to miss the morning walk and you can do it then," Len said after consideration. "And, of course, if you haven't finished in time, I'll explain to the staff."

"Oh, merci bien!" Brigit said fervently as she finished putting away her books. She hurriedly left the room and Len turned to the culprit, who was still sobbing tempestuously.

"Well, Fredrika?" she said. "Why did you lie about it?"

"I—I—" The sinner could get no further.

"Well, of course, you must tell Miss Moore why your map can't be judged properly with the others. Also, you must give this back to Val. Just what you can do about all those crumples, I don't know. I think Val must have a new book and that means it must go to Miss Dene. Tomorrow morning you must come with Brigit and do what you can of your prep. I will see that the staff concerned know why you have to leave part of it as I imagine you must. Now you may go. And another time when you are caught doing anything you ought not, own up. Don't make bad worse by telling lies about it. Put your books away and go to your commonroom."

Fredrika would have given anything *not* to have to go to the commonroom. She could guess the kind of reception she would have. But Len walked her there and saw her in, leaving her to her fate.

Chapter X

HALF-TERM ADVENTURE

UPPER IVb were very subdued after that evening. They took good care to let Fredrika know what they thought of her doings. The truth was that so much had been happening to them that quite a number of them had decided to turn over a new leaf and keep it clean, once it was turned. But that did not prevent them from showing Fredrika most unkindly their opinion of her.

"You *couldn't* expect us to believe a lie like that about Brigit!" Aimée Diderot remarked in shocked tones. "She may get into trouble, but she is *honest*!"

"She not only doesn't tell lies, she *can't*!" Val put in. "She always gives herself away when she tries. Anyhow, Fredrika von Gerling, we know that you can and do, so don't expect us to believe any tall stories in future."

After this they sheered off and left her severely alone. Fredrika wished that she had stuck to the truth and owned up to the map when Len asked them. She was not, normally, a dishonest girl as Upper IVb appeared to think. When she had lied she had done it in a moment's panic. She had sought out Brigit and apologised humbly and sincerely, and Irish Brigit, having calmed down by that time, accepted the apology, merely telling her not to be such a goop another time. However, the form kept the matter to itself. It did not wish to hear any more derogatory remarks about its manners, morals or work, and the whole thing blew over and was forgotten in an announcement of the Head's, made on the following Friday at Prayers.

"I have something to tell you girls," she said when the Catholics had taken their seats in Hall after Prayers. "This is a short term as Easter comes so early this year. We shall have no proper half-term. That is," as she saw the consternation in their faces, "no one will go away for it. Next Saturday, however, you will all have expeditions, weather permitting, of course. If not, there will be various entertainments arranged for you. Work will continue as usual until the end of Friday afternoon, but there will be no prep in the evening. Instead, you will have games, dancing and competitions. Also, you will be free to speak in your own languages. Work will begin again on Monday. *But*—" here, she paused and everyone listened eagerly for her next words, "*but* instead of coming back on the third Thursday after we break up, you will have until the Tuesday following, which will give you nearly a month's holiday at Easter."

She dismissed them after that, and from then on they spent every free moment in guessing what form the expeditions would take. Early in the next week the lists went up on the big notice-board in Hall, and the various forms knew their fate both as regards place and escort—that latter being always of supreme importance to them.

Upper IVb rejoiced to learn that they were scheduled for Geneva with Miss Armitage, Miss Burnett and their own Miss Ferrars as escort. The two Sixths were off for the day to Grindelwald and Va were to visit Sion. Vb were thrilled to hear that they were visiting Adelboden and Inter V were to go to Lake Lucerne with Stans as their ultimate goal.

"What's so important about Stans?" Samantha asked Ianthe Yetters who, as a Swiss, might be expected to know.

"About Stans itself, I do not know," Ianthe replied. "I have never been there. But at least three great men are associated with the town."

"Who?" demanded Jack Lambert who was listening.

"First, Arnold von Winkelried. You know about him, nicht?"

Jack was vague on the subject, but Wanda von Eschenau knew. "He was the hero who broke through the Austrian square by rushing at it and gathering as many of their spears as he could to himself, Jack. The Swiss army had been unable to break through before, but he made a path for it and the Austrians were defeated."

"Oh, *that* chap! Well, it was a jolly brave thing to do though quite mad," quoth matter-of-fact Jack. "Well, who else?"

"Niklaus von Flüe, who put a stop to a terrible war by his good advice," Emilie Gabrielli joined in. "He was a holy hermit and noted for his wisdom. When the Confederation—"

"The what?" interrupted Jack with some rudeness.

"The Confederation of Swiss States," Emilie said placidly. "They had just beaten the Burgundians after a fearful war and they could not decide on how to divide up the—the loot. They quarrelled violently about it until someone suggested they should send for Niklaus to ask for his advice. That was at the Diet of Stans. He refused to go himself, but he sent them a message and they agreed to do as he advised and so another war was avoided. He was canonised about twenty years ago because he was so holy as well as wise."

"And who was the third?" Samantha queried as Jack subsided for the moment.

Quite half a dozen voices answered her. "Oh, that was Pestalozzi!"

"Who under the canopy was he?" Samantha asked blankly.

"He was the true beginner of kindergartens," Renata van Buren told her. "During the invasion of Switzerland at the time of the French Revolution he gathered together as many orphans and lost children as he could and started a school for them. It was quite different from any of the schools at the time."

"How?" Samantha was interested.

"Oh, well, before his day school meant mainly reading and writing and arithmetic and grammar and—oh, mostly uninteresting things. Pestalozzi didn't agree with it."

"What *did* he think then?" Jack asked.

"He said you ought to start quite tiny children to observe things properly and learn to talk about them. Then he went on to drawing and measuring and only started them on reading and writing and number and things like that later," explained Meg Walton, who intended to be a kindergarten mistress and was deeply interested.

"Oh, and he was a friend of Mme de Staël," Wanda said. She hurried on, seeing yet another question in Jack's eye. "Lots of young men who were interested in education went to learn from him. One of them was Froebel, who carried his ideas much further and helped to establish kindergartens everywhere. But the man who began it all was Pestalozzi," she wound up triumphantly.

"He sounds quite an interesting bloke," Jack remarked.

"Can you see the original school?" Samantha asked curiously.

No one could tell her and she had to wait till she could ask Miss Annersley who was one of their escorts on the expedition. She was greatly disappointed to hear that during the Franco-Swiss invasion of 1798 the French had sacked Stans and more or less laid it waste.

"Well, it sounds very interesting," Arda Peik observed.

Saturday dawned fine and dry. Frühstück was early to enable those who had some distance to go to get off in good time. The authorities had decided to use the school coaches and 08.00 saw them filing into them, all excited and ready for anything. Samaris, though she was to be parted from Samantha for the whole day, was as thrilled as the rest.

"We'll have heaps to talk about later on," she told her friend when they met in one of the corridors. "I'll tell you everything I see, and you must tell me. Mind you take care and don't hurt your poor shoulder any more. Thank goodness your ankle is practically right again!"

"So is my collarbone if it comes to that," Samantha laughed. "Don't fuss, Sam! I'll be all right. Mind *you* don't get into any mischief!"

They laughed together and then Margot Maynard arrived and moved them on with the remark that there was no time for gossip just then.

"You can talk this evening and tomorrow if you want to. And don't forget that rules are rules, half-term or not, and talking in the corridors is forbidden. Off you go, both of you!" However, she forbore to give them order marks so they were not unduly depressed.

With the Head in charge, and Matey and Mdlle to back her up, it seemed unlikely that Inter V could get into mischief. It was another matter with Upper IVb, which contained its fair share of imps. However, Miss Burnett, Miss Armitage and Miss Ferrars were all experienced people, so everyone hoped for the best. In the event, Upper IVb spent an enjoyable and fairly normal day. It was to Inter V that the really startling experience came.

All went well at first. The great coach rolled off over the hard-packed snow into which the tyre-chains bit deep. The only cause for any rebuke was the loud chatter of the excited girls. The Head let it continue at first, but when they reached the great Autobahn running westward from the foot of their own mountain, she did call for lowered voices and they calmed down.

The route ran along the northern side of Lake Brienz from Interlaken to the little town of Brienz, whence it turned sharply north to Lucerne. At Sarnen it swung east to Stanstaad, famous for its wide view of the lake. Thence, they went on to Stans itself, where they left the coach. They clustered round their escorts in some eagerness to know what came next.

"What is there to see, Miss Annersley?" Mollie Rossiter asked.

"The town itself and an early baroque church which was built in 1647. At least," the Head corrected herself, "it was begun in 1641 and consecrated six years later. Next door to that is a sixteenth-century chapel with a monument to Arnold von Winkelried. Then there's the town hall which was built in the eighteenth century, and the historical museum which, until the Reformation took over, was a Capuchin monastery. Which will you have to begin with?"

"Oh, the church, please!" Jean Abbott said eagerly.

"None of them is very old," Renata commented. "Have they no really *ancient* buildings here?"

"I'm afraid not, Renata. Have you forgotten that the French sacked the town thoroughly during the wars of the French Revolution? They destroyed many buildings and massacred a number of people. That is not much more than a hundred and eighty years ago, so Stans has nothing much that is really ancient left. We may be thankful for what was spared. Come along, girls, and we'll visit the church."

Led by her, the form marched off to the church, where they paused to admire the Romanesque bell-tower before entering. They gazed at the windows and statues with delight and, following the example of their Head, most of them knelt to say a brief prayer before leaving the church for the little chapel next door with its monument erected to the famous fourteenth-century hero, Winkelried. A short walk then took them to the town hall after which Miss Annersley called a halt in favour of Mittagessen.

Mittagessen proved to be a minor adventure in itself. The Head had ordered previously and arranged for them to have a meal composed mainly of dishes peculiar to the Lucerne region. They began with Kässuppe or cheese soup.

"Queer flavour, hasn't it?" Jean murmured to her neighbour, Mollie.

Mollie wrinkled up her pretty nose. "I've tasted worse in my time—not much, though!"

However, they all approved of the next course, which was fried fillets of lake perch, served piping hot in a delicious butter sauce with creamy potatoes to accompany them. They finished up with slices of Krapfen, a rich fruitcake made with pears, nuts and almond paste as well as the more usual ingredients. To drink with their meal they had Limmat wine diluted with water. The Head knew well that it is not wise to drink plain water in a mountainous district. When they had finished, she proposed that they should take the funicular railway up the Stanserhorn for the sake of the magnificent views to be had from its summit.

"What shall we see from the top, Mdlle?" asked Michelle Cabràn of Mdlle who sat next her. "Have you climbed it?"

"But yes; many times. As for the view, you will see all our own mountains, including Mt Titlis, which is one of the snow-capped mountains, as well as a glorious view of Lake Lucerne."

"One has told me that it is possible to go up Mt Titlis by cable car," said Michelle, "but me, I should not like that. I do not altogether like even the funicular, though I know great care is taken."

At this point, the little train suddenly stopped short with a jerk and then began to slide slowly downwards. Michelle shrieked and Ianthe and Emilie joined her. The rest exclaimed, but held on to their self-control though it took some doing. Mdlle flung an arm round the nervous Michelle in an instant.

"But be quiet at once, Michelle!" she exclaimed. "There is no real danger! No screaming, if you please!"

Miss Annersley was also on her feet. "Girls, remain quietly in your seats! There is no danger!" she repeated Mdlle's words.

"Ah!" as the downward motion ceased with another jerk which nearly threw some of them off their seats to the floor. "It has stopped! You have been told over and over again how carefully the funiculars and chair-lifts are tested every three or four months. No need to be afraid!"

The girls kept their heads, but more than one looked shudderingly out of the windows to make sure that the cars were really still and not slipping again. Jack, who didn't know the meaning of nerves, was trying to calm Ianthe, and Matey had taken charge of the badly shaken Emilie in her own inimitable way.

"Now then! How many babies have we here instead of sensible girls?" she demanded, giving her charge a slight shake to bring her to her senses. "I hope there are no *cowards* among us!"

Emilie had been about to utter another shriek, but this bracing treatment made her shut her lips tightly on it. Matey said no more, but kept an eye on her white face, ready to deal at once with any tendency towards fainting. In fact, the three adults were far more upset than any of the girls. They were responsible for this young crowd and though all three spoke bravely, all three felt distinctly anxious. Nothing happened, however, except that they stayed where they were; nor was there any sign of the downward car coming.

"A failure in the electricity, I expect," Miss Annersley said. "We must stay here until they correct the fault."

"Couldn't we get out and walk down?" Jean asked tentatively.

"No, Jean; we must stay where we are. What's that, Samantha? Sweets? A good idea! Yes; hand them round. I'm only sorry I haven't any. I meant to buy them when we got back to Stans and treat you folk on the homeward journey."

Renata and Arda had also provided themselves with bonbons, and the mere fact of eating helped to steady the girls. Samantha even managed a slightly shaky laugh as she said, "I guess we'll have some tall tales to put into our home letters tomorrow. Wait till I get hold of young Sam! She'll be eating her finger-ends off with envy when she hears of this adventure!"

The Head was quick to seize on her idea. "More than one person will be thrilled to hear of it—Mrs Maynard for instance. She'll put it into her next book, I expect." A movement caught her attention. "Jack! Where are you going?"

Jack stopped dead in the gangway. "I just thought I'd take a dekko outside."

"Come back to your seat at once! Of course you can't. The doors will be sealed in any case. Girls! You hear me! You are to stay in your seats!"

Seldom had the Head spoken more firmly, and if any of the others had been minded to follow Jack's example, it was more than they dared do now. Jack returned reluctantly to her seat.

"Why did you want to look?" Samantha asked. "I should think it was enough to be stuck here, not knowing what may happen at any moment. How'd you feel if the brakes suddenly gave and we all went sliding down the hill?"

"Not knowing, can't say. But you needn't be afraid of *that* happening."

At that very moment there came another of those terrifying jerks and then the train began to glide smoothly and evenly downwards. The girls gasped and Michelle set up a smothered yell. The Head held them, however.

"Queer!" Jack muttered to Samantha. "I'd have thought it almost impossible to reverse the current like that! I wonder what they've done?"

"What do *you* know about it?" snapped Samantha, who found Jack's endless curiosity a little trying just now. "My guess is that they're taking us back to the nearest station. Do hold your tongue,

146

Jack, or Michelle, at least, will be having the screaming meemies!"—a piece of slang for which she would certainly have been hauled over the coals if anyone in authority had heard it.

"Not if the Head knows it! But it's interesting, isn't it?" Jack the mechanically-minded asked.

"It may be to you. I only know that once I get safely out of this it'll be a precious long time before I risk another mountain railway!"

The train continued its downward passage and finally glided, intact, into the station where the party was met by at least three officials, all excitedly apologetic, all desolated at what had happened, and all wondering what the Swiss authorities would do about it; likewise, the school.

Miss Annersley met them halfway. "I do not think it has harmed the girls," she said with lips that were still rather white. "We are all safe, and at least it has been an experience. A good meal will steady us all, and for the accident—"

A clear voice cut across her assurances. "But what did, actually, happen?" it asked.

"Jack!" said Miss Annersley awfully.

The leader of the railway party smiled at Jack. "We know that a great log fell across the line and caused a break in the current. How it got there, we do not know and it is something which must be inquired into. But it was more than that, for, as you know, once the log was removed, the line worked again, but backwards. That, gnädige Frau," he bowed to Miss Annersley, "is something else into which stringent inquiries shall be made. When we know the facts they shall be communicated to you. That is truly your right."

At the moment, Miss Annersley was not disposed to stand on her rights. All she really wanted was to get the girls safely back to school, where she could relax once they were all under its roof. However, that could not be for a time yet. She thanked the officials as charmingly as she could, and then marched her charges off to the pâtisserie where Kaffee und Kuchen had been ordered, and insisted that they make a good meal. It was not difficult for most of them, for the cakes were of the kind that they rarely saw at school and the coffee was blanketed with whipped cream. The three adults ate, too, but more as an example to their pupils than because they felt like it. In fact, all three were thankful women when at long last they left the girls surging down the corridors to the splasheries and themselves retired to their own room, where they might sit down in peace and try to recover from the strain on their nerves.

Chapter XI

NINA APPEALS TO JOEY

"WELL, Nina, my lamb, here I am at last!" Joey Maynard stooped over the bed where Nina Rutherford lay with heavily-bandaged head. She looked very thin and white under her bandages, but her dark eyes were alight as she smiled up into the delicately-featured face bent over her.

"Mrs Maynard! Oh, how nice! I've been longing to see you. How is everyone? Is your little Phil going on all right?"

Joey nodded as she sat down on the chair nurse had set for her beside the bed. "Making strides now. She's beginning to walk and she's getting back her old gaiety. And how are *you* after all this time?"

"Like Phil, I'm making strides. But oh, how this has messed up my programme! No tour of the Antipodes for me yet awhile, even when I'm on my feet again. I'll have a lot to make up. I'm most frightfully out of practice, you see."

"I understand. At the same time, my sweet, you've a lot to be thankful for! You might all have been killed. Your cousins might have been as badly hurt as you. As it is, even your Cousin Yvonne is almost fit again. Alix is all right and Anthea was only bruised. You and that poor young American were the ones who came off the worst. Now you're really pulling round and all the doctors say you will be your old self again before too long."

"How *is* Mr Dwight—isn't that his name?" Nina asked.

Joey nodded. Inwardly, she was feeling nervous, for young Dwight had died from his injuries. No one had told Nina yet and she had undertaken to break the news that day. Just how the girl would take it, no one could be sure. Nina, touched with the magic fire of genius, was an unpredictable creature. Her music came first, last and all the time with her, but after such an illness as she had had she might be more sensitive to the young man's tragic death than was expected.

Nina gave her no time to speak. "Just exactly what *did* happen?" she asked.

"He skidded on an icy patch and crashed into your car. He was going too fast, considering the state of the road, or it might not have happened. *Most* mercifully, Gaudenz saw it all, kept his head, and dashed out with one of the school's big fire-extinguishers and put out the flames in time to save you all from frizzling."

"I see." Nina said no more for the moment, and Joey began to summon up her courage to break the rest of the news. But again the girl was before her.

"Mrs Maynard, how *is* Mr Dwight?"

"He is quite well now," Joey said steadily.

"Oh? I'm glad—no; what do you mean? Not—not—"

Joey kissed her. "I mean that he is quite well. He will never have any more pain or grief—and he had had his share of grief. Listen, Nina! One reason why he was driving so recklessly was that his mother whom he adored had died very early that morning. She had been up here for some months, but she came too late. He refused to believe it and when the end came suddenly, he was badly shocked. I'm not saying that he had any right to lose his head like that and risk other people's lives, but that is the excuse. And after all, he wasn't long parted from her. He died a week after the accident, and since he did not fully recover consciousness, he had little time to miss her. For him, it was the best way in the end. *You* know what it means and you can sympathise."

"I see," Nina was silent again. Then she suddenly caught Joey's hand. "What about his father? Had he any other relations?"

"His father died when he was a baby and the only other relation he seems to have had was an elderly cousin of his mother's whom he had scarcely seen. He and his mother were all in all to each other. It was a waste of a life, but for him it was well." Joey kissed the quivering lips again before she added, "So you won't fret about it, will you, Nina? It was no fault of Lady Rutherford's. We all know what a careful driver she is. Young Dwight is at rest, and even you are making headway. Will you think of all that and, instead of fretting, try to be thankful for God's mercies?"

Nina pressed her friend's hand quickly. "Yes; I will. As you say, it's saved him a lot of grief. I—I know how I felt when Father was drowned. And I did have Cousin Guy and the rest of the cousins, and the Embury cousins came later. I'm not alone in the world and from what you say he *was*, so it's best for him. Thank you for telling me. I've wondered this last few days, but I didn't like to ask. I think I've been waiting for you to tell me. You—you understand so well."

"Thank you, Nina. That's one of the nicest things I've ever had said to me. And I'll add this. You feel sad about this, but remember that every new experience is of help to you. Your music will be stronger and better. And now," Joey changed the subject, "I've a message for you from your cousin Winifred. When you are really fit again she wants you to go to stay with them in Montreux. She'd have been up before, but the kids have had whooping-cough and she didn't dare risk the infection for you. All clear now, though."

"Sweet of her. She and Cousin Martin have been very good to me. So have the Rutherford cousins."

Nina stopped there. Joey nodded. "You must hurry up and get

well enough to go there. Montreux will be lovely in a few weeks' time when the narcissus fields are in full bloom, not to mention the other spring flowers. I admit," she went on with a glance out of the window, "that it doesn't seem very possible with the present weather. Look at that mist! It's just as well the term is so short no one bothered to think of more than the Saturday expedition. The school is hard at it at Monday's lessons as usual. By the way, they're all thrilled about your scholarship and essay prizes. That last was a brainwave. What made you think of it?"

Nina laughed softly. "All I learnt while at the Chalet School myself. You know, until I went there music was the greatest thing in life to me and I can see that I was growing one-sided. I've found that out more and more since I've been going about, meeting people of all kinds and hearing them talk. That was when I found out what a little ninny I'd been. Oh, how furious I used to be over having my practice cut down for other things! But if I hadn't been made to learn I should have found myself left out hundreds of times. Now it's different. Music still means the best of life to me and always will: but I do realise that there are other things as well. *You* made me see that first," she added shyly.

"Glad I've so much to my credit," quoth Joey, firmly keeping the conversation on a matter-of-fact basis. "Well, I've a request to make to you and then I must go."

"Oh? What is it? I'll do anything I can."

"We've a new girl at school this term—a child of thirteen or fourteen—called Samaris Davies. She's been living in Innsbruck and attended one or more of your recitals and was thrilled to bits by them—or so she says. She'd love to come and visit you now that you *are* allowed visitors. What do you say?"

"Bring her by all means. I'd love to meet her! Is she musical? What instrument does she play?" Nina spoke eagerly.

"Sorry to disappoint you, but I think the only instrument she knows is the mouth organ. I believe she had piano lessons in her extreme youth, but they were a complete flop. She loves music, however, and when I've time to talk it over with her, I mean to find out if something a little more classic appeals to her. Or she may have a voice. Not knowing, can't say at the moment. I'll bring her along on Saturday some time. Be prepared to be regarded with awe and reverence. Samaris, from all accounts, thinks you're the cat's bathmat!"

Nina giggled. "What rot! But I'd love to meet her. Samaris, did you say? What an odd name! I don't believe I've ever met it before."

"*I* certainly haven't! And to make it funnier, we have another new girl, an American, who is called Samantha. The two Sams are by way of being pals, though Samantha must be around two years older than Samaris. Oh, by the way, I must tell you of the adventure Inter V had on Saturday during their expedition," and Joey launched forth into a brisk account of the mishap to the funicular.

"What a horrid experience!" Nina exclaimed. "I'm thankful I wasn't there! Poor Miss Annersley and Mdlle and Matey! They must have felt stricken!"

"Oh, they're recovering. Such a thing happens only once in a blue moon on the Swiss railways. Well, I've had my half-hour with you, so I must say goodbye. I'll pop in again during the week and bring Cecil and the twins, shall I? Would you like that?"

"Love it! I always feel I've a special right in Cecil because I was the first of the school to see her—after her sisters, of course. Who is she like?"

"Con, mainly. She's darker, though. She has black eyes where Con's are brown and her complexion is darker. She's six in April and quite a little person on her own now. She's very proud of the fact that she's the only member of the family to have had music written for her especial benefit. Do you remember your little lullaby, *Welcome for Cecil*?"

"*That* thing?" Nina laughed. "I'll do something much better for her some time."

"Well, not for a while yet, please, or I shall have to buy her a new hat! The monkey is quite conceited enough about the *Welcome*! Now I really must go. I'll see you in a few days' time and meanwhile you can set yourself to getting well enough for the trip to Montreux."

"I'll enjoy it, I know, but—"

"But what?" Joey asked as Nina halted and looked at her eagerly.

"I don't mean to be rude, but—oh, may I come to you first? I remember what a lovely place Freudesheim is. There's a very special *something* about it. I'm very fond of the Embury cousins, but your place—well—"

"Come and welcome! We'll be delighted to have you. But you mustn't stay too long or Winifred will talk!"

"There's more to it than that, though, even though it's my main reason," Nina said. "You live next door to the school and I could go and see everyone there. I was so happy at the Chalet School once I'd got over my first stupidity—I'd love to be able to run in and say hello to them all."

Joey laughed. "So long as you don't do it in school-time you'll be as welcome as April showers and May flowers together. That's settled then. As soon as Jack gives the All Clear you shall come to us for a fortnight. That will help you to get properly on your feet before you go down to Montreux. I know the girls will be overjoyed to see you. In fact," she added plaintively, "I can see myself being overrun by visitors from the school whenever the girls have a chance. And now, for the last time, I must go.

Goodbye, Nina! Be sure you're looking more like yourself when I bring the babies!"

With a final kiss she went off to be picked up by her husband, who had been patiently waiting for her in Matron's room. On the way home to Freudesheim she told him about her visit, including Nina's request. He fully approved of the idea, and also of her suggestion that she should take Samaris along to the Sanatorium next Saturday.

"Take Samantha, too," he said. "Now that Nina knows about poor young Dwight's death it'll be just as well if we can fill her mind with other things. She's a sensitive creature, and if she broods over his death it'll do her no good. By the way, I've had a note from Guy Rutherford. He says that his own family are all well, even Lady Rutherford. Some of them are coming out in June and they want to take Nina back to Brettingham for the end of her convalescence. The tour is off for the present, so she might as well go. I'm impressing on her agent that she must take things very quietly for some months to come."

Joey nodded. "And I've just had a brain-waggle! When they come to collect her, we'll send them off to the Tiernsee for a week or two. *We* shan't want the house until the summer holidays, if then. Madge and her crowd will be home in August, remember, and I expect we'll be slated for Wales if she has any say in the matter. Somehow," she concluded as the car swept in at the gate, "I don't see us having much time at the Tiernsee *this* Summer!"

Chapter XII

The Sams Meet Nina

"Oh, Mrs Maynard, this *is* a thrill! How are we going—car, or walk, or what?"

Joey laughed down into the excited face Samaris lifted to her. "Neither car nor walk, my sweet. We're ski-ing. Much the best and quickest way, considering the state of the roads. That last blizzard we had *and* the black frost that followed have made ski-ing the perfect means for getting around. Miss Burnett told me that you both ski, so scram and get your skis strapped on. Don't forget your sticks!" She had to shout the last sentence, for the two Sams had scuttled off on the word. Her triplet daughters arrived at that moment, so she gave it up and hoped for the best.

"Oh, my goodness!" she exclaimed as she surveyed them. "To think that my cuddly first babies have grown into you three leggy creatures! And you've put your hair up, Len. Why?"

Len laughed and touched the heavy coils of chestnut hair at the back of her head self-consciously. "I thought it was time I did something about it. After all, we three are going on for eighteen."

"Lordy, lordy! How ghastly! It's time I thought of turning middle-aged when I have three daughters nearly eighteen."

"Don't you dare!" Margot exclaimed.

"Don't worry," said quiet Con. "She may talk about it, but it's beyond her. Besides, if she did that she'd have to stop being a Chaletian. Can't have middle-aged Chalet School girls, you know."

"Anyhow," Len chimed in, "she doesn't begin to look it. Even now she doesn't look very much older than us."

Joey laughed ruefully. "Goodness knows I've had enough to age me this past year or two! There've been times when I've felt as if I were *eighty*! Ah! Here come the Sams, all ready for the fray."

"When are *we* to see Nina?" Margot asked jealously. "After all, we're old friends. Why take the Sams to see her?"

"To give her something fresh to think about, ninny! I had to tell her on Monday about poor young Dwight and—well, Nina's a genius and no one wants her to go off at a tangent about him. Oh, I know she never knew him, but they were in the same accident and she's appallingly sensitive. Everything else being equal, I dare say you three can visit her next Saturday." She turned to the two Sams who had come round the corner of the building on their skis and were standing a little way off till she should be ready for them. "Ready? Then come on! Goodbye, you three! I'll be seeing you some time." She kissed her daughters and then set the pace down the drive and along the motor road.

"There's one thing I want to say," she said as they skimmed along. "Don't be too taken aback by all Nina's bandages. They'll come off in due course, and though they had to cut all her hair away at one spot, they haven't shaved her whole head and her hair is so thick it'll be possible to brush it over so that the place won't show before the new hair grows again. It's only a short visit you know. She still has to be kept pretty quiet. But she's making a good recovery and her colour is coming back. Not that she ever had much." She began to laugh. "What a little fright she was when she first came to school! She was skinny and white and her eyes looked like black saucers. I've been told that when her Rutherford cousins first met her she looked even worse for she was in deepest Continental mourning for her father. Lady Rutherford soon put a stop to that, however, and in school, of course, she wore uniform. By the end of the first term she looked a different creature."

"That would be this marvellous air," Samantha said wisely. "I guess it has something you don't get down in the valleys. I know I feel twice as fit as I did before I came here."

"Oh, so do I!" Samaris cried. "I like Innsbruck all right, but in the summer months I did feel limp; it was so deadly hot!"

"Innsbruck lies in the valley and is shut in by mountains. That's one reason why we have the school up here instead of down by the lakes. I'm just wondering how this new school that's opening next term will get on at Thun. Well, time will show."

"Why didn't you bring Bruno?" Samaris asked as they neared the railway. "I'm sure he'd have loved the run."

"Mainly because dogs aren't allowed in San. Don't bother about Bruno. He's had one good run already and he'll get another later on." She nodded towards a lane running down from the motor road. "More Old Chaletians live down there. Heard of Mme Courvoisier, either of you? She was one of our pupils at the Tiernsee.[1] Later she came to the school as history mistress. Mrs Graves was with us at the Tiernsee and in Guernsey and England. Then she went to Chelsea to train for P.T. and came to us as Games mistress. They share a big chalet down there. Biddy has a family of three—the twins Pat and Marie, and Petit Jean who is nearly two. Hilary has four now that her second boy arrived last Sunday. The two eldest are girls, Marjorie and Lois; young demons, both of them. Then comes Winkie whose real name is Philip after his dad; and now this new baby who, I understand, is to be called Frank. You'll meet them all some time. It's just as well we decided to start the kindergarten, for there are plenty of small fry coming along."

"They've quite a number now, haven't they?" Samantha

[1] *The Chalet School and Jo*

queried. "We don't come across them much, but I've seen them occasionally."

Joey nodded as she guided the girls past the head of a path leading down to the plain far below. "You're right Sammy. Oh, we shan't lack for pupils at St Nicholas now we've opened it. My own Felicity and her twin Felix were there till last term. Then Felicity came to the big school and Felix went off to prep school with Charles and Mike, my next older boys. Stephen, our eldest, is in his first year at public school, and enjoying life to the full. Let's see; you two have no brothers, have you?"

"Not me; but I've two kid sisters," Samantha said. "Ermina is nine and Menela is seven. They'll be coming here later, I expect."

"And you, Samaris?"

Samaris shook her head. "I'm a one-and-only. I've often envied girls with brothers and sisters, but Mam told me once that if there'd been any more we couldn't have travelled. We're not exactly rich, you know."

Joey glanced at her. "You say 'Mam'. But of course! Your name is Davies. You're Welsh."

Samaris nodded. "At least," she amended, "I'm part Welsh. Some of Dad's folks came from Australia and Mam is Canadian— French Canadian. My second name is Charlot. That was her surname."

Samantha exclaimed. "That's odd! One of my aunts married a Mr Charlot."

Samaris chuckled. "Not really? P'raps we're cousins of some kind and don't know it."

"Maybe we are. Say, wouldn't that be great?" Samantha gave the younger girl a warm look. "Pappa's pure American, of course. We hail from New York in the beginning. His folk were Dutch settlers, way back in the sixteen hundreds, but we reckon ourselves plain American these days. Mama came from Boston and her folk crossed over from England more'n a hundred years ago."

Joey laughed. "You'll have to go into pedigrees some other time. There are the San gates and in a few minutes more we'll be seeing Nina."

In the excitement of this, Samaris forgot about ancestors, but Samantha, less interested in the young musician, thought about it at intervals. Not just then, however, for they had reached the great doors of the Sanatorium and Joey was instructing them to remove their skis and leave them together with their ski-sticks with the porter. Then she took them through the doors into a long, white-tiled corridor. Halfway along, she paused before a door at which she tapped. A pleasant voice said, "Herein!" and they went into a small room full of flowers, with gay chintzes on the chairs and a little sofa. Seated at a table by the window was a tall woman whose black hair was turned grey. She greeted the visitors with a bright smile and a warm welcome.

"Joey! How nice to see you! How is Phil?"

"Coming along, thank goodness. She's laughing again and she's beginning to eat and not peck like a bird. Walking is slow. She can't take a step without hanging on to something; but it's coming. And oh, Helen, you don't know how thankful I am!"

"Good! Well, now, are these the two Sams I've been hearing about?"

"They are. This is Sammy, otherwise Samantha. But, of course, you two know each other already. And Sam II is really Samaris. Samaris, this is Matron—Miss Graves. It's all right, isn't it, Helen? They can go to visit Nina?"

"Quite all right. Like your Phil, Nina is making steady progress now. The doctors hope to be able to reduce her bandages in a few days, and then someone must break to her the news that she's been cropped."

"Leave it to me: I'll tell her. I'm sorry because she had such lovely hair—so long and thick. I suppose it hasn't given her curls like Mary-Lou?" Joey spoke eagerly.

Matron laughed, but she shook her head. "I'm afraid not."

"Oh, what a pity! Mary-Lou was thrilled to the marrow when she discovered she'd got curls out of that accident. I rather hoped it would be the same with Nina."

"Nina wouldn't thank you for curls. And I'm positive they wouldn't suit her in the least. Her straight, smooth hair is exactly right with that oval face of hers and her regular features. Curls would be all wrong."

"I suppose you're right. Oh, well, I must think up some other form of consolation. But I'll break the news tenderly, never fear!"

Matron laughed. "I'm certain you will! Now take off your coats and get thoroughly warm and then you may go to visit our celebrity. Don't talk her to death—that's all I ask. She can't stand much, even yet. Twenty minutes, Joey. Come back here and I'll have coffee and cake for you all. Where's my friend Bruno?"

"Not here. Jack took him for a good run earlier on, and as we ski-ed here, I left him behind. Come to tea tomorrow if you want to see him."

"I'll think about it. I may be full up. I'll give you a ring later and let you know definitely." She turned to the girls. "Are you well warmed up? Let me feel your hands. Yes; that's all right. Take them along, Joey, and mind you don't overrun your time. Nina still tires quickly."

"Don't worry! I'll see that we're punctual!" Joey laughed and then led the girls out of the room and along the wide corridor where they met an occasional nurse hurrying along. The two Sams noted that everyone of them had a smile and a greeting for Mrs Maynard and it was clear that she was a general favourite. At the end of the corridor, she turned into a short passage and at the end she stopped and tapped lightly on a door. A young nurse opened it and smiled broadly when she saw who was there.

"Bonjour, Madame," she said in rapid French. "Ah! Les deux Sams!"

Joey nodded. "As you say." She spoke in the same language. "How is Mdlle Rutherford this morning?"

"Oh, she is very well and looking forward to meeting her visitors." She stood back and, led by Joey, the two Sams entered the little private ward where Nina Rutherford lay. Her eyes lit up when she saw Joey.

"Mrs Maynard! So you did come!"

"Complete with the two Sams. Don't I always keep my word, Nina? How much better you're looking this morning! Very much more like your old self! Matron has allowed us twenty minutes, so we mustn't waste time. This is Samantha and this is Samaris. Girls! Miss Rutherford!"

Nina smiled and held out her hand. "What fun for you to have names so alike and to be new together this term, and yet no relation to each other! Come and sit down and tell me about school."

Nurse had set three chairs before she left the room. They sat down, the two girls feeling rather shy as they looked at the bandages which still covered most of Nina's head. She was pale, but her eyes were bright and she smiled at them gaily.

"Which forms are you in?"

"I'm in Inter V and Sam is Upper IVb," Samantha said. "Do you really feel better today, Miss Rutherford?"

Joey grinned to herself as Nina exclaimed, "Oh, for heaven's sake! Make it Nina, please! Much matier, don't you think?"

"May we really?" Samaris asked. "It *would* be matier, of course, but it seems rather cheek. After all, you are Somebody."

Nina laughed. "What rot! It's only a few years since I was at the school myself—four, to be precise. And even if I've left officially, I still reckon myself a Chaletian."

"Like me," Joey nodded. "I'll be a Chaletian till I die, even if I live to be a double centenarian!"

"Gosh! Wouldn't that be awful!" Samaris exclaimed. "Fancy living to be two hundred years old!"

"Methuselah in the Bible lived to be nine hundred," Samantha reminded her. "I'll bet he didn't enjoy the last part of it much," Samaris told her. Nina laughed and the faint pink in her cheeks deepened. "We can't tell at this late date."

"And in any case," Joey chipped in, "I've always understood that the Hebrew years were shorter than ours. However, even my first century is a good long way off, let alone the second one. All I'm trying to impress on you three is that whatever else I am or may become, I'm a Chaletian, first, last, and all the time. Now give it a miss! I understand they mean to remove part of your bandaging, Nina. That'll be a relief, I should think."

"I shan't be sorry to be rid of them. Mrs Maynard, will you tell me something?"

"If I can. I'm buying no pigs in pokes from you or anyone else. What do you want to know?"

"It's my hair. Have they cut it?"

"They have, and a jolly good job, too. If they hadn't you wouldn't be here now, my love. It was your hair or your life and, on the whole, we all preferred that it should be your life. Don't worry! A mop like yours will soon grow again. I hope, by the way, that you aren't expecting curls like Mary-Lou, for in that case you'll be disappointed. Matron says your hair is still straight and smooth. Anyhow, curls wouldn't suit you at all. You haven't the face for them. Mary-Lou has."

Nina laughed. "Oh, I don't mind. How short *have* they cropped me?"

"As short as Jack Lambert's—oh, but you don't know her; she's since your time. Boy's crop, then. It suits Jack's cheeky

little face almost as much as it will suit yours, which is quite
different. You'll like her, by the way. You'll probably meet her
while you're staying with me. I'll warn you of one thing. She's a
human question mark. Jack wants to *know*, and my goodness, the
things she wants to know are just legion! My poor Len knows
that!" She giggled softly.

Samantha and Samaris joined her giggles. They had been at
the school long enough to know that Jack Lambert seemed to
regard the Head Girl as her own special piece of property.
Samantha, in the same form, had seen plenty of evidence of it
and had commented on it to Samaris.

Nina chuckled. "It does seem queer that Len, who was just a
kid of twelve or thirteen when I first knew her is Head Girl, and
chased after by a—what is she? Junior—Junior Middle?"

"My dear, she's a Senior now and in Inter V with Sammy
here. It began when she was a shining light in IIIa—about eleven,
I suppose. Len was her dormitory prefect and Jack latched on to
her promptly. I'll see you meet her—Jack, I mean—before you
go to Montreux. She'll be a new experience for you."

"How?" Nina asked curiously.

"Well, she's a girl, but actually she's more than half a boy."

"When we were discussing your essay competition the other
day, Jack said that she meant to go in for motor engineering and
run a garage of her own later," Samantha said pensively. "Gee!
Is she mad about motors! I'll tell the world!"

"And what are *you* mad about?" Nina asked.

Samantha blushed. "Nothing in particular, really. Now Sam,
here, thinks she'd like an outdoor life with lots of animals. She's
mad about music, too."

"Sammy!" exclaimed the crimson Samaris.

"It's true, isn't it? She went to hear you, Miss—I mean Nina—
and she just raved about your playing."

Nina looked interested. "What do you play yourself, Samaris?"

"The mouth organ!" Samaris blurted out, redder than ever. "I did have piano lessons when I was a kid, but I couldn't get away with the piano. It's not my cup of tea. So Dad stopped my lessons. He said he'd enough to do with his money without wasting it like that. In some ways, I wish he hadn't. But I've got my harmonica. That's better than nothing."

"I suppose it is. But if that's the sort of thing you like, why don't you take up one of the wind instruments—woodwind for choice. What about the flute or the clarinet? You might do well with one of those if that's what you like."

Samaris's face lit up. "I say! What a whizzer idea! I never thought of that. Only—don't they cost the earth?"

"Good ones do, of course; but you wouldn't need a first-class one to begin with. I wonder—listen, Sam—that's what they call you, isn't it?—I know a man who's a brilliant flautist. He has three or four flutes, including the one he started on himself. When I'm better I'll write and ask him if you can borrow it for a while and then you could try it out and see how you like it. Oh, but what about lessons?"

"That's easy enough," Joey observed. "Plato—I mean Mr Denny—used to play the flute in his young days. He could start Sam off, anyhow, and we could see how she got on. It's a good idea, that. You write as soon as they'll let you, Nina, and if you get the flute I'll tackle Mr Denny and then—we'll see!"

"Gosh!" said Samantha. "Next thing you know we'll have Sam coming out as a—a flutist—if that's what you call it!"

"The word is 'flautist'," said Joey, glancing at her watch. "Well, our time's more than up and we must go. I, for one, have no fancy to be *chucked* out! It's goodbye for the moment, Nina. Go on getting well as fast as you can. Remember, Sam is now relying on you for that flute! Say goodbye, you two, and come on!"

They said goodbye and left the ward. Nurse, who had been coming to warn them, nodded and smiled and went in to look at her patient. She found that the mournful look which had been in Nina's eyes ever since she had heard of the death of young Dwight had vanished. She was tired, but she was quietly happy. Joey had not only broken to her the news that her glorious mane of hair had been cropped, but had also given her a healthy outlook on the poor lad's tragic end. Also, between them, she and the Sams had brought the patient an entirely new interest and that was just what the doctors had wanted.

Chapter XIII

THE JUNIORS IN TROUBLE

DESPITE her good intentions, Joey had contrived to upset more than one person by taking the Sams to visit Nina. Among the prefects Marie Hüber, the music prefect, was especially aggrieved.

"But I cannot understand why Mme Maynard should take those two to visit Nina Rutherford," she said to Margot. "They are not musical. Neither of them learns any instrument. Why should they be chosen?"

"Better ask Mum," Margot said carelessly. "It was *her* idea. And you're wrong about one thing, anyhow. Young Sam is very musical, even though she doesn't learn any instrument. I've seen her listening to the radio concerts. Don't be silly, Marie!" She laughed and went off without giving any more thought to it.

In a way it was a pity that Marie had not relieved her feelings to either Len or Con. Margot was clever, but she was lacking in the deep insight into character the other two possessed. Either of them would have explained Joey's motive in taking the two new girls to visit Nina Rutherford, and Marie, who was a reasonable girl, would have been satisfied. Margot merely decided that her mother's intentions were no business of Marie's and left it at that.

There was further discontent among the members of Inter V and Upper IVb. At least half a dozen girls in Inter V felt that they had more right to be allowed to visit Nina, seeing they had known her when she was at school. Among them Margaret Twiss, Barbara Hewlett, Arda Peik and Renata van Buren, all of them musical, felt that if anyone were chosen, it should have been one of them, rather than Samantha van der Byl, a newcomer that term and not particularly keen on music, anyhow. Barbara and Margaret said nothing, but both Arda and Renata gave voice to their feelings.

"If Mrs Maynard wanted to take any of us to San, why should she choose Samantha?" Renata demanded during the afternoon of the same day. "It isn't as if either she or Samaris knows Nina, though I believe that kid Samaris has heard her. Samantha can't really care—or Nina either," she added, none too lucidly.

Samantha shrugged her shoulders. "I guess it was Mrs Maynard's pick. She's a right to take who she chooses and she don't ask anyone else's opinion. I didn't *ask* to go, but I'm right glad I did. I like Nina a lot. Maybe I'll take to music after all."

"Huh!" was Renata's only rejoinder to this.

"Who said you could call her Nina like that?" Arda demanded.

"She did herself. Ordered us to, in fact."

"I don't believe it!"

"O.K. Go and ask Mrs Maynard. She was there and heard her."

In Upper IVb the reaction was quite different. Their main interest lay in the accident and they were wildly curious to know what the victim of it had to say about it.

"Does she look *very* ill?" Emmy Friedrich asked.

"Well, she's very white and her head's all bandaged, but she seemed to me fairly fit otherwise," Samaris replied. "It's a good thing she didn't injure her arms or her hands. That might have stopped her playing for ages."

"Did she tell you how she felt when the crash came?" Brigit asked eagerly.

"We never mentioned it," Samaris replied.

"Never mentioned it! Then what was the point of you going? What *did* you talk about?" Rosemary wanted to know.

"Music, principally. Oh, and Mrs Maynard told her they'd had to crop her hair."

"Did they? Oh, well, what does that matter? Lots of people have short hair nowadays," Clarissa Dendy pointed out. "Your own hair's short if it comes to that."

"Yes; but my hair has always been short. They say Nina had a real mane."

"Did she mind?" This was Robina.

"I don't think so. Mrs Maynard told her it had been her hair or her life and they saved her life—naturally."

"Well, why did you go, anyhow? You don't know her, do you?"

"I do *now*. But I've heard her play, of course. I was awfully keen. She's miraculous!" Samaris spoke with enthusiasm.

Lysbet eyed her severely. "I don't see why. You don't learn anything yourself."

"That's not to say I'm not keen. As a matter of fact, I am—awfully. What's more, I rather think I'm going to begin presently."

"Piano—or fiddle—or what?"

"Flute, I hope. And, by the way, I do play the harmonica."

"What's that?" Robina demanded.

"Mouth organ to you."

"Oh, that!" Lysbet spoke contemptuously. "That's not a proper instrument."

"'Tis, then! Someone's even written a concerto for it, so now!"

"What? I don't believe you! My kid brother has one and I *used* to. It's just a kid's toy," Rosemary put in.

"Oh, no, it isn't!"

"Well, *I* never heard of any real musician playing it. It—it's like the saxophone they have in jazz bands—that sort of thing!" Brigit spoke scornfully.

"You're wrong there. I know that the saxophone has been

used in some of the modern symphonies, anyhow." Samaris was becoming heated.

"Beethoven didn't use it—and nor did Brahms," Lysbet said. "They are the really great musicians."

"P'raps it wasn't invented in their day," Robina suggested by way of smoothing things over. "When did it begin? D'you know, Sam?"

"Haven't a clue; but I do know it's been used in at least one symphony if not more."

"Well, I still don't see why *you* should have gone to see Nina Rutherford. You didn't know her—just going to one of her recitals isn't knowing her," Celia Thornton took a hand. "Lots of *us* do know her. Why couldn't Mrs Maynard have chosen one of *us*?"

"Ask her, if you want to know all that badly!" Samaris snapped.

"Oh, don't be such an ass!" Celia snapped back.

Just what might have happened, there is no knowing, for they were all getting heated, but at that point a series of wild shrieks rang out from the Junior commonroom next door and they all forgot the promising squabble. With one accord they made for the door, wrenched it open, and dashed down the corridor just as a posse of prefects, headed by Len Maynard, came flying to the rescue.

Len acted swiftly. "Back to your room, all of you!" she ordered. "Stay there until you're told you may come out. Priscilla, and you Carmela, go with them, please and see they keep quiet!" Then, in a different tone, "Bother this door! I can't get the handle to turn properly."

Loud sobs from within and then the voice of Felicity Maynard.

"Oh, Len, is that you? Oh, please get us out quickly! We c-can't open the d-door!"

"Is that all? Then stop shrieking like a set of hysterical screech-owls and stop crying as if you were kindergarten babies!" Len said in her firmest tones. "The latch has stuck somehow; that's all. If I can't get it open myself I'll go for Gaudenz or someone and he'll deal with it." At a touch on her shoulder she turned to add relievedly, "Oh, Miss Ferrars! These little ninnies seem to have fastened themselves in and can't get out. That's all!"

Miss Ferrars, who had heard the shrieks in the distance and come post-haste to find out their cause, broke into a delighted giggle. The prefects stared at her in amazement. They could not know that the memory of a certain night when Matey had been shut in the bathroom and had had to yell for help had leapt to her mind. The staff had kept the episode to themselves, with the exception of telling Joey Maynard, who had laughed herself nearly sick over it. "Ferry", as the school called her among themselves, had no intention of letting that tale slip out, even if she did giggle.

A tearful voice recalled her to the business of the moment. "Oh, Miss Ferrars, shall we have to stay here forever?"

"Of course not! Don't be so silly, Margery!" she said bracingly. "Calm down, all of you, and get right away from the door. Find books and begin to read quietly. You'll be out before the gong sounds for Kaffee und Kuchen: I promise you that."

As she had a well-established reputation for keeping her word, the Juniors were soothed and were heard retreating from the door. Miss Ferrars twisted and turned at the knob, but to no effect. Whatever had happened to the latch it held fast. She finally gave it up and beckoned to Ted Grantley.

"Ted, I seem to remember that you have a pretty good grip. Come and see if *you* can free the catch."

Ted stepped forward and proceeded to put forth all her strength. Nothing happened for a minute or so. Then she stumbled and almost fell backwards, the knob of the door in her hand.

"Glorianna!" she exclaimed. "I've yanked the thing right off! *Now* what do we do?"

Fresh howls rose from the room where the listening Juniors had heard every word and now had visions of having to stay where they were for at least the rest of the day and possibly even the night.

Miss Ferrars acted promptly. "Girls!" she shouted, raising her voice to its fullest pitch, "Stop that noise at once—at *once*, do you hear?"

A shaking reply came from little Hortense Romande, a nervy child at best. "Oh, please, must we stay here all night? And have nothing to eat, or beds, or anything?"

"Of course not, goosey!" Miss Ferrars' tone was reassuringly matter-of-fact. "We'll get you out long before that."

"B-but if the h-handle's come off, h-how can we get out?" Felicity quavered. "We c-can't get through the windows."

"You can't—and don't any of you dare to try!" Miss Ferrars said sharply.

The Junior commonroom had ventilating shafts at the tops of the windows and she had horrid visions of the scared children inside trying to climb through them, smashing the glass and cutting themselves badly. "I *promise* you we'll get you out in a few minutes. Len, go and see if you can find Gaudenz or one of the other men. Tell him what's happened and ask him to bring his tools and see if he can get the lock off. If not, he must just break down the door. You children in there, stop crying and behaving like babies! You'll be all right. Kaffee und Kuchen isn't due for another twenty minutes."

"And if you're not out by that time," Con Maynard suddenly raised her voice, "you can let out lengths of string through the ventilators and we'll tie eats on to them for you to draw up."

This original idea helped to soothe most of them, though the mistress could hear that Hortense was still sobbing. Len had torn off to seek Gaudenz, the school's handyman. The other four or five prefects present were gathered in a bunch, making various suggestions as to how the prisoners were to be freed.

Miss Ferrars waited impatiently for Gaudenz, at the same time trying to remember who was on duty with the Juniors. The elder girls were left more or less to their own devices, but no one was going to trust such a set of featherheads as the Juniors to look after themselves. Before she had got round to it Miss Andrews, Head of the Junior school, appeared. She pulled up short at sight of the group in the corridor, then hurtled forward, demanding to be told what had happened *now*?

"Your little lambs appear to have locked themselves in," Miss Ferrars said with a grin. "Unfortunately, they couldn't do the *un*locking and took fright, with the result that Ted, here, has finished things off by wrenching off the door-handle."

Miss Andrews gave an exclamation of annoyance. "Oh, bother! I only left them for five minutes to get a handkerchief. I would have been back at once but I met Miss Dene and she held me up for a minute or two. What *have* they been doing to lock the door at all? They promised me they would play no silly tricks while I was gone."

"I don't think they've broken their promise. Actually, the latch seems to have caught on some obstruction—it's happened before, you may remember—" her eyes met Sharlie Andrews' and that young lady suddenly choked. "They couldn't free it and none of us could open it. I asked Ted to see what she could do with the result that no one can do anything until Gaudenz or one of the other men can remove the lock—or break the door down."

"What a nuisance! I hope it won't come to actual violence on the door. But what *were* they doing for the latch to slip like that? Let me speak to them for a moment."

"Delighted! Don't be too cross with them, though. We've had several wild shrieks of horror when they thought they would have to miss their meals and stay there all night. They're quieter now, but I don't suppose it would take much to set them off again."

Miss Andrews laughed and, duly warned, smothered her vexation at the situation her lambs had got themselves into and spoke in her usual genial tones.

"Well, you people seem to be adding another to our school legends. What did happen?"

"Léonie was going to be excused," said a tremulous voice. "She couldn't open the door and nor could we, and then s-someone said we m-might have to stay here all n-night—"

"Nonsense!" said Miss Andrews crisply. "As if anyone would allow that! What would Matey say—and Miss Annersley? It wouldn't be allowed. Now stop being silly, all of you and go and sit down quietly. I'll be with you in a few minutes and then I'll read to you till it's time for Kaffee und Kuchen. *Atishoo!*" She finished with a mighty sneeze and Kathy Ferrars gave her an unmistakeable look.

"You'll do no reading if you're starting a cold, my girl! What would Matey say?"

"This isn't a cold—just one of my sneezing fits. My nose started tickling and I knew this would happen. That is why I went—" she broke off with a perfect volley of sneezes and Kathy Ferrars, well imbued with Matey's horror of running colds, turned to the girls standing at a little distance.

"Better go back to your own rooms, girls. We'll run no risk of infection. None of you can do anything here until Gaudenz or whoever it is arrives. Miss Andrews and I are both here. Has anyone else been startled by this kerfuffle?"

"Upper IVb were here," said Ted, who was still rather red

after Miss Ferrars' remarks. "Len sent them back to their own room with Carmela and Priscilla in charge."

"Oh, good! Then you people can go back to whatever you were doing and I'll take charge here."

She waved them away and when they were gone, she turned to her colleague. "I'm sorry, Sharlie," she said in lowered tones, "but you'd better go, too. You know what Matey is about infection. Yes; I know you have these sneezing fits for no reason at all, but there's always a danger that it's a cold and we certainly can't risk letting germs loose on the Juniors. Have you forgotten that the Millies' pantomime comes off next week? A sweet set of elves and fairies we'd have if they were all red-nosed and sniffling! I'll take charge here and you, my love, had better go back to your own room until we're sure that it's nothing worse than one of your usual."

Miss Andrews opened her mouth to argue this, but another violent attack of sneezing rather spoilt the effect and she withdrew with a final protest that she felt all right, except for the sneezing.

Len arrived a few minutes later with Gaudenz. Miss Ferrars sent her off and then explained what was wrong to the big man who had brought his tools with him. At his suggestion, she ordered the Juniors to the far side of the commonroom and he set to work, first to try to free the lock and then, when that proved impossible, to force the door off its hinges.

It took some time to do that for the doors were all sturdy and well-hung. At last there came a splintering sound. The hinges gave under his steady pressure and the door burst open to show a mob of small girls, some still weeping, some looking apprehensive and the remainder, though half-frightened, yet half-delighted.

Gaudenz growled at them as they rushed forward, and they drew back.

"The latch, he was slipped and—ah! Here is something which

blocks him!" Gaudenz said in his native Schweizerdeutsch. He produced a fine-pointed tool and began to dig round the latch. A shower of fine, blackish dust came spurting out and two small faces went red as Jean Allison and Amarilla van der Kock looked at each other.

"There are naughty ones here, mein Fräulein!" Gaudenz roared. "They have filled the latch with dust—pencil dust. And here are wood shavings! That is why the latch has caught and the door would not open. Now we must put on new hinges and that is not easy."

"It looks like a new *door* to me!" Kathy Ferrars said as she surveyed the wreck. She swung round to confront the throng. "Which of you did this?" she demanded.

They owned up at once. They had had the bright idea of stuffing the latch with the pencil dust and shavings left when they had finished sharpening their pencils. They had done it while the others were getting out the table-games they favoured and before Miss Andrews had left the cupboard where the said games lived. They had closed the door and awaited results. Miss Andrews' own exit in search of her handkerchief had forced dust and shavings down, clogging the latch completely, hence all the trouble.

Of course there was more trouble for the sinners. They were condemned to a severe talking-to from the Head and the loss of nearly all their pocket-money until the repairs to the door had been paid for. What they minded even more, they were marched off to bed as soon as Kaffee und Kuchen was over, which meant that they missed the Saturday evening fun. Finally, the whole crowd were told that in future *two* mistresses or prefects would be with them in their free time until they had proved by their general behaviour that they really could be trusted to play no more tricks of this kind. As Jean and Amarilla alone were to blame for this, the rest of the crew told them exactly what they thought of them and for some days after that the couple were treated like pariahs by their own kind until something else happened to turn the current of their thoughts in another direction.

One good thing had come out of it all, however. Upper IVb were so enchanted by the Juniors' latest that they forgot their quarrel with Samaris and no more was said on the subject. This was as well, for excitements were never far to seek in the Chalet School and Samantha was to supply them with a really choice effort in that line.

Chapter XIV

MINETTE!

THE excitement caused by the Juniors' exploit might have made Upper IVb forget their grievance against Samaris. It was otherwise with Inter V. They remembered Nina Rutherford and were old enough to appreciate the fact that she looked like becoming a celebrity. They strongly resented the fact that Samantha van der Byl, the newest of new girls, and not even specially musical, should have been chosen rather than one of themselves to visit her. Joey's well-meant effort to give Nina something fresh to occupy her mind had gone badly wrong there. It is true that matter-of-fact Jack Lambert stigmatised the whole thing as "an idiotic kerfuffle about nothing!" and Wanda von Eschenau pointed out that the choice had been Mrs Maynard's and had really had little or nothing to do with the Sams. Quite a number of the others objected furiously and showed their objection by their manner to Samantha.

Samantha herself did nothing to smooth things over.

"I don't know what you're all making such a fuss about," she told Renata on the Monday when that young woman continued to treat her with icy politeness. "I'm very glad Mrs Maynard asked me to go, and I'm more than glad to have met Nina Rutherford; but why you should make such a bustle about it, I just can't see. I guess you're just plain jealous!"

This, being the truth, silenced Renata for the time being, but was hardly soothing.

"You do think you're someone, Samantha van der Byl!" she

fumed. "And don't you talk to me like that, either!"

"I'll talk as I please without asking you!" Samantha retorted, her temper rising under this treatment. "Anyhow, Nina was quite pleased to see us both, new girls or not. She don't seem as mad on you as you think. She never mentioned you, anyhow!"

"Oh, be quiet, both of you!" Jack broke in angrily. "No one can do a thing with you talk, talk, talking all the time! Shut up!" As she used the rather vulgar French slang, "Fermez les becs, toutes les deux!" both combatants were offended and Renata, remembering how often this phrase had been forbidden to them, rubbed it in.

"We are not permitted to say that," she said frigidly. "You had better attend to your French and your manners, Jack, and not interfere in what does not concern you."

Jack promptly retorted. Arda Peik instantly took up the cudgels for her compatriot, and soon a very pretty quarrel was boiling up in Inter V. The net result was that by the end of the morning the form was divided into two camps, most of the girls agreeing with Renata; while the others secretly thought that if Mrs Maynard had wanted to take someone from their form to visit Nina, she really ought to have chosen someone who knew the invalid previously. As for Renata and Co, they were making a most ridiculous fuss.

Samantha had got on well with her form before this, but now she found herself being cold-shouldered by the majority of them. She was quite unaccustomed to this sort of thing and she had a hot temper which rose under the treatment. She walked about, squaring her elbows and elevating her nose, making remarks about babyish jealousy and sentimental girls who went in for *grandes passions*. None of it endeared her to her fellows. If there was anything the school at large looked on with scorn, it was sentimentality. None of them felt that sort of thing for Nina, proud as they were of her and her achievements, and Samantha's observations got them on the raw.

To make matters worse, the weather had changed and a partial thaw had set in. Winter sports were ended for the moment and though they had their daily walks those had to be along the motor road for everywhere else was far too wet and slushy for them to be allowed to have even a minor ramble.

"Spring's coming early this year," observed Audrey Everett of VIb to her friend and ally, Ruey Richardson, as they set off for their morning walk on the Thursday. "I wish it would hurry up over this stage and get it over! I loathe all this wet, sloppy snow!"

"I don't suppose it'll continue like this," Ruey replied. "The wind will change and we'll get frost again. It's too early for the real end of winter. At the same time, I'm sick of these everlasting walks! I'd give something for a good ramble if we can't have any winter sporting. Besides," she added, "I'm more than sick of having to work so hard."

"But that's what always happens when we can't be out, and well you know it!" Audrey retorted. "Thank goodness we have the pantomime on Saturday! That will give the Middles and Juniors something fresh to think about. They're all on edge just now."

"It's more than the kids," Ruey said, dropping into English.

"Ruey, my pet, this is French day!"

"Sorry! What I was going to say is that there is trouble in Inter V."

"Oh? What is it?"

Ruey shook her head. "Not knowing, can't say. They seem to be at sixes and sevens—some trouble with that new girl, Samantha. What's more, there's trouble between Jack and Renata."

"Well, so long as they don't come to fisticuffs," Audrey said with a grin as she remembered sundry occasions when Jack's feuds had, literally, come to that very thing.

Ruey chuckled and forgot her French. "Far from it. After all, they're both fifteen and too old for that sort of thing. As a matter of fact they are being as snooty to each other as they can be."

"Silly little asses!" concurred Audrey, likewise speaking in English. At which point they turned in at the school gates and the subject was forgotten.

A member of the school who has not come into this story so far was responsible for the next episode. This was Minette, the school cat. During the spring and summer and early autumn she was free of the grounds, but in winter she was kept strictly in the house. The bitter winters of the Alps are not very suitable for little cats to wander outside, and Karen, head of the kitchen staff, usually took good care that Minette got no chance to slip out.

On this day, however, Liesl, a new kitchen-maid, had carelessly left an outer door ajar and Minette, with all the contrariness of cats, had seized her opportunity. Liesl had remembered Minette and rushed back in panic-stricken haste to shut the door. She did look out, but by that time Minette had vanished behind a snow-laden bush and, seeing nothing of her, Liesl trusted that the demon was safely somewhere on the premises. She dared not confess her sin to Karen, who was a tartar on occasion. Neither did she dare to go hunting for the cat for fear of questions. Minette was shut out in a cold, wet world which she hated. None of the downstairs windows was open and she had no means of reaching the ventilators. She found a door at the side of the house and stood there, mewing piteously for admittance, but it opened from a corridor used mainly by the staff who, by this time, were all hard at work in the formrooms. No one heard her and Minette, her heavy coat well soaked by the melting snow and shivering with the cold, mewed in vain.

Inter V were busy with Miss Wilmot and some particularly nasty arithmetical progressions. Only two girls in the form seemed able to tackle them—Jack and Samantha. Jack was keen on mathematics and Samantha had done progressions before she came to the school and at least understood what she was doing. The rest remained blankly ignorant of the whole rule.

"You two," said Miss Wilmot when Jack and Samantha had shown up work well done, "may start on your preparation. The rest of the form will pay attention to me and the blackboard."

The form at large looked disgruntled, but though Miss Wilmot was described by the school as being a complete poppet out of lessons, in them she could be a terror. They sat back and prepared to do their best to follow her. Halfway through, she suddenly decided she needed another textbook. She glanced round the room. Jack was working hard, but Samantha, who had finished her first example, was taking a breather. The mistress grinned to herself.

"Samantha," she said, "have you finished?"

"Only the first sum," said Samantha with a blush.

"Then you won't mind if I interrupt you to go and bring the blue-backed Godfrey and Martin from my shelves in the staffroom. You'll find it on the second shelf on the right-hand side. Go by the staff corridor and use the front stairs. It'll be quicker. Don't dally on the way, please. Now, girls!" And she turned to her victims.

Samantha got up and left the room, rather pleased by the break. She had been concentrating with all her might, and though she was growing accustomed to that sort of thing, it was coming slowly. She still found working to the speed of the others a little difficult.

She took the indicated route, found the book in short order and began to come back. Just as she entered the lower corridor, she heard a heart-rending yowl coming from outside.

"Minette!" she exclaimed, stopping dead.

She dived for the door, but at this season of the year it was kept locked as there was little need to use it. Furthermore, Matey had removed the key and it was hanging with a bunch of others in her room. Meanwhile, Minette had heard her name and was mewing as loudly as she could. Having found no open door or window, she had scrambled up a small tree near the building. Opposite a bough stretching to the house was an open ventilator. Minette had managed to jump from the bough to the edge of the ventilator and edge her way in. Unfortunately, having got there, she stuck halfway. Worse; she found when she tried to back out that she was caught. She could move neither way. The only thing she could do was to voice her woes at the top of her voice and she did it with all her might.

Samantha loved cats as much as she feared big dogs. She instantly tossed the book down on a nearby windowsill, pushed the window open and stared out, calling Minette at the same time. Minette was nearly exhausted, what with the cold, the wet, terror, and her yelling, but she managed to produce a squall which drew the girl's eyes upwards. She could just see the end of a bedraggled tail sticking out halfway down the wall.

"Oh, poor Minette!" she cried; and lost her head.

What she *should* have done was to report the occurrence at once. What she *did* was to scramble out of the window— mercifully, her arm was now out of its cage—drop down into the slushy snow and look round to see how she could reach the panicking cat. She saw the tree. She also saw the branch from which Minette had made her own wild leap. It was none too stout, but Samantha made nothing of that. She had always been fond of climbing and she felt sure that if she could get part way along, she could reach out, grasp Minette's tail and pull her free. Then she could take her round to the kitchens, where Karen would see to her. As for "Willy", as everyone called Miss Wilmot, and the algebra book, she never gave them another thought.

She looked carefully at the tree, discovered a branch fairly near the ground, leapt as high as she could and just succeeded in gripping it. It was slippery but she kept tight hold and by means of a complicated wriggle, got herself up on to it and saw where she could climb towards Minette's branch.

It was not easy work. She was shivering with cold and the wood kept sliding under her chilled fingers; but she had a strong vein of obstinacy in her which made her refuse to give up. Besides, Minette's howls were growing fainter. Samantha felt sure the poor little thing was suffocating—though why she should have connected suffocation with an open ventilator was something she was never able to explain. She reached the branch, straddled it, and began to work her way cautiously along it. Halfway along, it groaned. Anyone else would have taken warning from that, but not Samantha. She wriggled along, bit by bit, until she was within reach of that miserable tail. Then she lay along the bough, stretched out her hand, got a firm hold and yanked!

This was the final straw where poor Minette was concerned. With a terrific screech, she made a final effort and contrived to free herself, swinging round on whatever it was that was clutching her tail, all her claws out to do battle. Luckily, Samantha was wearing her blazer and though one claw caught her hand, the others stuck into the sleeve. At the same moment the branch gave up the ghost and parted from its parent trunk to throw girl and cat to the ground just as Joey Maynard, coming across from Freudesheim, arrived in time to see the whole business. She uttered a squawk that almost outdid Minette's best effort and leapt to the rescue.

It was well for Samantha that she fell into partly melted snow and *not* on to the iron-hard surface of the previous week. As it was, the breath was knocked out of her, but she still kept her grip on Minette's tail. Minette herself was also knocked breathless and by the time Joey arrived was only just beginning to realise that she was still alive.

Samantha got dizzily to her feet, her arms going round the cat's body in a firm clasp and Joey completed things by flinging *her* arms round the pair, nearly smothering them in the folds of her big cloak which had flown open.

"What *happened*?" she cried. "No; never mind telling me now. Come straight to Matron! You *can* walk, can't you? Here; give me that cat before she starts clawing everyone in sight! Now take my arm—that's it! Come on, Samantha!"

Samantha was too stunned to argue. She went meekly with Joey, who hustled her round the house and in at the big door. There, they encountered Miss Annersley and Matey in the entrance hall. To say that they were startled is to express it mildly. Joey, having slammed the door shut with a backward kick, let Minette slip and that abused animal, finding herself safe in familiar surroundings, bolted for the passage leading to the kitchens, where she nearly upset Karen who happened to be in the direct line of her flight.

"What on earth—" the Head began; but Matey interrupted her ruthlessly.

"Samantha, you look frozen to death! Upstairs with you and into a hot bath at once. Plenty of time later on to hear why you've been breaking rules wholesale!"

She rushed the shivering Samantha up the stairs and into the first bathroom handy, where she turned on the taps before hurrying off in quest of hot towels. She returned to find Joey helping Samantha to strip. The Head had been summoned to reply to an urgent 'phone call.

Samantha was plunged into a hot bath and scrubbed until she cried for mercy. Then she was dried with the hot towels and hurried along to a warm bed in the school san where Nurse administered a beaker of hot milk and a hot-water bottle. Matey waited until the milk-beaker was empty and then examined her for any injuries, but apart from the ungrateful Minette's clawing and a good shaking she seemed to have escaped unharmed.

Minette underwent the same treatment before Karen made inquiries as to how she had got out. Liesl tearfully confessed her sin and received a scolding the kitchen tyrant had never bettered. Samantha had to tell the full tale to the Head, after a long nap had returned her to her usual self. She was made to feel that a girl of her age should have known better than to tackle the problem as she had done. By the time the Head had finished with her she was feeling that what was left of her would go into a thimble. And *then* she had to run the gauntlet of Miss Wilmot's remarks on people who were sent on errands and did not return at once. However, Nancy palliated her comments at the end by saying, "I suppose you *couldn't* leave that dratted cat where she was so we'll say no more about it. Now tell me where you've put my Godfrey and Martin, and we'll let it go at that for the moment."

Chapter XV

THE UNEXPECTED HAPPENS

SAMARIS never knew what roused her at three o'clock in the morning. Usually she fell asleep almost as soon as she lay down, and slept soundly until the rising-bell sounded next morning. On this occasion, however, she woke with a start in time to hear the big school clock chime three.

"What's wrong?" she wondered as she sat bolt upright in bed.

Not a sound disturbed the stillness that followed on the clock ceasing to chime. There was only the quiet breathing of the eleven other girls in the dormitory, marred by an occasional snore or a muttering from Val Pertwee, who was given to talking in her sleep. Instinctively, Samaris turned to the half-window at the side of her bed. She looked out on to what Robert Louis Stevenson called "a wonderful clear night of stars". Then her eye travelled further and the next instant she was out of bed and yelling, "Fire—fire!" at the top of remarkably healthy lungs.

Her yells disturbed not only her own dormitory, but both dormitories on either side, and in less than ten minutes the whole school was awake. Such a noise had rarely if ever been heard in the Chalet School at that hour. People still half-awake and more or less dazed with sleep were demanding to be told what it was all about. The girls in Samaris's own dormitory were crowding to the windows to stare out and gaze at the red glow in the sky which was what had given rise to her shrieks. The mistresses, tumbling out of bed in a hurry, scrambled into dressing-gowns and slippers and hurried to quiet the din. Matey arrived with her official apron tied over her dressing-gown and her cap set cock-eyed on her brow.

"Where is this fire?" she demanded in tones which helped to quieten the excited girls in Geranium whence the worst of the noise was proceeding.

"Over there—look, Matron!" Samaris cried excitedly.

Matron stared at the glow over her shoulder. The next moment she was organizing things with her usual calm efficiency.

"I see. Well, it isn't likely to trouble us at the moment. Go back to bed, all of you, and lie down and keep quiet. Don't let me have to come back to you!"

They obeyed on the word and she hurried out of the dormitory to encounter Rosalie Dene, the school secretary, who had come racing up the stairs at top speed.

"Where is it, Rosalie?" she demanded.

"Somewhere near St Mildred's. I've rung up the fire guard and, to judge by the sound, most of the Platz is awake and rushing to the rescue. The Head sent me to say that the girls are to go back to bed and stay there. The school itself should— Drat! The telephone!"

She turned and fled downstairs to the telephone. Joey Maynard had been roused and was demanding to be told what was wrong.

"Fire somewhere near the Millies! Not the house itself, I fancy. You keep cool! It isn't as if this was high summer with everything tinder-dry and ready to take fire at a spark. Where's Jack?"

"At the San—as you might expect. You're sure it's all right, Rosalie? I needn't wake the babies and get them up?"

"Don't be silly! If your family isn't awake already, let them sleep. I must go now. Can't stop to natter!" And Rosalie hung up and turned to go and report to the Head only to be summoned back by another ring.

This time it was Miss Wilson—"Bill" to the school at large—

ringing up to say that the fire was in a shed at the side of the garden. The fire guard were already there and the girls were up and dressed and helping to pack and carry out important papers and other valuables. Everywhere was wet with the melting snow, but St Mildred's was built of wood like most of the other houses on the Platz and no one was going to take any chances.

"Is it bad?" Rosalie asked anxiously.

"Blazing! The shed's done for! But so long as we can confine the fire to it, it's no great matter. That is with one exception."

"What's that?"

"Practically all the pantomime dresses were in there—in cases, of course; but I'm afraid we shall find that cases and dresses are just pitiful heaps of ash when we can get down to investigation."

"*What?* But we always leave the dresses in the dressing-rooms at the hall."

"Couldn't be done this time. There's a leak in the roof and the rooms are so damp it wouldn't have been safe to leave anything there—oh, half a minute!—Yes, Gill? What is it?"

Rosalie held on, guessing that the St Mildred's secretary, Gillian Culver, had arrived in the study. She heard a murmur of voices. Then Miss Wilson spoke again. "That was Gill. She tells me that they've got the fire under control, but the shed and its contents are finished. Let Hilda know, please, Rosalie, but say nothing to anyone else. I'll come over early in the morning and give her all the news. You can see for yourself what this means, can't you?"

"No—what?"

"Use your wits, girl! I can't stop now!" And Miss Wilson hung up on her final word, leaving Rosalie to puzzle over what she had meant. Suddenly it dawned and she exclaimed.

"Oh, my goodness! No clothes—no pantomime!—Or I wonder?"

She went quickly out of her office and along to the Annexe where the Head appeared as she opened the communicating door to the school.

"What was that, Rosalie?" she asked anxiously.

"First Joey to ask if there was any danger and ought she to get her babies up. I told her to have more sense. Then Nell Wilson to say that the men have got the fire under control, but the shed is completely gutted."

"Thank God it's no worse!" Miss Annersley was pale but her face had lighted up at Rosalie's words. "What about the girls?"

"All quite safe and very busy. Our own crowd seem to be calming down now. But you don't know the worst yet. There's been a leak in St Luke's roof over the dressing-rooms, so they brought all the pantomime dresses back and stored them in the shed in their cases. The lot have gone up in smoke with the shed. You can see what that may mean, can't you?"

"Good heavens! No clothes, no pantomime!" The Head paused there and thought for a few moments. "Come along to my salon, Rosalie—or no; go and fetch Mdlle and Frau Mieders, and—well anyone else who likes to come. I'll go and ask— Ah, I see I needn't! Here comes Karen, to the fore as usual!" as that worthy lumbered into sight, bearing a tray loaded with cups, coffee percolator and a heaped-up basket of bread-twists.

"Bitte, mein Fräulein, a little coffee," Karen said, beaming. "I bring him to your salon, nicht? I have milk heating for the young ladies; and Gaudenz has sent word that all is now safe. The danger is at an end, Gott sei Dank!"

"Danke schön!" The Head moved to let Karen carry the tray over to a table. "Please see that everyone has a hot drink—yourself and all the maids as well as the girls."

Karen nodded and went off, followed by Rosalie. The appalling din had died down and the school was clearly in no danger. The Head, sitting down at the table to pour out the coffee, gave her mind to the question of whether the school could possibly help out with enough dresses. She doubted it. St Mildred's had already ransacked the acting cupboards to supply their needs and what were left would probably be all the smaller dresses. Would it be possible to alter enough to enable the Millies to give their pantomime that afternoon after all? She must consult the needlework specialists before she decided finally. She was almost certain that it couldn't be done. And then she turned her mind to the question of how the school had known about the fire. Who had told them?

She had not solved this problem when Rosalie and the others arrived; but on her asking the questions it was soon explained by Mdlle de Lachennais.

"It was the little Samaris who woke up and saw the red glow in the sky," that lady said as she took her coffee. "It seems that she cried the news aloud for all to hear and so the school was awakened. And tell me this, Hilda, chérie, is it true that all—but *all* the dresses for the pantomime have been burned? But what will happen this afternoon?"

"That is what I wanted to discuss with you all now. Anna," she turned to Frau Mieders. "You have charge of the acting cupboards. Can you tell me—roughly—if we can possibly find enough to dress the girls?"

Frau Mieders shook her head. "I do not think it possible. It is fortunate that all the fairy dresses are here. They came back with the children this afternoon. But how to dress the principals—ah, that I cannot tell. They had taken almost all the robes except some of the Chinese ones. What else are left are too small to be of much use."

The telephone rang again and Rosalie picked up the receiver of the Head's private 'phone. "What—oh, my dear, we're in

Hilda's salon considering what we can do to help you out. I can't tell you for the moment, but—"

"Let me have it, Rosalie." The Head held out her hand for the receiver. "Who is that?—You, Nell? Tell me; is everyone safe?"

"Quite safe, thank God! The girls were never in any danger, and thanks to the fire guard the house is safe. The shed is ruined and all the acting dresses in it are gone; but that's the extent of our losses— Oh, some garden-tools, including the electric mower, but it can't be helped and we're well covered by insurance. Thanks be, everywhere is as wet as can be. This thaw seems to be going on. If you ask me we're due for an early spring. In the meantime, unless you can help us out, I'm afraid the panto is off! I wish now I'd risked the damp in the dressing-rooms and left the cases there—"

"You couldn't possibly have done that! You'd have had an epidemic of chills and colds if the girls had had to wear damp dresses all the afternoon. As it is, all the fairy dresses are safe. Listen, Nell! I have the staff here and we're going to see if we can possibly manage to provide dresses of a sort for this afternoon. I doubt it, I may say, but we'll do our best. Are you going back to bed now?"

"Talk sense! I've sent the girls back with hot drinks and a light meal to quiet their nerves; but Vi Norton, Gertrude Rider and I aren't likely to get to bed for some time, if at all."

"Right! Then we'll go up to the acting cupboards now and see what we can find and what we think we can cobble up. I'm afraid that's the best we can do. I'll ring up when we know."

"Well, thanks," said Miss Wilson's voice in a melancholy tone. "It's good of you, but I doubt if there's much to be done about it. Oh, well, what can't be cured must be endured; but I do feel furious when I think of the best part of our quite good theatrical wardrobe going up in smoke!"

"Do you know what started it, by the by?"

"Not yet. I suppose it's been a fuse somewhere. That's the most probable thing at this time of year. I expect we shall have to wait to know that."

"A fuse seems to be the likeliest thing," the Head agreed. "I'll have the electrician up as soon as I can and have all *our* wiring inspected. Yes; I seem fussy, I know, but I've no wish for any kind of holocaust here."

"I don't think you're fussy at all. I'm going to do the same myself. One can't be too careful when one lives in a wooden house. Well, I must ring off. I've plenty to do before I can think of snatching an hour or two in my bed."

"Let us know if we can be of any help."

"Oh, of course!"

"And as soon as possible we'll tell you what we can do about the dresses."

But when, an hour later, she did ring up it was with the melancholy news that it would be impossible to dress the pantomime. St Mildred's had borrowed heavily, and with all the will in the world no one could hope to provide enough dresses. Nor would there be time to hire from the nearest theatrical wardrobe. That was in Berne, and by the time everyone's measurements had been taken, someone had gone down to collect the dresses and bring them back and they had been fitted it would be late afternoon.

"I'm afraid you must cancel," Miss Annersley said.

"Not if we can help it. We must postpone till the end of term. Oh, well, it can't be helped. We must be deeply grateful that it is *only* the dresses that have gone. It might have been the house. As it is, the fire guard have been able to confine it to the shed and it's a lot to be thankful for. By the way, has Joey rung up?"

"She has, but I gather that Rosalie was most crushing to her and I only hope she went back to bed like a sensible creature."

"What a hope! Look here, Hilda, ring up Freudesheim, will you, and tell her it's all over. I don't want her plunging along here before Frühstück. She can do nothing to help. And, by the way, the St Hilda girls were coming. You might ring up Miss Holroyd and break the sad news to her. She'll sympathise all right! She had enough of fire when she came up here herself!"

"I'll see to all that. Anyone else we can ring up for you while we're at it?"

"Yes; the Rösleinalp. Some folk were coming down from there. Ring up the Gasthaus and ask them to broadcast it. Gill can deal with the rest."

"Very well. Now I'm ringing off or neither of us will get any sleep and we'll be limp rags during the day. Don't worry about the girls. We'll find some sort of substitute for the pantomime."

"I'm sending down all my crowd to Interlaken this afternoon. They can't do any good up here and the fire guard will be busy clearing up the mess. Early bed this evening to make up for their loss of sleep; and I'd advise the same for your little lot."

"It's already arranged—trust Matey! Then I'll go, Nell. Let me know if you want any more help from us." She rang off and went along to the office to seek Rosalie Dene and set her to letting various folk know about the catastrophe after Frühstück.

"Right!" Rosalie said. "Well, I'm sorry for everyone's disappointment, but I'm more than thankful it's no worse. Ready, Hilda? Then you go and I'll switch off the lights."

Chapter XVI

To Celebrate St Patrick

"No panto! Oh, what a swizz!" exclaimed Valerie. "Are *all* the dresses gone up in smoke? But what about when *we* want them? There's the Sale next term and the Christmas play the term after. We can't do them if we have no dresses."

"Keep calm—keep calm!" said Len who had brought the news to Inter V. "Naturally we'll have to make new dresses. No need to worry over that."

"That mightn't be too bad," said Celia Everett musingly. "Some of those dresses were beginning to look shabby after all these years."

"Eight years or more. We brought a lot of them from England. We've added to them, of course, but we were still using quite a number of the old ones." Len smiled. "No use crying over spilt milk, anyhow. We can be thankful nothing else more valuable went."

"How do you mean?" Samantha asked.

"Supposing everything had not been drenching with the thaw? What about St Mildred's itself catching fire—and, just possibly the rest of the Platz?"

"Surely that couldn't happen?" Samantha looked horrified.

"It's been known," Len said drily. "You've heard what happened to St Hilda's the term they began up in the mountains, haven't you? The whole place went and the Head was seriously injured."

"But that was the summer term," Wanda reminded her.

"It was; and so might this have been."

"If there's no pantomime, what do we do this afternoon?" queried Michelle Cabran. "We cannot go out, for look at the rain!"

Len glanced through the window at the rain, which was coming down in sheets. "I expect we shall hear after Prayers what is being arranged. Meanwhile, I must go and tell some other forms. If I were you I'd try to drum up some ideas in case we are asked to produce anything." Len finished with a broad grin and left them to it.

"Does this mean there will be no pantomime at all?" Arda Peik asked.

"It looks like it," Celia said gloomily.

"Well, it may be hard luck on us, but it's a lot harder on the Millies after all their work," Jack Lambert reminded them.

"That is true," Emilie Gabrielli agreed.

"What about asking if we could give a party for them instead," Jean proposed. "We could ask Frau Mieders if we might make cakes and jellies and things this afternoon—"

"It would be the Sixths if it came to that," Celia reminded her.

"But we might decorate Hall," Wanda suggested.

"Nothing doing, my love! All the trimmings will be at St Luke's. How could we get them here in that downpour?" Margaret Twiss demanded.

"It surely is a problem," Samantha said thoughtfully.

Renata swung round on her, their silly feud forgotten in this much greater disaster. "Sammy! You have all sorts of ideas for parties in America, don't you? Can't *you* think of something?"

Samantha shook her head. "I've been trying, but I can't think of a single thing. If only it had been fine and frosty we might have had ski-ing and coasting, but the thaw seems to have set in good and hard. Does it always come so early in these parts?"

"Not as a rule," Jack said thoughtfully. "We usually have

winter sports up to the end of the term. Of course, Easter is early this year."

"What on earth has that got to do with the thaw?" Valerie inquired.

Before Jack could reply, the gong sounded and talk had to cease. They marched off to the Speisesaal, where they found that Karen, at least, had done what she could to make up for their disappointment. Instead of their usual plain, solid fare she had provided wafer slices of ham, hot, crisp rolls and great dishes of honey. Towards the end of the meal, the Head's bell rang and all chatter ceased as they turned to the high table to hear what she had to say.

"I'm sorry the weather is so bad, girls. I'm afraid even walks are out of the question. However, we are planning something to make up for your disappointment. Miss Wilson has asked me to say that the pantomime is only postponed. If they can get new dresses, it will be given on the last Saturday of term. I've told her I was sure some of you would want to help with the sewing—" She paused here and laughed, for a forest of hands was waving in the air. "I see I was safe in making that offer. We'll accept your help with pleasure. Meanwhile, this morning I propose you do your mending and letters as usual. After that you may read or play games. This afternoon, I propose we have a session of the Hobbies Club. As for the evening, the mistresses have it all planned out, but it's a deadly secret for the moment. But I *think* you will enjoy it." She gave them one of her flashing smiles as she ended, and Jack the irrepressible began to clap. The rest took it up and for a moment or two she gave them their heads. Then she struck her bell, and when silence fell, she nodded to them.

"That is all I can tell you now. Finish your meal and then go and attend to dormitory duties. This will be a short morning." She sat down and the girls set to work to finish off their meal.

But she had said enough. They were full of curiosity to know what the staff's latest might be.

One good thing had come out of the blaze. Renata and the rest had given up their ill-feeling against Samantha, and Inter V were once more a united form. They chatted together amiably, mainly trying to guess what was coming in the evening. Even when duties were out of the way and they were free to amuse themselves, it continued and Valerie, for one, heaved a secret sigh of relief. She had felt responsible for Samantha and she hated being at odds with the rest of her form.

Halfway through the period, Con Maynard arrived. "I've just come to remind you all about Nina Rutherford's essay competition," she began. "Time is getting short now. If you've any spare time, I'd get on with them. That's all!"

She grinned at them and departed. She had a very good idea that quite half of them had done nothing about the said essays as yet.

"Glorianna! I'd forgotten all about the ghastly thing!" Jack said when the door closed on the prefect. "Well, I know what I want and what I hope for, but what sort of an essay I can produce on it is anyone's guess!"

The others laughed, but more than one girl sat turning the subject over in her mind during what remained of the morning.

The afternoon was spent as the Head had suggested in a session of the Hobbies Club. The girls were encouraged to enjoy all kinds of handwork. They had two small handlooms and some of the Seniors turned out quite delightful scarves and head-handkerchiefs. Quite a number of the Swiss girls went in for pillow lace, and one or two even tried their hands on point and thread lace.

Fretwork accounted for a number of the younger ones. Jack, in particular, produced most ingenious toys of various kinds.

Others made scrapbooks on stiffened muslin, and when the pages were finished, they were varnished to make them more or less imperishable as well as washable. Some of the Fifths had taken up bead-weaving and produced waterfall necklaces and bags which everyone admired. Len Maynard cut jigsaw puzzles and Margot had lately taken up stencilling and was busy with most attractive cushion-covers and tray-cloths.

Samantha had learned various embroidery stitches from her mother's French maid and was working on a tapestry fire screen. It had been left to Ailie Russell of Vb to take up one of the most original hobbies. She made papier-mâché trays and bowls and her two friends, Janice Chester and Judy Willoughby, who were both artistic, helped her with painting them.

Miss Carey, the handcrafts mistress, oversaw the younger girls, but as a rule the girls were left to get on with their work by themselves. Hobbies Club belonged to them and, apart from the Junior Middles and Juniors, there was as little supervision as possible.

They had been informed at Mittagessen that Hall was out of bounds for the whole of the afternoon and most folk were agog to know what the staff proposed to do with them in the evening. For that they had to wait until after Kaffee und Kuchen, but once they were sent upstairs to change into their usual evening velveteens, they could scarcely contain themselves.

"What do you think they're going to do with us?" Samantha asked Valerie.

"Goodness knows! You never can tell with them," Valerie replied.

Whatever it was, it is safe to say it was nothing that anyone had expected. When the summons came and they marched into Hall, they found the place transfigured. All the green curtains the school and Joey could muster between them had been hung round the walls. The forms were set back against them and here and there were tables loaded with all sorts of trifles, every last one having some reference to Ireland or St Patrick. Here and there were clusters of hastily made paper shamrocks, and every mistress wore at least something green, though the Head, Miss Dene, Miss Ferrars and Miss Wilmot were gracing the scene in green frocks.

When the last girl had found a seat, the Head, who was on the dais with Matey, Mdlle and Miss Denny, rose and smiled on them all.

"This is a St Patrick celebration," she said. "I know it is rather early. His feast-day is March 17th. However we *are* actually into March, so we are celebrating him this way. The programme will now begin."

She sat down and a sextette, consisting of Miss Derwent, Miss Moore, Mdlle Lenoir, Miss Ferrars, Miss Charlesworth and Miss Andrews, appeared on the dais and proceeded to give the delighted audience a rollicking *St Patrick's Day in the Morning*. The girls applauded vociferously and only desisted when Miss Burnett appeared, attired as an Irish colleen, and danced a jig. This was followed by a complete surprise for even the triplets. Joey Maynard, dressed in appropriate green, slipped through the double doors to come and stand on the dais and sing to the old Londonderry air, the charming words of the poem, *Would God I were the Tender Appleblossom*. Joey had been the school's prima donna during her own schooldays, and though through the years her voice had lost its chorister's beauty, it had gained immeasurably in maturity and fullness. She was cheered to the echo and had to come back to give an encore, though she said firmly that this was the only one as she must get back to Baby Phil who was not quite so well. She sang *My Love's an Arbutus* and, with a smile all round the room, then slipped out again. Nor would the Head agree to allowing her to be recalled. Instead,

Miss Lawrence went to the piano and gave them Percy Grainger's *Molly on the Shore* with a verve and rhythm that made a number of people long to get up and dance it.

Two choruses, *Phil the Fluter's Ball* and *St Patrick was a Gentleman* brought this part of the programme to a close and then the Head called on them to march to the Speisesaal where a feast of what Brigit Ingram called "real Irish eats" awaited them. They had boxty bread, sliced, and then fried in butter. With this came herrings—Karen kept a goodly supply of frozen foods for just such emergencies—and fried bacon. Potato-apple cake followed with dollops of whipped cream, and griddle cake, smoking hot and soaked in butter.

"Not in the least like our usual feasts, but jolly good!" was the verdict of the school as the heaped-up plates emptied in short order.

The girls insisted on helping to clear away and then they all went back to Hall and waited for the next surprise. It came in the shape of small cardboard discs—green, of course—which some of the younger mistresses carried round in bags. Each girl was invited to take one and then followed a distribution of gold discs. That done, they were sent to the tables, hitherto untouched, where they exchanged the discs for a tiny parcel and a bag each of pale golden toffee. Frau Mieders had an old Irish recipe for Yellow Man and had spent most of the day making great panfuls of it with help from Miss Burnett and two of the junior music mistresses. The parcels contained mere trifles, but were a delightful surprise, nevertheless. Six of the prefects had Irish-linen handkerchiefs with shamrocks embroidered in the corners. These, as they later discovered, were the offering towards the gaiety of the evening of Miss Ferrars, who had sacrificed her whole half-dozen for the occasion. Joey, who collected beads, had contributed a whole bunch of green necklets. Miss Carey

201

had spent her day framing coloured views of Ireland in passe-partout and produced more than a score of really delightful pictures. There was something for everyone, including paper dolls dressed as Irish colleens which delighted the hearts of the small fry.

All in all, as everyone agreed, the staff must have slaved throughout the day to produce so much. Len called for three cheers for them, and they were given with a will that nearly brought the ceiling down in Hall.

Prayers came next, and then bed. Matey insisted that after their disturbed night even the Seniors must have early bed. On the whole, no one was sorry.

"Well, I think we've managed to entertain them," observed Nancy Wilmot as she flung herself into an armchair in the staff sitting-room with a prodigious yawn.

"I'm sure we have," Kathy Ferrars agreed. "And to crown all, they still have the panto to look forward to at the end of term."

"And that," said Rosalind Yolland solemnly, "is more than *we* ever had when I was a pupil at this establishment. Oh, I'm tired! But it's been well worth it. Let's hope the rain is over by tomorrow. They will at least go to church, which will be an 'out'. Too much of being housebound always means trouble, especially with the Middles. Well, there seems to be nothing else for us to do, so I'm for bed!"

"So am I!" It came as a chorus as the staff rose and began to gather up sundry belongings.

Nancy ended it with a chuckle. "Let's hope no one else gets up a blaze tonight! I can do with at least eight hours of solid sleep. In fact," she added, "I'll be just as pleased if the Millies' bonfire is the last of our excitements. I'd like a few days of peace and quiet for once!"

Chapter XVII

A FLUTE FOR SAMARIS

"THAT you, Hilda? Good! I'm coming over if you're not tied up with visitors or teaching or what not. Can do?"

"Apart from my endless correspondence, I'm quite free," Miss Annersley replied. "What's the excitement, may I ask?"

"Ask nae questions and ye'll be tellt nae lees!" Joey retorted. "You wouldn't be having elevenses, I suppose?"

The Head glanced at her clock. "It's ten minutes early, but I don't mind. Wrap up well, Joey. The rain may have ceased, but this heavy mist is just as wetting. I'll expect you in ten minutes' time." She rang off and turned to the inter-com 'phone to the kitchens to give her order. She had just finished when she heard light, springy footsteps coming along the corridor and knew that her self-invited guest was on her.

Her greeting was not exactly a welcome, for as Joey entered, she threw off her big cloak and tossed it down on the nearest chair. "Joey Maynard! You careless creature! Your cloak is wet and you've flung it down on top of my Sixth Form essays! Take it up and put it on one of the hangers in that cupboard. Really! At your age you might have more sense!"

"Sorry!" said Joey with her usual insouciance. "There! Will that do you?"

Her friend looked at her sharply. There was something not quite normal in her manner. All Miss Annersley said was, "Quite; but why not do it in the first place?"

"Didn't think about it. Hark! I hear footsteps! Miggi with

elevenses, no doubt. Can't anyone ever teach that girl to walk like a Christian and not trample like an elephant?"

As Miggi appeared at that moment with a tray, the Head had no chance to reply to this sally. Joey bestowed a vivid smile on the maid.

"What have you brought us, Miggi?" she demanded in easy Swiss German. "Chocolate and some of Karen's pastries? Oh, good! I'm ravenous. We had Frühstück extra early and have been on the go ever since."

Miggi returned the smile, set down the tray and departed. The Head poured out the chocolate and handed her guest a steaming cup. "Wrap yourself round that," she commanded. Then, as her fingers touched Joey's, "Joey! You're like ice! Pull up your chair to the pipes and get yourself warmed. You'll be down with a chill next!"

"Not I! It's only my hands. I didn't bother with gloves or mitts. Otherwise I'm as warm as toast. Thanks, Hilda! This looks just the job." Joey sipped her chocolate and sighed. "Some day I'm going to steal Karen from you. Her pastries are out of this world."

"You'll have Anna to deal with if you try that on. Not that Karen would come. The school is her very life, I believe. Now stop talking nonsense and eat your pastry."

Joey bit into her pastry and munched thoughtfully for a minute. "Hilda, I want Samaris Davies, please."

"At this hour of the day? Certainly not!"

"Oh, Hilda, I thought you lo-oved me!" Joey wailed.

"Not to that extent," Miss Annersley said firmly. "Anyhow, why do you want her?"

"Well, for two reasons." Joey finished her cake and then went on. "First, I have a little present for her. Yes," as the Head raised her eyebrows, "the flute's come. Nina sent it along this morning and I want to give it to the kid myself and watch her face."

Miss Annersley laughed. "She'll be thrilled, I know. Well, I can't spare her this morning, but you may have her after afternoon prep for half an hour or so, only she must be back for Kaffee und Kuchen at the proper time. Why didn't you bring it along with you and present it to her here?"

"Because I know you! If I had brought it you wouldn't have let me hand it over in the middle of morning lessons—or afternoon ones, either, if it comes to that. Besides I have another reason for wanting her at Freudesheim."

Something in her tone put Hilda Annersley on the alert.

"What reason?"

"Phil wants her."

The Head's face changed. "Nothing wrong with Phil, is there?"

"No-o—at least, I hope not. She's not been so well this last day or two." The forced gaiety had left Joey's voice. "I really am worried about her, Hilda. She's lost her appetite and has to be coaxed to take every scrap of food. What's worse, she doesn't want to walk. She cried when I tried to persuade her to yesterday."

"What does Jack say about it?" Miss Annersley demanded, knitting her brows.

"Says he *thinks* it's only a temporary set-back, probably owing to the weather. I hope so, I'm sure; but I don't like it."

"Jack is probably right, I think. Oh, I know it's desperately worrying—"

"Worrying? It's driving me up the wall! We so nearly lost her and now, just when we all thought she was making such good headway this has to happen. *Why* should it? We've always taken such care of our babies. The rest are sturdy enough—even Chas now. Phil was as bonny and well as could be until last spring. But first mastoid and then polio! My poor baby! I'd give ten years of my life to see her fit again!" Joey's voice shook and her friend sprang up and came to put an arm round her.

"Joey, for Phil's own sake you must keep up your heart. Oh, I know it's easy to talk and this relapse is horribly disheartening, but Jack *has* said he thinks it's only temporary. Probably when this wretched weather clears up Phil will go ahead again. Meantime, if Phil wants Samaris, she shall have her—as far as I can manage it. Let me look at the timetable."

She left Joey and went to study the timetable pinned up on one wall.

"If you *can* let her come to us, even if it's only for a short time, please do! Phil seems to have taken a violent fancy to her and keeps on asking if Sam can't come and play with her."

The Head nodded. "She may come after needlework this afternoon and she may stay till Phil's bedtime. I can't do more today, Joey. Samaris's people sent her to us for her education."

Joey looked up. She had gained control of herself, but her friend saw the terror in her eyes and knew how bravely she was trying to suppress it. "I've sent Cecil to Biddy's for the moment. Geoff is too little to be badly affected if—if anything should go badly wrong, and Phil would miss him. But Cecil is nearly six and she's a sensitive scrap. By the way, don't let my other girls know about all this, will you?"

"Certainly not. Now finish your chocolate—I'm filling up your cup, for that lot must be lukewarm by this time. Take another pastry. Yes, Joey; I mean it. For Phil's sake you must eat properly. You never know when she may need all the strength you can give her."

Joey obeyed, and when she was nibbling at the pastry, Hilda came back to sit down beside her. "Joey, darling, don't despair. Phil is in God's hands. She *could* not be safer."

"I know, but it's not a lot of comfort at this moment." Joey swallowed the last of her chocolate and stood up. "I've been away from her long enough. Anna's there, of course, and the

Coadjutor, but I feel I can hardly bear to let her out of my sight. Where's my cloak?"

Joey dashed her hand across her eyes while Hilda brought her cloak and wrapped her in it. Joey kissed her.

"I—I feel a little better. Thanks, Hilda: you always do me good. Don't tell Sam about all this, by the way. She mayn't notice how the baby's gone back and if she knew it might make her self-conscious. Thanks a lot for everything."

She went off through the French window in the salon, and hurried back to Freudesheim, feeling, as she had truly said, better for the brief visit. Left alone, Miss Annersley went to find Matey and confer with her. What Matey had to say gave the Head a measure of hopefulness, and when she sent for Samaris at the end of the morning, she was her usual self. "Mrs Maynard wants you to go over to Freudesheim this afternoon, Samaris," she said. "Your flute has come and she wants to give it to you herself."

"O-oh!" Samaris slowly flushed and her eyes lit up like stars. "Oh, how—how *miraculous*! And how sweet of her to send for me!"

The Head smiled. "You may have permission to cut afternoon prep and go over after needlework. Change into your velveteen first. You may stay till 17.30 hours for once. Little Phil has been asking for you and this weather makes things very dull for her, poor baby. When you come back you must work hard at your preparation and try to finish, but if you can't, anything you have left will be excused for once. Now run along and make yourself tidy."

"Yes; I will. And thank you for saying I may go to Freudesheim. You don't know how I'm looking forward to that flute!"

"I can guess. But remember this, Samaris. If I find you neglecting your other work for it I shall insist on your leaving it in whatever music-room you use for practice and you won't be allowed to touch it except during practice periods."

"Oh, I won't neglect my work for it, I *promise* you!" In her earnestness, Sam came close to the Head and touched her arm. "It's just that I do love music and I have so wanted to be able to play *something*: only the piano didn't seem to be what I want."

"We'll hope that the flute is. Tomorrow Miss Dene will discuss your practice timetable with you. Mr Denny will give you lessons. You know, he used to be a flautist himself, and a very good one, too. Now run away!"

Samaris skipped to the door, only pausing there to perform her curtsy. Then she went off to the splashery where she was met by Robina, who demanded to be told why she had had to go to the study.

"What have you been up to?" Robina said severely.

"Nothing! Only, you remember I told you that Nina Rutherford said she was going to try to borrow a flute for me so that I could learn? Well, it's come! It's over at Freudesheim and the Head sent for me to tell me to go over there after needlework this afternoon to collect it."

Robina chuckled. "It's just as well this is Wednesday. I'm certain you could never have said all that in French!"

"I couldn't," Samaris agreed with truth.

"What's all this?" asked a fresh voice from the doorway as Len Maynard looked in. Her tone altered. "Samaris Davies! What on earth have you done to your hair? It's positively wild! Hurry up and comb it into decency or you'll be late for Mittagessen. The gong will sound any minute now. Why didn't you do it before?"

"The Head sent for me," Samaris explained as she produced her brush and comb and began to belabour her curls. "I've just left her. And we had gym last lesson."

"I see. Give me that brush and I'll straighten it for you or you'll never be ready." Len took the brush and with a few scientific strokes reduced the rampant mop to neatness. "That's better! Have you washed? Good—and there goes the gong! Hurry along, you two, and join your line."

It was just as well that the midday meal was always followed by a half-hour of rest and silence. Otherwise Samaris could never have calmed down. As it was her flushed cheeks and sparkling eyes drew Samantha's attention and when they were clearing away their deck-chairs at the end of the period, she contrived to have a word with Samaris.

"Sam! What's biting you? You look ready to fly off the handle!"

"Oh, Sammy! Such gorgeous news!" And Samaris poured it out to her at top-speed. "The flute Nina promised me—it's come! I'm to go over to Freudesheim after needlework to collect it. I'll show it to you when I come back. Isn't it *gaudy* of her to have remembered?"

"I guess Nina Rutherford isn't the kind that forgets," Samantha said. "Good! I'm mighty glad for you!—Here! Margot Maynard is glaring at us. Pick up your chair and come on or we'll be hearing *all* about it!"

Thus urged, Samaris picked up her chair and cushion and they hurried to the cupboard where chairs and cushions were kept when not in use. But she remained strung up though she managed to control herself outwardly on the whole.

"You *are* revved up about your old flute!" Robina murmured to her during needlework when they might talk if they did it quietly and without neglecting their work.

"I've always wanted to learn music, but I couldn't make a thing of the piano," Samaris explained, taking careful stitches round the buttonhole she was working. "Somehow I feel I'm really going to do something with the flute."

"Rather you than me!" Robina was not especially musical, though she had a pleasant little voice for singing.

"Besides, I'm to stay to tea and play with little Phil, and that's good, too."

"What? Oh, you lucky wench! How *is* Phil, do you know?"

"The Head said she was finding things dull this awful weather. I s'pose they won't let her go out in the fog."

"Bobby, may I borrow your scissors, please?" came a pleading voice behind them and as Robina turned to hand the scissors to Erica Standish, the subject was dropped.

When the lesson was over, Samaris raced upstairs to change into her evening velveteen before going down to the entrance hall, where Matey was waiting to escort her to Freudesheim. The mist was beginning to thin a little, but it was still thick enough to make Matey hasten her charge along the soaking paths and across the Freudesheim lawn to the salon window, where Joey was waiting to let them in. In her hand was a narrow leather case and as soon as Samaris had discarded her oilies and wellingtons, it was put into her hands.

"Your flute!" Joey said, smiling down into the dancing eyes. "May you do really well with it and enjoy every lesson you have on it. Now take it upstairs and show it to the twins. They're waiting for you. I'll send for you when teatime comes."

"Oh, thank you—thank you!" Samaris cried, flinging her arms round Joey in her excitement. "Thank you most terribly much!"

Then she was off to the playroom, clutching her new treasure, and thrilled, as she would have said, to the very marrow.

Chapter XVIII

A SURPRISING DUET

THE playroom at Freudesheim was at the top of the house. It was a big room with three windows guarded by bars. In this room stood the two big dolls' houses—La Maison des Poupées which Jack had made for the triplets when they were tiny girls, and an even more magnificent affair which Con had won at one of the earlier Sales of Work run annually by the school in aid of the free children's ward at the Sanatorium. There was Jack's own old rocking-horse; a big Noah's Ark, also home-made, and a farm. Bookshelves held books of every kind appealing to children of all ages, some old-fashioned stories inherited through three generations of Bettanys and Maynards; others the latest products of modern writers.

Tables and chairs of the kindergarten variety gave plenty of scope for the small folk to draw or crayon, as well as play such games as Ludo, Snap, and Snakes and Ladders. A couple of comfortable chairs and a big nursery table supplied the needs of the grown-ups, and in one of the two cupboards built in between the windows were nursery crockery and other needful articles. The other held toys and games not in present use. Joey very wisely kept putting away selections of everything, to bring them out later when they were fresh again.

Samaris had been up here two or three times before and she always loved it. Now she opened the door quietly and peeped in to find Rösli, the Coadjutor, seated in the rocking chair, little Phil on her lap. Geoff, Phil's twin, was playing with the farm, but as soon as Sam's bright face appeared round the door, he jumped up and ran to clasp her round the knees.

"Tham!" he lisped. "Oh, *hath* you come to play?"

Before Sam could reply, Phil had sat up and was holding out her poor little sticks of arms.

"Sam—oh, Sam! Tum to Phil!"

Sam ran across the room to kiss her. "Phil, darling! See what's here!" She opened the case and produced the flute, handling it almost reverently.

"What ith it?" demanded Geoff.

"A flute—something to make music with. Listen!" She raised it to her lips and blew. The resultant awful squeal made Rösli jump and the tiny pair giggle.

"*Funny* noise!" said Phil delightedly. "Do it adain—p'ease!"

Sam did it again and as her fingers had moved over some of the holes, she produced an even more heart-rending sound.

Geoff chuckled. "Thoundth like Poothy when you twead on her tail," he pronounced. "Let me twy, Tham—p'ease!"

It hurt Sam a little to hand it over, but she had been horrified by the look of illness on Phil's little face, so she handed it over without demur. "You hold it to your lips and blow."

Geoff did his best, but nothing happened. Nor could Phil manage any better. She gave it back to Sam.

"Sam p'ay it."

Sam was quite agreeable. She blew and another eldritch shriek followed. In fact, anything less beautiful it would have been hard to imagine. Rösli was giggling as she stood up, the baby in her arms.

"Now I go to bring rolls and cakes and milk," she said. "Mein Blümchen will be a good girl and eat her share if Fräulein Samaris will play the long whistle for her, nicht?" She set Phil into a little armchair.

Sam was on to this at once. "Of course I will. I'll play all you like, Phil, if you'll drink your milk and eat a big tea."

Phil nodded. "I p'omise," she said sweetly.

Rösli slipped out of the room, still giggling, while Samaris, with the flute at her lips, tried again. She warmed to her task as she went on and the appalling noises that ensued made Joey, coming upstairs with Matey, cover her ears. "Heaven preserve us! What is the school in for?" she exclaimed. "Poor you, Matey! You have my deepest sympathy!" She paused at the head of the stairs. "And I thought Nina loved us!"

Matey gurgled. "Awful! Still, I expect when she has had a lesson or two it won't be so bad. But I shall warn Dorothy Lawrence to give her her practice times in the most secluded of the practice-rooms," she added as she followed Joey into the playroom.

They were also followed by Bruno. He entered just as Sam, trying her hardest, evoked from the long-suffering flute a sound that outdid everything she had produced before. Geoff screamed with delight and Phil clapped her hands.

"Do it adain—oh, do it adain, Sam!"

"For pity's sake *don't* do it again!" their mother exclaimed as she advanced to pick Phil up. "It sounds like a soul in torment!"

Sam giggled. "It *is* rather awful till I get the hang of it, but they love it. I've promised to play if Phil will take her tea properly."

"Oh, well, a promise is a promise. In that case my lamb, you *must* do it again." She looked down at the chuckling tiny in her arms. "It seems to appeal to these two, anyhow. Does my Philly really like it?"

"Ezzer so much," Phil said, snuggling against her mother. "Mamma, tan us have a flute, too?"

"Yes, if Papa says you may and you two are good and as soon

as Sam can play a proper little tune on hers for us. Hear that, Sam? You'll have to work hard, honey girl, for these two are going to give no one any peace until they get their flute."

"Oh, I'd do that in any case," Sam said. She regarded her precious flute gravely. "You know, I did think that being able to play the harmonica would make it easy to begin on this. I never imagined it would be so hard!" She lifted it and produced another piteous squeal.

"It isn't quite the same method," said Matey, her eyes scanning Phil's little thin face carefully. "Now don't do it again, Samaris. We've heard quite enough to assure us that at least the thing works. Phil, aren't you going to say how do you do to Auntie Gwyn?"

Phil was gazing at the flute, but she gave a tiny smile. "How do?" she said.

"Vat's yude," Geoff remarked virtuously. "You's a yude girl. Mamma, may we have dam tartth for tea—*pleathe*?"

Joey sat down in the rocker, waving Matey to another chair, and taking her youngest daughter on her knee. "It's time you learnt to drop that lisping, my boy," she remarked. "Jam tarts aren't for boys who lisp."

"Tan't help it," he said briefly; and Joey gave it up. He had always been much slower in his speech than Phil. "All right, sonny. But only one each, and Phil must eat all hers herself. No giving half of it to Geoff, my precious."

"I p'omise," Phil nodded; but her eyes were fixed on Sam and the flute. "Sam p'ay adain," she begged.

Sam glanced at the elders and Joey giggled. "Oh, go on! I dare say neither of us will expire on the spot. Or no! Here comes Rösli with tea. Will you have yours up here, Sam? I see Rösli has provided for you. Do you mind?"

"I'd love it," said Sam, who felt that she would enjoy the

meal far more with the babies than with Matey as company. Like all the rest of the Chalet School people she held that redoubtable person in deepest awe.

"O.K., please yourself," Joey said easily. "Phil and Geoff, no more flute until you've eaten a good tea and drunk all your milk. Understand?"

Like all Joey's children the twins had been brought up to be obedient, so both nodded. Joey laughed as she stood up. "Good! And you set them a good example, Sam. Only one jam tart each, Rösli, for the twins. Sam, I'll come and fetch you when you have to go. Come on, Matey! Back to the salon for us! We'll leave these hungry hounds to clear the plates up here."

She led the way while the "hungry hounds" settled down to their meal. But when she and Matey were sitting by the fire, partaking of tea and hot cakes and pastries, she looked across at her friend. "Bless Nina for her inspiration! I know she was only thinking of young Sam, but those truly ghastly noises seem to have set Phil off again and you don't know how thankful I am for the tiniest thing that does that."

"I can imagine. I don't quite know how we're going to manage about Samaris, though. She was sent here to *school*!"

"I'll make Phil understand that Sam playing to them is a treat for good little girls who eat properly and can only happen now and then. Oh, Gwyn! If this should prove to be a real start once more!"

The soft black eyes were swimming with tears. Matey nodded. "Quite likely it is," she said. "Don't fret, Joey. I think this last phase has been only a temporary setback, and now that Phil has been jolted out of it, she will go on. Don't cry, you silly girl! Be thankful!"

"Oh, I *am*!" Joey mopped her eyes. "I've felt so disheartened and anxious these last few days. Sorry, Gwynneth! I didn't mean to treat you to a scene! I must be tired, I think." She gulped and then picked up her cup and drank. "There! I feel better now! Have another Welsh cake. Anna makes them to perfection."

"She certainly does," Matey agreed, helping herself. She looked round. "Where's Bruno?"

"In the playroom, probably. He adores Phil." She went on with her tea. Suddenly she looked up. "Gwyn! I've had a most awful thought!"

"What now?"

"Those two! They loved the excruciating noises Sam was making. You *don't* think it means they've no ear for music?"

Matey stared at her and then burst out laughing. "An awful thought indeed! Of course not! Small children do like noise of almost any kind, as you ought to know by this time. In fact," she added as she surveyed the dish of pastries before her, "I've known older people who do. Have you forgotten Corney Flower's concert at the end of your last term at school?"[1]

Joey laughed. "I have not! Neither have I forgotten the morning when Frieda Mensch and I caught that crew practising on their varied instruments! Corney on her sax really was something! Talk of the tune the old cow died of. It was more like the death agonies of an elderly bull!"

"I've always been sorry I missed that," Matey said. The next moment she jumped violently and nearly overturned her teacup into her lap.

Joey bounded to her feet and made for the door. "What *is* happening? Heavens above! We'll have the whole Platz along to inquire who's being tortured! Come on!" And she shot out of the room and upstairs, Matey following.

The most outrageous sounds were coming from the playroom and Sam was *not* responsible for all of them. Tea there had

[1] *The New Chalet School*

finished, Phil faithfully keeping her word to eat as much as she could besides drinking all her milk. Rösli had watched with a beaming face. During the past few days it had been a case of coaxing Phil to take anything, and this was the first really good meal she had had since she began to go back. But once the meal was over, both children had begged for "More flute, p'ease!" and Sam was only too willing to oblige them.

What no one had bargained for was Bruno's reaction to the fearful noises she evoked from the flute as she went on. He winced violently at the first sound or two. Finally, he could bear it no longer. Raising his nose to heaven he howled mournfully and the resultant duet between him and Sam reduced Geoff to rolling on the floor with laughter while Phil chuckled and even Rösli laughed though she covered her ears with her hands.

Joey and Matey arrived to find the playroom party all in fits, for Sam was unable to go on for laughter. Bruno was still howling and Geoff was crimson with mirth. Even Phil's pale little face was faintly pink.

It ceased when the door opened and Bruno saw a way of escape from those terrible noises. He stopped howling, plunged heavily to the door, and literally skidded down the stairs to seek refuge in Anna's kitchen. In his passage he pushed so violently past his mistress that she lost her balance and sat down heavily, luckily on a big nearby pouffe. Matey saw him coming and skipped nimbly out of the way, collided with a chair and sprawled on the floor. The exploits of her mother and "Auntie Gwyn" put the finish to Phil's piteous mood. Smiling sweetly at Rösli, who was wiping her eyes, she held out her mug and said "More milk, p'ease!" And drank it up when she got it.

Matey marched Samaris off after that. It would be bedtime for the twins before long, and Sam had prep. But before she went she had to promise faithfully to come again soon.

"A *soon* soon!" Phil pleaded, lifting her milky mouth for a final kiss.

"Sunday if we can manage it," Joey promised. "Meantime, Sam must go back to prep and I'm coming for bedtime stories."

"Want Sam to stay an' listen, too."

"I can't," said Sam. "I've got heaps of prep to do. But I've had a lovely time and I'll come again as soon as I can." She kissed the twins and ran off, followed by Joey, who called back her promise to come and tell them bedtime stories in a minute.

When they were in the hall where Matey was waiting for them, she took the girl in her arms. "Thank you more than I can say. Between you and your flute I believe Phil's on the right road again—though I think we'll keep you and it and Bruno well apart for the present. What a scene that was!" She laughed again as she thought of it. "Ready? Then you must go and I must keep my promise to the small fry. Thank you once more for Phil. I really do think she'll go ahead now."

Matey cut the farewells short. "Come along, Samaris. Goodbye, Joey. I don't think you need worry much over Phil now. I honestly believe the worst is over." Then she took Samaris's arm and ran that young woman out of the house and through the gardens where the mist was steadily thinning, and so to school and prep.

Chapter XIX

News for the Sams

It was Monday morning and Inter V were in their formroom, reading their letters. Samantha gave a sudden exclamation and jumped up.

"What's biting you?" Jack Lambert queried, looking up from her mother's letter.

"I must go and speak to the Head at once. She'll be in the study, won't she?"

"Use your wits! Where else, at this hour?"

"Thanks a million!" Samantha dashed out of the room, leaving the form to wonder what on earth had happened.

Meanwhile she sped along the corridors to the study, where she tapped. She heard the Head call, "Entrez!" and went in, red with excitement. Miss Annersley was busy sorting out the Seniors' essays but she looked up with a smile.

"Well, Samantha?"

Samantha paused to collect her French. "I have had a letter from Mama and she says she and Papa are coming to Interlaken on business for a few days. She wants to know if I may join them on Saturday and stay till Sunday night and take Samaris Davies with me. She is writing to you today."

The Head thought for a minute or two. "I can't give you an answer at this moment, Samantha. I expect it will be all right for you, but I am not sure about Samaris."

Samantha's face fell. "Oh, Miss Annersley, I do hope she can come!"

"I have not said she may not. But why are you so anxious to have her?" The Head looked at the girl with real curiosity.

"Because Mama says Papa thinks Sam's father may be a distant cousin of his. He's not dead sure, but he thinks it's so. It'll be real exciting if she's kin of mine," Samantha explained.

Miss Annersley smiled. "That explains it. How has he discovered it?"

"Partly from our names—Samaris and Samantha. I got my name from my great-grandmother, you know, and so did Samaris—from hers, I mean. Great-Grandma was one of twins and her twin was Samaris. Papa thinks our Sam may be descended from the twin. Anyway, it's set him hunting up records—"

She had to stop there for the bell for Prayers pealed out. The Head nodded, got up and pulled on the M.A. gown she always wore in school hours. "I understand. Well, Samantha, as I said, I can't give you a definite answer now, but I will think about it. I'll see you later. Meanwhile, say nothing to Samaris until I give you leave."

"No," said Samantha reluctantly. "Only, I've got so fond of Sam, and I wondered if maybe it's because we *are* kin."

"It very well might be. We must wait until your father has his records." The Head picked up her books. "At the moment, dear, you must go."

There was no more to be said. Samantha made her curtsy and left the study. Miss Annersley sat down to await the second bell.

For the rest of that morning, Inter V spent any spare moments they might have in wondering what had happened to Samantha. She seemed completely *distraite* and some of her answers in lessons made the staff wonder, too. She was not a student type, but usually she worked well enough.

When morning school was over, Valerie, who still felt a certain responsibility for her, asked her, "Is there anything wrong, Sammy?"

"Nothing," Samantha said. "I've had some interesting news from Mama and if it's all right it really is exciting. But the Head forbade me to talk of it."

With this they had to be satisfied. At least they grasped the fact that the news, whatever it might be, was giving Samantha thrills of the highest order. Samaris, when they met at the end of school, was also given reason to wonder. Samantha threw an arm round her shoulders and gave her a hug.

"What's the why of that?" Samaris demanded.

"I'm so excited. My folk are coming to Interlaken and I'm to go down on Saturday week to stay with them," Samantha said quickly.

"Next weekend? Do you mean a week on Saturday? But you can't! That's the day of the Millies' pantomime. You don't want to miss that, surely?"

Samantha's face dropped. "Gee! I'd forgotten all about it! No; I surely do not. Oh, what a mix-up!"

"How long are they staying? Couldn't they come up for the panto and take you back with them?"

Samantha brightened. "You've got something there, Sam. I guess that would be best." To herself she added, "And then they'll see you right away."

"Write and tell them," Samaris urged. "It would be miraculous if they could! I've been hearing reams about it from our crowd and they all say the Millies' pantos are stupendous!"

"Guess I will at that. It's a fine idea, Sam."

"You must get leave first," Samaris reminded her.

"I'll get leave all right," Samantha said. She gave Samaris's shoulders another squeeze and left her to wonder to herself what on earth had happened to make the elder girl so unlike her usual self.

The next thing that happened was a letter to Samaris herself from her father. Mr van der Byl was not given to dallying and he had made it his business to break the journey from Vienna where he and his family were staying and he and his wife had gone to Innsbruck. There he had sought out Mr Davies and together they had gone into the matter at length. The result was that they had discovered that they were second cousins and the girls were, as Samantha expressed it, kin.

"Mam and I hope that your Samantha can come to spend a week or ten days with us during the Easter holidays," Mr Davies wrote. "Her people say it will be all right, so if she likes the idea, ask her. Both Mam and I would like to know her. Her father, your cousin Silas, and I have plenty in common and Mam and your cousin Estelle got on well."

Samantha also had a letter from her father, describing the visit to his cousin Ivor. "We got on just fine," he wrote. "In fact we were buddies at once. If your Sam is anything like him I guess you two are buddies, too."

The pair exchanged notes and Samantha said with a giggle, "Well, he's dead right. I guess they've been buddies from the start, just like you and me. I just knew there was some reason for it."

Samaris laughed. "It struck *me* as weird. After all, it isn't even as if we were in the same form or the same age. I'm nearly two years younger than you and two forms lower."

"I guess if you're blood kin it makes all that much difference," Samantha said wisely. "But there's one thing, Sam. I want to know why Papa never knew about all this before."

Samaris was unable to tell her and they had to wait until the van der Byls turned up for the pantomime before they knew; and before that happened, the pair had an adventure that everyone could well have done without.

It began early on the Sunday morning when they walked to church together. The mists had ended three days earlier and a stiff breeze was drying up the land rapidly. After the service, the girls were given permission for a short ramble before Mittagessen. By this time the whole school knew that the two Sams were related. No one was surprised when they begged leave to go together to visit Nina Rutherford. Samaris wanted to thank her in person for the flute, though she had written a very charming thank-you letter days before. Samantha was delighted at the idea of meeting again the girl to whom she had taken a great fancy at their sole meeting. Miss Ferrars and Miss Wilmot were going to spend the day at Adlersnest, the chalet shared by Mme Courvoisier and Mrs Graves, both Old Girls of the school, and both former mistresses. The Görnetz Sanatorium was little more than ten minutes' walk further on. Samantha had more than once shown herself capable and responsible, so the pair were told that they might finish the short distance by themselves. Dr Maynard, who was at the Sanatorium that morning, would run them back to school in time for Mittagessen.

It was a three miles' walk, but both girls were good walkers. The fresh air was invigorating and when they bade the mistresses goodbye at the end of the little lane where Adlersnest stood, no one could imagine that they were likely to come to any harm.

At this point the path ran fairly near the edge of the cliff which fell almost sheer to the valley below. Just beyond the lane an opening led to the path which at one time had been the main way down. It was very steep, but went down in a series of zigzags—which was just as well. On one occasion, this pattern had saved Bruno from a nasty fall.[1] It also acted as a drain-off for much of

[1] *The Chalet School Triplets*

the superfluous water on the Platz during the thaw. The last of the water had got away the previous day, but the rocks lay glistening wet and, if the Sams had but known it, as slippery as ice.

At the head of the path, Samantha paused to look across the valley at the great wall of the northern Alps which had been shrouded in mist most of the last week. Today was clear and the girls gazed at the mountains with delight.

"Aren't they marvellous?" Samantha breathed.

"Fabulous!" Samaris agreed. Then, in a different tone, "I wonder what it's like further down this road?"

"Pretty bad, I guess. Look at the pitch," her new-found cousin remarked.

"We've heaps of time. We were out of church earlyish. Let's go a tiny way down and see where it leads to," Samaris suggested.

Samantha shook her head. "No. It just goes down to the plain, anyway and we can't go that far. Come on, Sam!"

Samaris gave it up and they went on to the Sanatorium. Here they were met with a snag. Nina's Embury cousins had come up from Montreux unexpectedly. They had arrived barely ten minutes previously and were with her now. Neither Samantha nor Samaris felt like intruding. They left lengthy messages at the office and then came away reluctantly.

"What shall we do now?" Samantha asked. "We're to go back with Dr Jack so we can't just trot home by ourselves, even if it wasn't against the rules. We'll have to wait for him."

"Yes, but where?" Samaris queried.

"Oh, I guess we'd best go for a stroll around until it's time to meet him—well, now what?" For Samaris had looked up suddenly.

"The path! Let's go down it a little way! Come on, Sammy!"

"I don't think we ought," Samantha began.

"Oh, rot! It's safe enough. Why, I've heard Len Maynard say that at one time they used to bring cars up and down it. It must be safe enough and I'd love to try it."

So would Samantha. Also, she felt no desire to walk on grass that was still on the sodden side. There was nowhere where they could sit down and the receptionist, new on Thursday, had given them no encouragement to stay in the Sanatorium. Her predecessor would have kept them and sent word to Matron Graves, who would have taken charge. As it was, there was no one to put a stop to their doings, so they set off.

They soon reached the head of the path and there they stopped and Samantha surveyed it carefully. "It looks mighty slippery, but I guess we can go a little way down," she said. "We'll have to be careful, though. Our boots aren't nailed and we haven't our alpenstocks. If you feel yourself going, Sam, grab a hold on me and I'll steady you. And we're not going beyond the first turn, either," she added.

"O.K. I just want to see what it's like," Samaris said.

"I'll go first," said Samantha.

"Oh, no, you won't! It's wide enough for two. Besides, if I skid behind you, how are you going to grab me?" Samaris asked with some point.

"I hadn't thought of that. O.K.; together, then, and mind how you go."

"Hadn't you better mind how *you* go? Don't forget your collarbone," Samaris said. "I've always wondered how on earth you managed to climb that tree and yank Minette free so soon after you did it in."

Samantha laughed. "My bones knit quickly—like Papa's. Anyhow, I was mainly using the other arm and my knees. If that bough hadn't come down, nothing would have happened. Well, if we're really going down we'd better start in."

They started, finding it hard going. The limestone rock was terribly slippery and they had to catch at knobs and juts more than once. However, they negotiated the first part of the path safely. Samaris was all for trying the next, but Samantha refused.

"It's taken quite a time to come down this far and it'll be worse getting back," she said. "I'm just going to climb up to that little ledge and take a peek over the edge. You can have a shot when I come back. Wait there, Sam. I won't be a minute."

Samaris stood back and Samantha scrambled up to her ledge and stared out over the rock wall which came nearly up to her chin. She decided that it was no use to let Sam try it. She was much shorter and would see nothing. She turned to tell her young cousin so just in time to see the tail of Sam's coat disappearing round the second corner.

"Sam! Come back!" she shouted; and scrabbled her way frantically down the side and followed just in time to see Sam slip, sit down heavily, and go sliding on her tail down to the next turn where she brought up against the rock with a crash and a shriek. At the same time a boulder, loosened by the thaw, heaved up and rolled down. Mercifully, it caught against a jutting out piece of rock which halted its progress, but it completely blocked the path. The two Sams were thoroughly separated.

Samantha made a valiant effort and kept her head. "Sam!" she yelled.

"Ye-yes!" came back clearly but rather faintly. Sam was more than a little dazed by the unexpected happening.

"Are you O.K.? No bones broken or anything?"

"I—I don't think so."

"Can you get up and move right over to the lefthand side?" Samantha kept an anxious eye on the boulder. If anything happened to dislodge it and it rolled on to Samaris, she would certainly be badly injured if not killed outright.

"Yes—*ouch*!"

"What's wrong?"

"Nothing! I'm only a bit bruised and stiff where I sat down. I'm up now."

There was a pause as Samaris looked round. She didn't feel in the least like climbing. Something in Samantha's voice, however, forced her to suppress a groan before she looked up at the sloping sides of the path. She gave a cry.

"There's a shelf here. I think I can reach it."

"You surely must—unless you want to be squashed flat as a pancake. There's a big rock come loose and rolled down—a *mighty* big rock. If it rolls on you there won't be much of you left!" Samantha said bluntly.

Samaris gave a squawk of horror and tackled the short climb on the spot. Luckily, apart from bruising, she was practically unhurt. She set her teeth and after two or three minutes which seemed to the anxious Samantha like hours, she called out, "O.K. I'm up!"

"Can you stay there a bit? I must dash to get help."

"I'll be all right. You—you won't be long will you?"

"Not a second longer than I can help. Once I'm at the top I can run. Keep your heart up, Sam! It won't be long!"

She turned back and set to work to toil up the slippery slope. Fear for Samaris forced her on, and arrived at the top she took to her heels and raced as fast as she could to the Sanatorium. In fact she concentrated so much on her speed that she never looked where she was going and ended up by burying her nose into Jack Maynard's chest as he came out of the big doors.

"Hi! Steady on!" he exclaimed, steadying her on her feet. "What's all the hurry?"

"Samaris! Oh, get men to help and come!"

"What? Where is she?"

As briefly as she could, Samantha gasped out her story. He acted at once. He handed the girl over to Matron with the curt command, "See to her!" Then he dashed off to seek some of the men who work at the Sanatorium, as well as some of the younger doctors. He assembled half a dozen in short order and then, armed with ropes, ice-axes, and jacks, they set off at a run for the path.

Samaris, perched most uncomfortably on her shelf, heard them coming and burst into tears from sheer relief. All the time Samantha was gone she had been watching the path with strained eyes, dreading to see the boulder come rolling and bounding down towards her. But the jutting side held it and shortly after the arrival of her rescuers it was securely roped and held by ice-axes driven into crevices and cracks in the wall. Then the doctor strode past it and arrived beneath the weeping prisoner.

"Stop that bawling!" he said severely. "This is your own fault. Now stand up—go carefully!"

No need for him to tell her that. Samaris moved in such a gingerly way it took her three full minutes to get to her feet. She looked down at him, her face smeared with tears, her hat gone, and her hair in a tangle. But she was up. Jack Maynard felt thankful for that. She had clearly done herself no great harm. He held out his arms, straddling the path firmly.

"Jump!" he ordered.

Samaris jumped and landed safely in his arms. He carried her to the top and along to the Sanatorium where, in one of the accident rooms, he examined her thoroughly. He smiled at her when it was over. "Well, you've a bruise the size of a saucer at the base of your spine, but you seem to have broken no bones or damaged yourself apart from that. You haven't got off scot free, but there's nothing that a day or two in bed won't cure. I'll take you two back now and hand Samaris over to Matey to deal with. Then I must report to Miss Annersley, so I don't suppose either of you will feel too happy about things for the next day or two."

"But what about this afternoon?" asked Samaris. "I promised to bring my flute and play to the twins."

"The twins will have to get along without you. Don't worry, Samaris. Phil is making real headway again and all *my* children have learned not to fuss about what can't be helped—even the twins. I'll explain to them that you've hurt yourself and can't come for a day or two and that will hold them. Now we must get this young woman into the car and home to bed." He stooped and picked up Samaris, smiling at Matron who had come along to see what the damage was. "Thanks for your help, Helen. The boulder is secure for the moment and I'll report to the authorities. The whole of that wall should be examined. Meantime, send one of the men to put up danger notices above and below the rock. That's all! Come along, Samantha!"

And that, as Joey said when she heard the full story, was that.

Chapter XX

BUDDIES!

No one said very much to either Samantha or Samaris until the next day. Samaris was put to bed in the school san on an air-ring. She had given herself a really nasty bruise. Samantha was also ordered off to bed, for as soon as she saw the Head she burst into tears and wept and wept. Miss Annersley, wise in her generation, knew that this was sheer reaction and handed her over to her House Matron, who brought her a beaker of hot milk, once she was between the sheets, and saw that she drank it to the last drop. She had slipped a small tablet into it and when she peeped into the girl's cubicle an hour later, Samantha was sound asleep as she had expected.

Nemesis came next day. Samaris was still in bed and very sorry for herself, for she was most uncomfortable. Samantha's nerves had more or less recovered and she was summoned to a painful interview with the Head. Miss Annersley pointed out firmly that she knew the rules about wandering about the Platz by themselves. She, as the elder of the pair, should have insisted on Samaris obeying them, however much that young person wanted to try the path.

Samantha had not a word to say in excuse. She only begged to be assured that Samaris had not hurt herself badly.

"She is very sore and bruised," Miss Annersley said severely. "Serve her right, too! I'm not sorry for her."

"I—I'm real sorry I forgot about the rule," Samantha faltered. "I guess it was more my fault than hers. Will—will she get up today?"

"Not until the doctor has seen her. Possibly not then. We must be sure that she has done no damage to her spine."

"I—oh, surely not!" Samantha paled a little.

Miss Annersley was secretly very sorry for her, but she felt that the lesson must be impressed on her, so she only said repressively, "I can say nothing about that until the doctor has seen her again."

There was a short pause. Then Samantha, summoning up her courage, asked shakily, "Will—will she be able to—to go to the pantomime on Saturday?"

She got a look that nearly froze her. "Do you think that she—or you, either—deserve to be allowed to go?"

"I—I—"

The Head relaxed a little. "I can't tell you yet, but I doubt it. As for you, since your parents are coming, you may go with them; but I am very disappointed in you. I thought you had more sense of responsibility than you have shown. You are well past fifteen and a Senior. Samaris is a Middle and nearly two years younger. You should have looked after her better. That is all I have to say to you now. You may go, but be more thoughtful in future, my dear."

Samantha almost literally *crawled* from the room. Miss Annersley had contrived in that ten minutes' interview to make her feel less than the dust; and this in addition to the very real anxiety she was feeling about her young cousin. In one way it was very good for her. Owing to the wandering life she had led hitherto and the fact that she was six years older than her next sister, she had come to school feeling she was someone of much importance. She had had the sense to suppress her ideas with the other girls, but it was there. Now she realised that she was regarded as merely a naughty, heedless girl who was not to be trusted with her juniors.

As for Samaris, she had punished herself well and truly, for not only was she in a good deal of pain from that bad bruise, but it lasted for some days and she had to miss the pantomime in consequence. She was kept in san and was allowed very few visits from the other girls for she ran a slight temperature for the first few days and Nurse ordained that until she could manage to sit comfortably with only a cushion, she must stay where she was.

On the Sunday after the pantomime, however, when she was sitting up in a well-cushioned armchair, she was allowed a number of visitors, including not only Samantha but Robina, Brigit, and Emmy in the morning. In the afternoon her parents arrived, having been brought by the new cousins for the weekend. They did not say much about her escapade, but her father did suggest that in future it would be as well if she tried to be rather more obedient. However, they were delighted to hear about the flute and promised that she should have time to fit in as much practice as she liked in the holidays.

When they left, Samantha arrived, bringing *her* parents, and Samaris made the acquaintance of the grown-up cousins. They made no allusions to the affair and Mrs van der Byl—Cousin Estelle, as she was to be called—set a huge box of what she called "candies" on her lap. Samaris had never had such a big one before, and its size made her open her eyes. Mr van der Byl also informed her that he had booked rooms for himself and his family in an Innsbruck hotel for the whole of the Easter holidays—he called it "va-cation"—so that they could all get to know each other.

"I want we should be real friends," he explained. "I guess we'll have a busy time of it at that."

The next visitor was Joey Maynard, complete with twins, and Samaris noted with delight that Phil was looking much better, with pink in her cheeks and the beginnings of dimples in them. Joey, too, made no remark about the cause of Samaris's incarceration. Instead, after Phil and Geoff had finished their rapturous greetings to Samaris, she handed them over to Matron, who bore them off to her own quarters, and then settled down to describe the pantomime to Samaris.

The Millies had elected to produce *Dick Whittington*, and by the time the invalid had heard of the scene in which the Cook had chased Dick all round the stage with a soup cauldron in one hand, an outsize of ladles in the other, and how the Cat got in her way whenever she came near his master, Samaris was literally crying with laughter.

"And the scene in the palace of the Sultan of Morocco was almost as funny," Joey said, chuckling as she recalled it. The rats had been played by six small people from IIa, and Joey's account of how Léonie Dubois and Hilary Simpson had contrived to get their very long tails twisted together, and bring down a pile of cushions on top of themselves while the Cat, played by Francie Wilford, magnificently ignored them and chased the other four, made Samaris regret more bitterly than ever that she had insisted on trying that path.

"Oh, I *wish* I could have seen it!" she mourned. "And it was all my own silly fault!"

Joey looked very straight at her. "If you realise that, you've learned your lesson," she said. "I'm sorry you had to miss it, Sam, and more sorry still for the reason. However, it's over and done with now. You won't do such a mad thing again."

"I jolly well won't!" Samaris said with fervour. Then, "Oh, Mrs Maynard, did you know that Sammy and I are cousins? Isn't it utterly *fab*?"

"Gorgeous!" Joey agreed as she stood up. "Well, I must go and collect my offspring. The others can tell you about the other highlights of the pantomime; but I must take my twins home to bed now. Phil is much better, but we can't play any tricks with her yet." She bent and kissed Samaris and left her.

But the cream of everything came the following Tuesday when Samaris and Samantha heard the whole story of how they came to be cousins. By that time she was back in school—with a cushion to sit on!—and breaking-up in two days' time and everyone was very busy with end-of-term chores. It was Mr van der Byl who told the story in full to them. They were in the Head's salon, that lady having offered it for the purpose, and as the two girls listened they became more and more absorbed, for it really was a thrilling story.

Their great-grandmothers had been twins, born in New York in 1870. Unlike many twins, they were not in the least like each other. Samantha, the elder, had grown up into a quiet, biddable girl, fair like her great-granddaughter, and law-abiding in the extreme. Samaris, on the contrary, had always been "agin' the government". She and her twin had quarrelled continually from baby days, and when at the age of seventeen Samaris had fallen in love with a young Englishman who was working in the American branch of an English publisher's office and who had nothing but his salary, the elder girl had done her best to persuade her twin to give him up. Samaris had insisted on becoming engaged to him, despite her parents' refusal to hear of such a thing, and finally the twins quarrelled so bitterly that they had refused to speak to each other for some weeks.

One night, however, Samaris had appeared in Samantha's room after they had gone upstairs to bed. She was still fully dressed, though Samantha was between the sheets and already half-asleep. Samaris said she had come to make up the quarrel. Samantha had used the opportunity to try to coax her twin to break off her engagement in obedience to their parents' wishes, but Samaris had only laughed and shaken her dark head.

"Not I! I guess I'll choose my own husband!" she had retorted. "Well, I'm going now, so I'll say goodbye. I'm the bad girl and you can be the good obedient daughter!"

That was the last any of them had seen of her. Next morning, Samaris was gone, bag and baggage. That goodbye had been for all time. All they could hear of her was that she and her lover had slipped off, first to Canada and thence to Australia, where he had obtained a post with a similar firm to his old one. They had been married early in the morning of their elopement and Samaris, writing home, had informed her family that unless and until they forgave not only her but her husband, they would hear no more from her.

"Your great-great-grandfather was furious," Mr van der Byl informed the enthralled girls. "He vowed he would never forgive either Samaris or her husband. All her belongings were packed up and sent off to the Australian address from which she had written and he forbade her very name to be mentioned in the family."

"Didn't she ever try again to get him to forgive her?" Samaris asked.

"Not as I know of. She was as proud and stubborn as he and when, later on, Samantha tried after her own marriage to get into touch with her twin, her letters were returned with 'Not known here' stamped on them."

"I guess Great-Grandma was sorry she'd quarrelled with her twin," Samantha said shrewdly.

"I guess that's so," he agreed.

"But couldn't they have sent detectives after them or advertised in the newspapers or something?" Samaris asked.

"They could; but he wouldn't. Anyway, they had lost touch. My grandmother died when she was in her early thirties and my father was brought up by his father's sister—your great-aunt Nancy Forrestal, Sammy. She knew the story, of course, and she told it to him when he was a young man, but he just wasn't interested. He was in the family firm and keen on his job. What's more, he was just engaged to your grandmother and I guess he forgot the most of it. But my mother heard the tale somehow and told us kids about it."

"Why didn't you try to find out yourself?" Samantha queried.

"It was all so long ago and no one had heard anything of the Davies for more'n fifty years at least. So far as I knew they were still in Australia."

"I see. But it does seem a shame no one did anything about it after Great-great-grandpa died, anyhow," Samantha said thoughtfully.

"Well, you know now and you two girls will help to make up for that old quarrel, I guess," he said with a smile.

"Well, it's all very thrilling," Samantha said. "I'm glad we two have met."

"Oh, so am I!" Samaris agreed. "I did know that Granddad Davies came from Australia. He came over with the Anzacs in the first world war and met Grannie in England—she was a V.A.D. in the hospital where he was after he was wounded—and they married and he decided to stay in Britain. His people were dead, you see, and he'd got a decent job in the firm Dad's with." She turned to Samantha with shining eyes. "Anyhow, Sammy, it's all come right now! But isn't it *odd*?"

"How's that?" Mr van der Byl demanded.

"Why, Mam and Dad came out to Innsbruck because of his job and I went to a school there; only they didn't want me to grow up Austrian. Fräulein Hamel told them about the Chalet School so they sent me here and when I came, Sammy was almost the first girl I met and we liked each other at once."

"And your Cousin Estelle and I had decided that it was time Sammy was at school and in some place where she stayed put. I guess too much wandering about the world isn't good for kids."

Samantha laughed. "You've said a mouthful! I've enjoyed going around with you, but now I feel mighty glad I'm settled for a year or two. I'm free to confess I wasn't too pleased about it at first, but now I'm very, very glad. I've got my Cousin Sam out of it and we might never have met otherwise."

"And I've got my Cousin Sammy. Oh, and there's my flute! I'm fearfully bucked about it and I mean to work as hard as I can at it for I want to play really well. Only think! If we hadn't come here I'd never have met Nina Rutherford and she wouldn't have given me my flute. I heard her play and was thrilled by it, but I'd never have dared to speak to her if Mrs Maynard hadn't taken Sammy and me to see her in the San that first time!"

Samantha laughed again. "I can see we're in for a queer time with you tootling about on it, but I'm glad you've got it. And I'm glad we both came here together and made friends at once. Buddies—that's what we two are!"

Samaris chuckled. "The two Sams—Two Sams at the Chalet School!"

HOME IS WHERE THE HEART IS
A Short Story by Katherine Bruce

This story, which opens some eleven years before the start of the Chalet School series, has its final scene during the term described in Two Sams at the Chalet School.

"Here you are, Margaret."

Looking up, Madge found that Guardian had come slowly into the drawing room, Josephine in his arms. He came over to where she was sitting in the window seat, looking out at the falling snow which formed a thick, white blanket over the wintry garden.

"Is there something I can do for you, sir?" asked Madge. She was not quite used to this stern, quiet, grey-haired man who had come to care for them after the deaths of their parents in India, now a little more than six months earlier.

One thing that was slowly becoming less peculiar was the house in London that Madge and her twin brother, Dick, were at present calling home. During their first weeks in the bustling capital, they had been taken to see some of the most famous sights of London. Then, when the weather became too bad for them to go out, they got to know the house.

Much as she appreciated the grandeur of the drawing room, Madge had quickly decided that her favourite room was a small sitting room with windows that looked out on to the bustling streets below. She could spend hours watching people walk to and fro, increasingly, as Christmas neared, carrying piles and bags containing objects of varied and interesting shapes. Although Guardian had warned that they would soon be going back to school, and that home in the future would be his house in Cornwall, he had consented to their having some familiar pieces of furniture from their home in India in the sitting room, which had been all but empty until the children's arrival. And so the old writing desk and the chesterfield had been placed close to the fireplace. Madge had also begged for an armchair that had been her mother's favourite seat and, to the poor orphaned girl, represented her loving and now absent parents. It wasn't a particularly striking piece of furniture, consisting of a body upholstered in dark green satin, with wooden legs in the Queen Anne style, but the twins' guardian had understood how important it was to his new charge and allowed her to give it pride of place.

Major Williams' face broke into a gentle smile as Madge crossed the room to join him in the doorway. "Your brother asked if you could come and help him wrap Christmas presents. Could you take Josephine to Nanny for her nap before you go to the sitting room to join him?"

"Of course, Guardian." Madge accepted the warm bundle and looked down into her sister's face. She drew the blanket closer round the tiny child. "Your first Christmas in London, Joey," she breathed. "And mine, too."

"Pah!" replied the little girl with a cheerful, toothless grin.

Madge smiled and then left the rather chilly drawing room, heading for warmer parts of the house. Once Joey was settled in her cradle, Madge turned to the sitting room, where she found her twin brother frowning as he tried to form crisp, neat edges round a misshapen parcel.

"What on earth is it?" demanded Madge as she sat opposite him.

"A ball," said Dick as he gave up the attempt and the paper sprang back to reveal the parti-coloured object. "It's for Joey, but it's jolly hard to wrap!"

Madge smiled. "I got her a rag doll," she confided. "Guardian said perhaps I could try to make a dress for it later, but," she added with a gurgle, "that will have to wait until I can sew a jolly sight better than I can now!"

"I should say so!" Dick joined in the laugh. "I haven't forgotten when you tried to sew up my shirt sleeve so Mummy wouldn't see I'd torn it, and it burst open right in the middle of breakfast as I was reaching out to get some more kedgeree!"

The children giggled appreciatively at the memory. Then Dick turned once more to the task of trying to wrap Joey's Christmas present and Madge took a sheet of paper from the writing desk and began to decorate it.

Major Williams found them still hard at work when he came up to join them two hours later. A small heap of neatly wrapped gifts stood on the desk and Madge was busy with one final object for which there was not quite enough paper.

"Almost finished?" asked the Major.

"Just about!" Dick rammed a colourful card into an envelope and placed it atop the little pile. Then he stood up and crossed the small room to where his guardian was standing.

"What happens this evening, sir? Do we go to church as usual?"

"May I come in?" inquired Major Williams, who remained in the doorway. "Then I shall endeavour to answer all of your questions."

"Of course!"

Dick stood back and indicated the Queen Anne armchair, which happened to be standing closest to the fireplace. Madge looked up as he approached and made a sudden protesting movement.

"P-please, sir, not there!" She pulled another chair close to the fire. "Th-that was Mother's," she added in a shaky voice, by way of explanation, and Major Williams, who had grown very fond of these poor children in the seven months he had known them, as well as being very understanding, at once took the seat she indicated.

"Come here, Margaret," he said gently.

As she rather laggingly approached, he held out his hand and drew her closer. Her eyes were fixed on the floor, but he slid his finger beneath her chin and raised her head so that she met his gaze. Dick had already sat down in the rocking chair, leaving the armchair for his sister. However, Major Williams drew Madge on to his lap instead.

"My child," he said gently, "don't be afraid to tell me if something upsets you. I have no intention of doing anything that would make you angry or sad." His voice deepened a little. "I do not want you to think that I am here in any way to take the place of your mother or father. I only mean to care for you until you are of age, or else to give you a good start for someone else to take on the task in time."

"I—I didn't mean to be rude," stammered poor Madge, on the verge of tears, "but only Dick and I have sat in that chair since we came here and it would have been too hard …"

"My poor girl!" Major Williams held Madge close. "Of course it would! I wouldn't dream of doing anything that distresses you, only you must be sure to tell me so that I don't do anything of that nature by mistake. Now," he went on, to give Madge time to recover herself, "what was it you were saying, my lad? Church? Not this evening, I'm afraid. Have you forgotten that your aunts are coming? And as they will bring their families, you are not likely to lack for companionship this Christmas, I can assure you! Your great-uncle speaks of coming tomorrow afternoon to see you, but that will depend on a great number of things, I imagine, not least the fact that he has to come from his home in Devonshire."

The Major looked stern as he spoke the final sentences, for William Bettany, a bachelor who travelled for many months at a time, had been unwilling to settle down in England and accept responsibility for the Bettany children. In the end, Major Williams, who had been the Bettanys' loyal family friend for many years, had been appointed their guardian.

"Shall the aunts stay here?" demanded Dick. "We haven't a great deal of room!"

Major Williams chuckled, for his home, while comfortable, was certainly not large enough to hold another two families with some dozen children between them.

"Certainly not," he agreed. "They will stay in their own homes here in London. But I expect them at almost any moment, so you two must hurry and wash. Come along now."

But he gave Madge a gentle hug before letting her slip off his knee and she cast him a shy smile before running off after her brother with the comforting thought that perhaps their guardian and their new life in England would not be such a bad thing after all.

*

It was the evening of the first full day of the holidays and the pretty sitting room at Die Rosen seemed rather more full than usual. Stacie sat in her invalid chair, the back raised only a few inches. Grizel was curled up on the window seat, looking out over the lake as the sun set. Biddy and the Robin were playing with Rufus in front of the empty fireplace while Madge watched from the sofa, where she was darning one of Jem's socks. The doctor was sitting beside her, ostensibly reading a medical journal, but actually teasing Joey. As the sun sank lower, there was a lull, broken by Grizel, who crossed the room to sit opposite Jo.

"Only a few days until we go off to camp," said the former Head Girl. "Isn't it wonderful?"

"Gorgeous!" declared Jo, who had settled into the Queen Anne armchair and was now thoughtlessly kicking her feet against the legs.

"Jo, I have asked you before not to do that," protested Madge. "You know how fond I am of that chair."

"Better not let Rufus near it again, then," replied Jo with a giggle, although she did cease her movements. "You remember what he did to it two years ago."

"I should think I do," agreed Madge with an attempt at sternness, though she had to join in the laugh at the end.

"Please, Madame," asked Grizel eagerly, for she and the other girls were wild with curiosity, "what was it?"

Madge smiled at her. "It was the Christmas before last," she began. "You might remember that I came down with mumps just before term ended and so you had to go to England with Miss Maynard instead of coming here. Well, one morning Jem had to go to the San and I was in bed. Rufus had been outside, but as it was raining, Jem left him in the kitchen with Marie. Somehow he escaped and, as I had to get up to answer the 'phone, I heard him downstairs. When I came down to take him back to the kitchen, there were scraps of fabric from one end of the passage to the other and the door to the salon was standing half open."

"That was my fault," admitted Jem shamefacedly, although his eyes were twinkling with laughter. "I had left my bag on the table and had to rush in to get it."

"So I understood," replied his wife. "Marie has said on more than one occasion that she takes very good care to close every door when Rufus has to be inside, in case he slips away and causes trouble."

"You mean like the time he got into my room and destroyed

my old rag doll?" asked Jo, and there was a gleam in her eye. "The one you gave me when I was only a baby?"

"Exactly," said Madge. "I could hear Rufus in here, growling at something, and I walked in to what seemed to be a snowstorm. Not only had he ruined the chair, but several cushions had also been torn to pieces. Of course, I bundled him back into the kitchen in short order, but that wasn't going to save the chair!"

Stacie looked at it. "It does not appear to have been badly damaged, Madame. Did Rufus only ruin the cover?"

"I wish he had," said Madge with a rueful smile, "but unfortunately he also scratched the legs very badly. In the end I sent the chair to Innsbruck and they repaired it as best they could. There are still some marks on it, but most have been well hidden." She grinned at her sister. "I made Jo help me with the new cover for the seat. After all, Rufus is her dog!"

"Are you really so fond of it, Madame?" queried Grizel.

"Rufus, d'you mean?" teased Jem. "Or the chair?"

"I am, Grizel, yes," agreed Madge, ignoring the interruption and answering the question as seriously as it had been asked. "It was my mother's chair. She always sat in it of an evening once the work was done. She would read to us, or sew while Father told us about what he had done that day. So you can imagine, Grizel, why I was so cross when I saw what Rufus had done to it."

"It's a well-travelled chair, that," Jem remarked. "Came from India in the first place; then it went home with you to London, didn't it, darling, and on to Cornwall when you moved there."

"Yes, we were only in London for a few months," said Madge. "Guardian had to make arrangements for us to live in his house in Cornwall. It was fortunate he did, because London during the Great War was no place for children."

"I should love to visit India and see the house where I was

born," said Jo wistfully. "Do you think I shall get there some day, Madge?"

"I expect so, Joey," replied her sister. "Perhaps when you have finished school, you could go and visit Dick and Mollie. Then you'd see baby Bridget again."

"That would be gorgeous!" declared Jo.

"And me, too, Tante Guito?" begged the Robin. "May I also go?"

"We shall have to see about that," said Madge, after exchanging glances with her husband. "It will be a long time before that happens, though, so we have plenty of time to think about things. And now," she added as the clock on the bookcase chimed, "it's almost time for Abendessen. Jo, you take the Robin and Biddy to wash. Grizel, you see to Stacie, please. Off you go!"

Everyone scattered on the word and when Madge came back down, after having checked on her son and the other children in the nursery, she found them gathered round the table and chattering like so many magpies about the shopping they meant to do before they packed to go away to camp.

*

Madge watched as Sybil and Jacky cleaned their hands, which were sticky from the work they had done on their scrap-books, and then dismissed them to the nursery. With a sigh, she went back to the kitchen to continue her cooking.

"Madame, Mrs Ozanne is here to see you," a voice announced from the doorway and Madge turned to nod to Marie.

"Thank you. Is she in the sitting room?"

"No, indeed!" exclaimed Elizabeth Ozanne's voice from behind the maid. "Sit in there like a prim old spinster when I can help you here? Certainly not!"

Madge laughed. "Well, come in, then. I admit, this room is lovely and warm, thanks to my labours. Jo herself said as much when she was here half an hour ago. However," she dusted the flour off her hands, "I'm almost finished. If you can put that tray into the oven for me," she gestured with a wave of her hand and Elizabeth did as she had been directed, "I will finish making the tea."

Ten minutes later, the two women were settling themselves in armchairs in the small summer room that Madge used when she had friends or family to visit, and which was cosier than the somewhat stiff sitting room where Jem entertained his colleagues when they came to call.

"So," began Madge, "when are you going to leave for Armiford?"

"Next week." Elizabeth sighed. "You can't imagine—well, actually I suppose you probably do understand how difficult it's going to be. We all love Guernsey so much."

"I know." Madge gave a sympathetic smile. "We felt the same about having to leave Austria, and now we have to move again." She sighed. "Still, at least this time we can plan things a little more carefully and take our belongings with us. Last time, when we left Die Rosen, we had to leave a good part of the furniture behind, though I managed to bring along several of our favourite pieces, including that chair you're sitting on."

Elizabeth at once stood up to look at her seat. "Yes, it is very lovely," she agreed after she had examined it for a moment. "I can see it's been well used, of course. One or two nasty scratches, particularly on this leg here, but on the whole it's charming, and matches the room very well with the different patterns!"

"I made a new cover for it just before Josette arrived," said Madge. "It was some leftover material that I found in one of the boxes we brought over with us. I had kept all sorts of scraps from different clothes and things I had made over the years—it was a habit I picked up from Mother, I believe—and the colours went together perfectly. There wasn't enough for a quilt or anything of that sort, but I did get the cover for that chair and some cushion covers out of it. The ones I had used in Austria were rather worn in places and the sewing was beginning to come apart. It seemed like a very good time to make something new for it."

"True enough." Elizabeth sipped her tea. "You said it was your mother's, didn't you? I wish we had something like that from my mother, but then she passed away so soon after Anne was born. Our stepmother was very kind, of course, but nothing can ever really compare with one's own mother."

"I do understand," said Madge warmly. "Although our guardian wasn't married, we did have a lot of visits from Aunt Josie—actually, she was our great-aunt. She was very kind, particularly when Jo was ill."

"On which occasion?" queried Elizabeth, and although there was something of a teasing twinkle in her eye, Madge failed to notice and answered the question seriously.

"When she was four years old. Dick and I were away at school and she began a cold. I've never been quite sure about what happened, but we came home for the holidays to find her very ill. They had forgotten about us—Dick and me, I mean—and there was no one at the station to collect us. I remember we left our cases and trunks there and walked home, wondering all the time what had happened. When we arrived, we found that Jo was so bad that no one thought she would live until the next day."

"I remember you once saying that you went to Austria in the first place at least partly in the hope that it would help Jo," said Elizabeth, in an attempt to distract her friend. "And it has done her a great deal of good from all you say. I think you'll find that the air here on Guernsey will also have done her good."

"Oh, she's strong enough now," said Madge comfortably. "She's thrived since the arrival of the triplets. Have more tea, Elizabeth?"

"Thank you." Elizabeth held out her cup and, while it was being filled, changed the subject to other matters.

*

"Here, Mother," said Josette. "Post's come!"

"Excellent, thank you, darling," said Madge, who was seated at the foot of the breakfast table. It was several months since the birth of the latest members of the Russell family and Madge was able to take her place at the table now that the girls were home from school for the holidays. "Hand them out, please, dear. Put anything for your father by his place. He said he would be here soon."

"Here, Margot," and Josette, obeying her mother's direction and looking through the bundle of envelopes, gave one to her cousin, "letter from your sisters, by the look of it!"

"Jolly good!" Margot all but snatched the letter and then cast an appealing glance at her aunt. "May I go, Auntie Madge?"

"Yes, dear, run along," came the sympathetic reply. "Don't forget, though, that we are going Christmas shopping and I want you to be ready to leave by half past ten."

"I'll be ready!" The comment came back through the half-open door, which Josette closed as she went to the other side of the table to put several envelopes down next to her father's plate.

There was silence for the next few moments as Josette opened the letters she had received: one from her sister, and several others from girls with whom she had been friendly before coming to Canada. Madge, meanwhile, glanced over her own correspondence, leaving a package from her sister until last.

Before she could open it, however, she was interrupted by a yelp of laughter from Josette.

"What is it, darling?" she asked.

Josette replied as well as she could for giggling. "Sybs is just about ready to eat her finger-ends off with jealousy that she isn't here to meet Kevin and Kester," she answered. "She says Auntie Jo just told her, and left her to tell Pegs and Bride. However," she went on, reading more of the letter, "she does say she can at least be happy that there are six Russells as well as six Maynards and Bettanys."

"Yes, I thought she would be as pleased about that as you and Ailie are," laughed Madge.

"And you, too, Mother," grinned Josette. "I know, whatever you might say, you're only too pleased to have caught up."

"What a terrible thing to say!" exclaimed Madge, although her eyes were dancing. "Really, Josette!"

"What has she done now?" Jem wanted to know as he entered the dining room. His tones, however, belied his words and he was smiling as he teased his daughter. "Josephine Mary Russell, what mischief have you been up to?"

"None!" declared the indignant Josette. "'Tisn't me. It's Mother. She's trying to tell me that she isn't secretly glad to have caught up with Auntie Jo and Auntie Mollie with their families."

"Well, if she isn't, I am," grinned Jem as he poured himself some coffee. "Perhaps your Aunt Jo will have to pipe down a little now."

"Not at all," said Madge. "Jo still has triplets and that's a feat neither Mollie nor I have attempted, let me remind you—and nor are we likely to at this late date."

"Speaking of which, where is young Margot?" demanded her uncle. "I've just arranged for her to 'phone her parents for Christmas and I want to pass on the good news. It will have to be quick, of course, but it will be better than nothing."

"I should say so!" agreed Madge. "But Margot has a letter from her sisters and I let her go off to read it somewhere private. Josette, go and find her, would you, dear? We shall have to be off soon and I don't want to miss the bus." Then, as Josette left the room, she turned her husband. "That was kind of you, darling. Although she doesn't let us see it, I know poor Margot has had times of missing her parents dreadfully and that should help."

"Yes, I rather thought so myself." Jem had slit his first envelope and now drew out the letter. He nodded at the large packet Madge was still holding. "That looks interesting. What's in it?"

"I've no idea," replied his wife. "I haven't opened it yet, what with your and Josette's nonsense. Pass me the letter opener, will you? Thanks."

She slit the top of the envelope and drew out several sheets of stiff cardboard, which she lifted with a cry of delight to find charming photographs of the Maynard family and also of Sybil and David Russell.

"Oh, how lovely! Look, Jem, Jo has sent us the photographs I suggested. Doesn't she look well?" she commented, dwelling on the picture of her younger sister, who was seated in a chair and holding baby Mike. Margot's triplet sisters stood on either side, each holding the hand of one of their brothers, and their father stood behind the group.

"Sybs seems to be the picture of health!" her father declared. "She certainly does look lovely, doesn't she?"

"And David is looking very like his father," said Madge, with a smile at her husband. "I can scarcely believe that he's fourteen! He will be thinking about his future before long, I suppose."

"I imagine he has a few ideas," said Jem. "But there's plenty of time for that, at least until we're back in England and can discuss it."

"I suppose so." And Madge turned back to the photo of the Maynard family. For a moment she studied it before giving a yelp of surprise. "Jem! Goodness, look at that! How *could* she? I hope nothing's happened to it."

"What are you holding forth about now?" demanded Jem, twitching the picture from her fingers. "Well, what is it?"

"Look at Jo," his wife demanded, as she gave her mouth a final wipe on her napkin and then rose from her seat. "Look what she's sitting on—my favourite chair! Well, if she thinks that with me over here she can calmly commandeer it for her own use, she'll soon find that she's mistaken."

Jem chortled. "I imagine she couldn't resist the chance to see if you would notice, my dear! You must write and tell her your thoughts on the matter—I don't see why I should have to listen to them!"

"Certainly not!" came the indignant reply, as Madge paused in the doorway. "I shan't give her the satisfaction of knowing!" And she swept out of the room to get ready to go shopping.

Jem laughed to himself as he examined the photo, noticing that the cover on the chair had been changed from the floral pattern that it had had for some years, and now had wide vertical stripes instead. With another chuckle, he slid the photographs back into the envelope and made a mental note to write to his sister-in-law himself to tell her the results of her very successful joke.

*

"And how do I look, Mother?"

Madge cast an appraising glance at her second daughter, dressed all in white, and smiled. "Lovely, my dear. Simply lovely."

"You're lucky to have such a fine day for it," declared Sybil from her seat by the window where she was putting a final gloss on her chestnut hair. "Particularly in April. The weather can be so chancy."

"Well, I had to be married before Mother and Dad left for England," argued Josette. "And you know they're going next week."

"And I'm thankful to be here for one family wedding at least," exclaimed Madge. "I do seem to have an appalling history where such things are concerned. I wasn't there for Daisy's, thanks to German measles. Then we were in Canada for Primula's big day. I was at Peggy's wedding, but we were here in Australia when Bride got married. And then, of course, we were here for yours, Sybs, but really I do think it's most unfair that I should have missed so many."

"Suggest to Auntie Jo that her three have a triplet wedding once you get back," chuckled Sybil from the folds of the sky-blue dress she was struggling into as matron-of-honour.

"Jo would shriek with horror at the suggestion," declared Madge as she came to lend a hand to her eldest daughter. "There, Sybs. That looks lovely. Now, if you two are ready, we will go down to your father."

"Wait a moment, Mother." Sybil turned to Josette. "Do you have the traditional four 'somethings'—old, new, borrowed and blue?"

"Hmm." Josette thought for a moment. "There's Mother's veil—that's old. My shoes are new. I borrowed your pearl necklace—and you were a gem to loan it to me! As for blue," she glanced at her sister and giggled, "that's you! Now, let's go!"

Madge linked arms with her two daughters, and they descended the stairs to where Jem was waiting for them. He rose as they came into the living room and crossed the floor to kiss his younger daughter.

"You look lovely, my darling," he told her. "be very happy."

Josette met her father's gaze. "I know I shall, Father, said simply.

"Yes, I believe you will." And he turned his attention to the others. "Madge, the car is waiting for you and Sybil. Josette and I will be there soon."

"Of course, dear." Madge smiled at him and then turned to Sybil. "Are you ready, Sybs? Let's be off, then."

"Ailie will be just raging at not being here," said Sybil as they went down to the car that stood at the foot of the front steps.

"Your father and I discussed it," said Madge, "and we felt it would be better if Ailie didn't miss any more school than she did for your wedding. She's really very lazy and it wouldn't do her any good."

"I suppose not, but it is hard lines on her."

"But then she was at Bride's wedding, which we missed," Madge told her as they got into the car. "She must just be satisfied with that."

Sybil smiled, but said nothing for several moments before looking up at her mother once more.

"Mother?"

"Hmm?" Madge had been looking behind to see if the car containing her husband and the bride was visible, but she turned back upon hearing Sybil's voice. "What is it, Sybs?" She frowned a little. "You look very serious, child. What's the matter?"

"I have some news for you, Mother." There was a tiny smile playing round Sybil's lips. "I didn't want to tell you in front of Josette. After all, it's her big day and I'd hate to spoil it for her."

"And what is it, Sybil?" Madge began to look worried. "Is it so important that you were afraid it would overshadow Josette's wedding?"

ı Sybil. "Very much so, I should
ldy—at least not until Josette has
"

once what it is! I promise, I shan't
ıst tell me, Syb …" And then her voice
daughter's shy expression and guessed
ıling!" She threw her arms round Sybil's
shou_   ɔ care for her dress or hair, embraced her
fiercely. "Aı   ′t be here for it! How dreadful! But when is
it to be—and how ₁ong have you known?"

"I've rather suspected for some weeks," said Sybil, smoothing
her hair. "But I've only known for sure since yesterday. I expect
it will happen in November—not that we need another family
birthday in that month," she added with a laugh. "Still, it's God
who makes these decisions, not me. I, I mean."

"Oh, Sybil, I'm so glad for you, dear!" Madge gently caressed
her daughter's cheek. "I certainly won't say a word about it until
after the wedding is over and the happy couple have departed.
Listen, I have a few things to arrange at Josette's new home this
evening. Come and help me with them, and then we can discuss
it all. But here we are at the church and we can't talk about it any
more. Still, your father will be one enormous thrill when he
knows! You're a wonderful girl, Sybil, and your father and I are
so proud of you! Now go and get ready. I must find my seat—
mercy, what crowds of people there are!"

And Madge had perforce to turn and answer the host of
greetings that came at her from all sides, while Sybil, her heart
lightened at having shared her secret, entered the church to await
her sister.

The afternoon simply flew by after that. Almost before Madge
realised it, Josette was married and all manner of toasts were
being proposed to the happy couple. Then they were gone for

their honeymoon to Adelaide, and at last Madge could escape to the peace and quiet of Josette's future home.

Even with Sybil's help, arranging the remaining bits and pieces took some time, so that it was dark when, at length, Sybil went home and Madge was left with the final things to tidy up. Eventually she entered the sitting room to place the last item, a delicate Chinese vase, on the mantel.

A sofa and two armchairs stood in front of the brand new television set that waited in one corner to be switched on. However, not everything in the room was new. Madge and Jem had arranged to have a sofa and chair made in the same style as Madge's old armchair, which had stood in so many different houses with such different histories. Now, with a fresh, crisp new cover, it stood proudly in a new home, waiting for a new owner and a new story.

With a satisfied nod, Madge slid her hand along the back of the chair as she left the room and closed the door behind her with a soft click.

APPENDIX II: ERRORS IN THE FIRST EDITION

In republishing *Two Sams at the Chalet School* we have kept to the text of the first edition. We have neither edited nor updated it, but have corrected obvious typographical errors wherever it was possible to be sure what the author intended. In accordance with our usual policy we have not corrected French or German usage. We hope we have not allowed any new errors to creep in.

Punctuation

We have changed a full stop to a comma and vice versa, and replaced a hyphen with a dash where the context required it; and we have added a couple of missing dashes. We have removed some spurious punctuation marks, and have also added missing ones, chiefly apostrophes. We have altered double quotation marks to single and vice versa where appropriate.

Misspelled words

As stated above, we have corrected obvious typos:

manoeuvering to manoeuvring
preven to prevent
Aldersnest to Adlersnest

Variant usages

We have standardised these where there is a clear majority usage:

Dr, not Dr.
entrance hall, not entrance-hall
everyone, not every one (where it is a pronoun)
formroom, not form room

Grantley, not Grantly (although there is no very clear majority
    in this book, this is the usual spelling of Ted's name)
Henriette, not Henrietta
Junior/Middle/Senior, not junior/middle/senior
Mr, not Mr.
outdoors, not out-doors
Samaris's, not Samaris'
san, not San (for the school san)
ski-ers, not skiers
timetable, not time table
van der Byl, not Van der Byl

We have not standardised the following, as there is no clear
majority:

    Abbot/Abbott
    finger-print/fingerprint
    notice-board/noticeboard

Missing or incorrect words

There are several places where it seems clear that a word has been
omitted, inserted or used in error, and we have corrected these:

page 83, paragraph 1, line 1: 'we don't to lose any'—'we don't
    want to lose any'
page 89, paragraph 1, line 2: 'To one side of its stood the house'—
    'To one side of it stood the house'
page 89, paragraph 4, line 5: 'Then come long and meet her!'—
    'Then come along and meet her!'
page 165, paragraph 3, line 1: 'sort of things'—'sort of thing'
page 183, paragraph 3, line 11: 'only thing she could to was to'—
    'only thing she could do was to'

page 215, paragraph 4, line 3: 'partaking tea and hot cakes'—'partaking of tea and hot cakes'

page 226, paragraph 2, line 2: 'going to to climb'—'going to climb'

page 226, paragraph 3, line 1: 'started out'—'stared out'

In other places it is not clear what was intended, so we have left them:

page 69, paragraph 3, line 7: 'We ought to be in our formroom'—'formrooms'?

page 89, paragraph 2, line 3: 'where what appeared to be two steps leading up to the front door'—This clause lacks a main verb.

page 163, paragraph 3: It is not clear whether there are two or three speakers in this paragraph.

Ruth Jolly and Adrianne Fitzpatrick

Girls Gone By Publishers

Girls Gone By Publishers republish some of the most popular children's fiction from the 20th century, concentrating on those titles which are most sought after and difficult to find on the second-hand market. We aim to make them available at affordable prices, thus making ownership possible for both existing collectors and new ones so that the books continue to survive. Authors on our list include Margaret Biggs, Elinor Brent-Dyer, Dorita Fairlie Bruce, Gwendoline Courtney, Monica Edwards, Antonia Forest, Lorna Hill, Clare Mallory, Violet Needham, Elsie Jeanette Oxenham, Malcolm Saville and Geoffrey Trease. We also publish some new titles which continue the traditions of this genre.

Our series '**Fun in the Fourth—Outstanding Girls' School Stories**' has enabled us to broaden our range of authors, allowing our readers to discover a fascinating range of books long unobtainable. It features authors who only wrote one or two such books, a few of the best examples from more prolific authors (such as Dorothea Moore), and some very rare titles by authors whose other books are generally easy to find second-hand (such as Josephine Elder).

We also have a growing range of non-fiction: more general works about the genre and books on particular authors. These include *Island to Abbey* by Stella Waring and Sheila Ray (about Elsie Oxenham), *The Marlows and their Maker* by Anne Heazlewood (about Antonia Forest) and *The Monica Edwards Romney Marsh Companion* by Brian Parks. These are in a larger format than the fiction, and are lavishly illustrated in colour and black and white.

For details of availability and ordering (please do not order until titles are actually listed) go to www.ggbp.co.uk or write for a catalogue to Clarissa Cridland or Ann Mackie-Hunter, GGBP, 4 Rock Terrace, Coleford, Bath, BA3 5NF, UK.

Founded 1989

— an international fans' society founded in 1989 to foster friendship between Chalet School fans all over the world

Join Friends of the Chalet School for
Quarterly Magazines over 70 pages long
A Lending Library of all Elinor Brent-Dyer's books
Le Petit Chalet (for those aged 13 and under)
Collectors' Corner Booklets
Dustwrapper and Illustration Booklets

For more information send an A5 SAE to
Ann Mackie-Hunter or Clarissa Cridland
4 Rock Terrace, Coleford, Bath, Somerset BA3 5NF, UK
e-mail focs@rockterrace.demon.co.uk
www.chaletschool.org.uk

You may also be interested in the New Chalet Club.
For further details send an SAE to
Rona Falconer, Membership Secretary,
The New Chalet Club, 18 Nuns Moor Crescent,
Newcastle upon Tyne, NE4 9BE